Praise

'What [Balestrini] narrates is not a fairy tale, but a terrifying experience. Not just his own, but also that of a lost generation who thought possible another world beside the world, who dreamt of workers' power, of autonomy, who revolted against everything, school, family, clergy, political parties, "historical compromise", State, police, boredom . . . *The Unseen* is, perhaps, the first true novel of the European Left.' *Libération*

'Balestrini offers a very lucid document, which is both the memory and the assessment of a disoriented generation. The Left now has its novel.' *L'Événement du jeudi*

'*The Unseen* isn't documentary writing, but it tells us far more than any documentary about a troubled phase in our history; how it was experienced, and most of all how it was lived in the imagination.' *Corriere della Sera*

'We should be grateful to Nanni Balestrini for having engaged his writing with this cruel sentimental education of a young man living in the seventies.' Rossana Rossanda, *il manifesto*

'The political passion of the rebel Balestrini is equalled by his literary vocation . . . the finale is not unworthy of Bontempelli or Calvino.' *Il Giornale*

'A work of high literary quality. Among many novels and elegantly crafted pieces of fiction . . . *The Unseen* has the courage to face an incandescent matter of reality, rich in implications that involve not only the literati but also a wider public.' *L'Unità*

'Not just a beautiful novel . . . it is the story of part of a generation in our country, who dreamed a different future and believed in it, believed in the possibility of making it real.' *Linus*

NANNI BALESTRINI was born in Milan in 1935 and was a member of the influential avant-garde Gruppo 63, along with Umberto Eco and Eduardo Sanguineti. He is the author of numerous volumes of poetry, including *Blackout* and *Ipocalisse*, and novels such as *Tristano*, *Vogliamo Tutto*, and *La Violenza Illustrata*.

During the notorious mass arrests of writers and activists associated with Autonomy, which began in 1979, Balestrini was charged with membership of an armed organization and with subversive association. He went underground to avoid arrest and fled to France. As in so many other cases, no evidence was provided and he was acquitted of all the charges.

He currently lives in Rome, where he runs the monthly magazine of cultural intervention *Alfabeta2* with Umberto Eco and others.

The Unseen

Nanni Balestrini

TRANSLATED BY LIZ HERON
WITH A FOREWORD BY ANTONIO NEGRI

VERSO

London • New York

First published in English by Verso 1989
This updated paperback edition published by Verso 2011
This updated edition © Nanni Balestrini and Derive Approdi, Rome 2005
Translation © Liz Heron 1989, 2011
Foreword © Antonio Negri 2011
First published as *Gli Invisibili*
© Bompiani, Milan 1987

3 5 7 9 10 8 6 4 2

Verso
UK: 6 Meard Street, London W1F 0EG
US: 20 Jay Street, Suite 1010, Brooklyn, NY 11201
www.versobooks.com

Verso is the imprint of New Left Books

ISBN-13: 978-1-84467-767-2

British Library Cataloguing in Publication Data
A catalogue record for this book is available from the British Library

Library of Congress Cataloging-in-Publication Data
A catalog record for this book is available from the Library of Congress

Typeset in Janson MT by Hewer UK Ltd, Edinburgh
Printed in the US

for Sergio

Foreword

Nanni Balestrini's book, now republished here, tells of unseen actors in the class struggle between the 1970s and '80s, particularly in northern Italy, and inside the jails of the Realm. These subjects are invisible because they are elusive, mutating beings in the act of metamorphosis. But what can we say about them today (and also about this novel) if not that rather than being an old, outdated story this is now very much of the present moment, one caught sight of at that time and followed in the course of its unfolding? The republication of *The Unseen* therefore has the advantage today of telling us about proletarian subjects whose class nature has finally been revealed: the unseen individual of yesterday is the proletarian of today, the immaterial worker, the cognitive precariat, the new figure of the worker as social labour power in the movements of the multitude. Those poor wretches did it, they managed to get through a revolution in the composition of labour and a ferocious political repression and to struggle on from the factories to society and (still productive) from society to the jail (still fighting back). And now where will they go? The elite of the working-class movement who betrayed and dragged the unseen into prison now look around, fearful and unable to build a politics, afraid of losing out if they do not resume contact with that age-old movement of transformation; but that elite will never win! Indeed, regardless of this betrayal by the working-class movement (which has been so serious, especially in Italy), the unseen have gone forward. In the '80s, they were organizing prison revolts and the first autonomous social centres in the cities; in the '90s they organized the Panther movement; in the late '90s they turned into Zapatistas and *tute bianche*, the anti-globalization movement and everything else that has happened and will happen.

It is interesting to note that each one of these movements always sought to give itself ambiguous, hard-to-pin-down names that could have been white but also dark in the shadow that the white produced, that could have been soft like the tread of a feline, that could moreover position itself as tireless resistance precisely in the name of the singular ambiguity of its disobedient behaviour. Since the '70s, these movements have all understood that starting all over again doesn't mean turning back but rather expanding, reaching into new spaces and new times, being coordinated and coordinating, seeking confrontation in the measure of consensus and consensus in the measure of confrontation. The fact is that, in contrast to the parties and the survivors from the *ancien régime*, the unseen place themselves in the here and now. Balestrini's unseen, right from the early '80s, were beginning to give shape to a multitudinous, singular, transversal subject that wanted never to be reduced to a mass but wanted in every case to be a whole. And even when ideological reminiscences drew them inside names and terminologies that sounded out of date, at that same moment this subject was able to invent itself anew. Think of the scene where the prisoners in the Trani revolt are locked up in their cells after the bloodbath and shed with their flaming torches a light that illuminates the night of every proletarian prison of the decade. This is the language of the multitude. But if it were no more than this, this reality in its biting descriptions, Balestrini's book might only be a piece of historical or sociological documentation. What is great about this novel is that the unseen individual becomes a literary subject. *Larvatus prodeo* – the proletarian advances masked by his invisibility. And with this transformation in those years of the '70s – which the bosses and their servants within the working-class movement failed sufficiently to curse – he represents the invisible yet powerful transformation from material work to immaterial work, from revolt against the boss to revolt against the patriarchy, along with the metamorphosis of bodies brought about within this movement, and the imagination that this new historical condition (social and political to be precise) brings to speech.

Balestrini's book is a great new experiment (the first was *Vogliamo tutto* [We Want Everything]) that shows us the body of the exploited as an actor in the revolutionary process. And we can add: in the passage from modern to post-modern, from the era when socialism dreamed of itself to the era when communism is beginning to be lived. Without a doubt this is a didactic novel; but who learns from whom? The novel of the Real or – this seems the mark of revolutionary literature – the reality of the novel? It pleases me to bet on the second hypothesis and ask the anatomist/physiologist of the language in question (Balestrini) to agree with me: in its ambiguity, in the difficulty it registers, this book has nonetheless anticipated reality and transformed the Real. In this case the ambiguity is between the real actor and the author of the narrative, a key connected to a mechanism of political and constituent potency, one poor in its genesis and yet of great richness in the series of effects it produces.

An act of love? This book is dual in character; it is a biopolitical tissue of postmodernity, another of the great concepts of contemporary revolutionary thought that Balestrini intuits and invents, along with the idea of the multitude. One could discuss this at even greater length and most of all one could insist on the question of the function, the vocation, the joy of the writer! How frequently lumpen proletarians reproach writers or intellectuals for describing phenomena they have not endured. This time there is great satisfaction in being able to acknowledge that Balestrini too has been invisible, that he has suffered the transformation to trace long years of poverty and love.

Antonio Negri, 2011

Translator's Note

The Unseen is anchored in the social movements of Italy in the second half of the 1970s and, especially, in the rise of Autonomy, a widespread network of extra-parliamentary alliances involving school and university students, the young unemployed and various groupings of the socially marginalized and economically disenfranchized (the *emarginati*).

Autonomy's political origins can be traced back to the factory strikes and occupations of 1969's 'Hot Autumn', but a number of immediate issues spurred its growth: price rises and cuts in public spending, a series of neo-fascist shootings and bomb attacks, rising unemployment, dissatisfaction with the education system. This was also the time of the Communist Party's attempted 'historic compromise', the move towards a hoped-for partnership with the ruling Christian Democracts. The party's tacit support for the government's economic policies and refusal to oppose legislation drastically extending police powers were the object of fierce criticism from the left.

Protests reached their height in 1977, when street demonstrations and violent, often armed, clashes with the police occurred almost daily in some Italian cities. It was also a year of explosive cultural opposition – through alternative radio stations and magazines, and through the theatrically staged actions of the 'Metropolitan Indians'. An outbreak of posters and slogans re-invoked the surreal challenges of 1968.

As divisions and tensions multiplied within Autonomy, especially over the question of organized violence, terrorism escalated.

The wave of repression which followed made few distinctions. Mass arrests, guilt-by-association and the imprisonment, frequently without trial, of hundreds of people, had profound consequences for an entire generation.

Of the many prison revolts during this period, the one whose events are most closely paralleled in the novel took place at Trani, near Bari, in December 1980.

Translation of the protagonists' names in the text would have resulted in excessive artificiality. So that their literal meanings are not altogether lost, I offer the following glossary:

Aglio	Garlic
China	Quinine
Cocco	Coconut
Cotogno	Quince
Donnola	Weasel
Gelso	Mulberry
Lauro	Bay
Lince	Lynx
Lupino	Lupin
Malva	Mallow
Mastino	Mastiff
Menta	Mint
Mora	Bramble
Nocciola	Hazelnut
Ortica	Nettle
Pepe	Pepper
Scilla	Squill
Spinone	Griffon
Talpa	Mole
Valeriana	Valerian
Verbena	Vervain

THE
UNSEEN
NANNI BALESTRINI

Part One

I

The cellars are a maze of passageways lit every twenty or thirty yards by dusty fluorescent strip-lights swinging from long ragged electric wires that hang from the ceiling its rough cement fissured by long deep cracks it seems to go on for ever and here and there bulges downwards as if pushed by some enormous weight up there crushing buckling breaking through and every four or five yards props made from great beams hold it up the wood rotten mouldy the ground covered in a film of putrid water the cloying sickening stench of putrefaction mingling with the stench of mould every so often at a turn-off or the junction of two passageways are little piles of sand of cement sodden collapsed trampled shovels and other rusty tools left lying there the air is damp and from our mouths come little puffs of vapour as we breathe that nauseating air

the irregular shuffling of the small silent procession merges with the continuous jangling of the chains the sound echoes whenever the gangways of rotting wood are crossed the shadows lengthen behind each step whenever it gets close to the sections lit by strip-lights they disappear and all of a sudden reappear ahead and the steps lengthen they move forward slowly paying attention to where they tread and to the chains so that they don't drag too much in front or behind trying always to leave the same distance between the one in front and the one behind taking care not to brush the right shoulder against the slimy wet wall and on the left keeping clear of the sub-machine-gun barrels levelled straight as the small procession turns repeatedly to the right and the left to the left and the right until all sense of direction is lost

then we climb a narrow stairway semi-darkness suffocating with long flights high steps aching tugs at the chains hurting the wrists and at the end of the last flight the light of a small door and we come out high up at the top of a stairway tiers spreading into an enormous room brightly lit full of people moving down there beneath us all of a sudden against my leg I feel an animal muzzle that growls threateningly the black pupils dilated the large eyes protruding two long very white teeth bared by the tight red mouth a huge massive dog the smooth black fur on end on its back arching its ears pointing up quivering all the time the *carabiniere* holding its leash is impassive in his bullet-proof overalls the latest in anti-terrorist style

from where we are the tiers fall away steeply to the floor of the room and from there rising all around up to the ceiling thick cylindrical iron bars varnished in gun-metal grey the enormous cage is full of officers in bullet-proof overalls in gun-metal grey everywhere we turn with more big black dogs growling and nervous one after the other the *carabinieri* remove our chains take the handcuffs off the sore red wrists the photographers' blinding flashlights flare on our faces they too are dogs no jackals and they writhe they bend they stretch up on tiptoe an anxious ballet arms raised straining higher and higher with the sleeves of their jackets slipping back to the elbows higher and higher

we rub our red wrists we light cigarettes we walk up and down the steps a bit we wave to relatives we sit down together in twos and threes talking quietly the photographers below us get on

their knees they jerk their torsos to right and left like contortion-
ists in the circus they lean towards the animals inside the cage
they try to get their heads sideways through the bars sliding
their long lenses between the legs the arms of the *carabinieri* who
form a motionless barrier their fingers twitch in a frenzy they
jiggle the cameras up and down they shoot pictures and let off
dazzling flashlights at the faces inside the cage then in a faraway
corner an even more dazzling light goes on and the whirr of the
television cameras starts up

I sit down on the highest step of all and far beneath me I can see
the lawyers with their black gowns thrown carelessly back on
their shoulders chatting calmly among themselves in small
groups behind the tables of peeling wood on the right parallel to
the cage the court is assembled with the investigating judge dour
lost in thought sitting in the middle on a high-backed chair so
high it rises well above his head then the assisting judge perched
sideways on another great high chair and to the right and left the
jurors men and women nearly all with their faces hidden behind
wide dark glasses the broad tricolour sashes across the pale pull-
overs the puffed blouses with their starched collars the double
breasted jackets in various shades of grey the ties greenish blue-
ish yellowish and at the far end on the right there's the public
prosecutor's solitary little stand

above the heads of the court millions of small fragments make
up a vast mosaic dusty and faded reaching the ceiling and depict-
ing a scene of confusion a furious battle on the left are the forces
of evil represented by strange beings contorted monstrous
entangled in dominant colours of green and mauve and on the
right the forces of good angelic transparent harmonious blue
and feather-light clashing in the centre in a furious battle but the
forces of evil are already clearly defeated they are beating a
retreat pursued by the implacable forces of good below in a
gilded oval stands the imposing figure of justice blindfold

holding in one hand the sword in the other the scales a little lower the legend in relief says the law is equal for all

on the left behind the barricade of *carabinieri* are the wooden screens behind the screens is the public gallery it's almost totally empty but for some relatives mother father sister brother cousin uncle sister-in-law no friend no comrade because they're all afraid because seen from outside the law-court looks like a stage-set for war metal screens and barbed wire cordons of police and *carabinieri* a succession of barriers and armoured cars in strategic spots while other armoured vehicles circle the building continually then dogs and metal detectors at the door and searches questioning files threats warnings hints and all the rest

the small door behind us opens once again and in the midst of another swarm of *carabinieri* emerging at the top of the steps are the women they too in chains and all of them handcuffed we all get up and go towards them the cage is filled with shouts with greetings with smiles with different perfumes all of them have dressed in the brightest of colours long skirts bright shirts bright scarves rings on their fingers necklaces chains brooches bracelets pendants on their wrists big fantastic earrings clasps in their hair in the chaos the *carabinieri* get edgy they shout orders the dogs growl menacingly the photographers' flash guns burst into light again the journalists make frenzied notes in their notebooks the handful of relatives wave and shout hello behind the screens and other shouts and greetings answer them

one after another the *carabinieri* slip off the chains and remove the handcuffs the girls run to us we run to them on the steps we mingle we entwine we entangle in a mosaic of embraces of hugs of kisses of voices all that interests us now is to talk talk about so many things talk about everything at last to talk to talk as long as we can to touch and hear one another as men and women

6

together everything vanishes around us the courtroom the *cara-biniseri* the photographers the dogs the judges everything that's on the other side of the bars is alien to us it doesn't exist presents get passed across good luck tokens small objects everything that could be brought there right into the cage we exchange clothes too shirts sweaters kerchiefs scarves

a bell rings out from the court bench and the investigating judge dourly begins reading the long list of individual charges this one that one charged with etcetera etcetera with having etcetera etcetera this one that one charged with etcetera etcetera with having etcetera etcetera in accordance with the law in an unvarying monotone hurried offhand this one that one charged with etcetera etcetera with having and so on and so on he rushes through it he slurs his words in his haste this that armed band association and so on and so on you can follow none of it he hurries to the end and then come the preliminaries and the lawyers with no conviction and as pure formality bring the usual futile objections therefore recess and the court's withdrawal to decide on the defence's objections and a few minutes and they're back already and the bell's rung again to say that of course all the defence's objections are overruled and the bell's rung again and the court declared in session and the investigating judge declares debate open

2

The agreed day arrives and early in the morning before they open the gates we'd put up a big poster to announce the mass meeting and inviting everybody to come along we are taking the meeting not asking for it it says in big letters and underneath Gelso had added as well as everything else we need the headmaster Mastino gets in first as usual and he starts reading the poster then his face turns ugly and he scowls at us stares at each of us as if to say I'm marking you down and I'll see to you later then the teachers get there and they read it without saying a word just look at us as though we're crazy a few minutes later out come a bunch of janitors that Mastino has told to pull down the posters

the bravest janitor who was also the stupidest one reaches up to remove the poster but Cocco gets in front of him in a rage with his arms raised with his long black overcoat with the scarlet lining and he lets out a scream at him the janitor stops in his tracks taken aback and then the rest of us get in front of the janitors they don't know what to do they look up at Mastino who looks down at them from the window of the headmaster's room but in the end they decide to go back inside because they realize if they push it it'll come to blows the first students to arrive have seen what happened they start talking it over with us and they don't go in and gradually the group gets bigger then Mastino decides to make a move himself and he comes out under the arcade so we can see he's there and he starts pacing up and down

I feel as if I'm watching the boss pacing in front of the factory in those stories I've read about the first workers' struggles the first strikes the same kind of intimidation and in fact the students get scared somebody starts saying he wants to go inside they come up with no end of excuses even though we keep explaining that if we all stay outside Mastino can do nothing he can't suspend us all but there's too much wavering and too much fear and a first little group heads shamefacedly inside it's like a general signal and the others all rush in too within a few minutes nearly everyone's gone in only twenty or so are left outside along with the six of us and Mastino goes back in too with a smug grin on his face

we're left in the lurch Malva's upset but Cocco's determined we'll go in and do it just the same those of us there are he says we have to do it just the same anyway we've got nothing to lose now he shouts and that way we'll persuade the others to hold the meeting just the same we all go in together and we install ourselves in an empty classroom on the ground floor and we've only been there a minute and we haven't even started speaking when Mastino arrives yelling what are you doing here you you and you you're all suspended come to my room one at a time and he walks out leaving the door open Scilla kicks the door and then he barricades it we shove two benches in front of it we're silent for a moment we must do something we eye one another but we don't know what to do we feel trapped

then in a flash I can see as if it was in front of me the page of a pamphlet I've read this summer about forms of struggle in the factories and all that stuff I can see that page in front of me with the heading in bold print indoor demo and I say indoor demo we must have an indoor demo what say the others yes an indoor demo we'll go into all the classrooms and we'll get all the others to come out at least we can try we'll start with the top class and we'll go through them all everyone agrees we go out and form a small procession in the corridor and we reach the first classroom the lesson has already started we burst in we all go into the classroom together in silence the teacher notorious as Mastino's toady takes fright and doesn't say a word all the students are facing the door

Valeriana is firm when she talks she is nervous of course but clear her voice carries well and her words are distinct the headmaster says he has suspended us all because we wanted to hold a mass meeting without his consent everyone knew it you all knew it too that this meeting was planned we've been talking about it for a fortnight now today you came inside out of fear but if you're scared today you'll be scared tomorrow as well and always and we'll never be able to settle our problems ourselves so you've got to make a start now right away we must all hold the meeting right away to show that in this school we aren't slaves we have to do it so we can do what they're doing in all the other schools to show that we're the ones to decide because the school is ours it's not Mastino's

Cocco and Scilla give the teacher threatening looks as if to say don't you dare open your mouth and he doesn't he keeps quiet all right some people at the desks stand up and the first comments start coming that's right let's get out there let's all get out there yes we'll go round all the classrooms Mastino arrives from the other end of the corridor and runs up against the procession he starts screaming but now nobody's scared any more Cocco stops right in front of him and shouts in his face mass meeting mass meeting Mastino goes on shouting purple with rage and threatens them all with suspension and screams to go back into class but the procession bursts into another classroom the method is to enter en masse without warning

by the time Valeriana's halfway through the speech they're all up and ready to walk out there's no need any more even to talk they've got the idea already the noise is bringing everyone out from the rest of the classrooms the procession swells and the whole ground floor is swept in we take the stairs in procession up to the first floor and go into the first classroom we come to by now there are so many people that they can't all get in and there too all the students come out right away the ones pushing in collide with those pushing out we don't even go into the other rooms the students come out by themselves all over the place on the second floor too we see some leaning over the banisters screams of everyone out and we climb up the stairs to the second floor and when we reach the corridor they're already all out of the classrooms and they join the procession

the procession has come to a halt up on the stairs they're all crowding up the whole length of the stairs you can hear Mastino below screaming something but it's unclear it's hard to make out what he's saying there's an incredible din then we lean out and see Mastino down on the ground floor in the centre of the stairwell tearing his hair desperation on his face all you can hear is him screaming the stairs the stairs paper pellets are raining from above and landing on Mastino's head then from the first and second floors come a hail of biros erasers pencils then exercise books and textbooks too they're all throwing things down at Mastino who is down there alone in the centre of the stairwell he's not even trying to shield himself his hands are thrust in his hair but not as a shield and he keeps on screaming the stairs the stairs

the teachers are nowhere in sight the janitors have vanished some teachers have run into the empty classrooms and locked themselves in in one classroom after another the glass door panels cave in and the teachers can be seen standing scared stiff with their backs to the wall down below Mastino delivers one last desperate shout that succeeds in being audible the stair's giving way the shouts quieten down less because of Mastino's words than because people have now let rip enough Gelso looks at me from behind his little round glasses he asks me what the fuck's the shit shouting and Cocco says he's bluffing he's got nothing else left beneath us Mastino lifts his outstretched arms imploring boys and girls boys and girls stop the stair can't hold all that weight calm down and walk down the stairs at an orderly pace no running no noise

but these are orders don't you hear him he's still giving orders shouts Cocco now you can take back all your threats take it all back in front of everybody no more suspensions and mass meetings whenever we want them there's a great rumbling roar mass meeting mass meeting everyone's shouting below Mastino holds out his arms and then lets them drop and when he manages to speak he pants out yes yes all you want but come down here at once I entreat you I'm saying it for your own good come down here come down quietly don't run I beg you there won't be suspensions you can have your own meetings but come down I beg you everyone's shouting victory victory but no one's going down nobody believes all that about the stairs collapsing nobody takes the least bit of notice

Gelso is cleaning his glasses contentedly Malva and I hug in delight and you can still hear Cocco's great hoarse voice yelling so that's the end of your big-talk now eh and then he adds Mastino you're suspended permanently go to the headmaster's room when we send for you Valeriana's voice can be heard saying we ought to go down to the yard now to hold the meeting because it's the only place where there's room for us all together and everyone shouts in agreement everyone shouts mass meeting mass meeting yard yard and they start coming down the stairs and instead of coming down at an orderly rate as Mastino wanted they all run down and what's more thudding along with leaps and bounds to spite him and all shoving Mastino is still there motionless with his arms raised and his head down shouting no no quietly quietly and then everyone knows how it ended

3

In town the youth groups have organized a festival in the cathedral square China and I take the train on our own we get there earlier than we've arranged with the rest of our comrades and there's already loads of people the police are turned out in force all around there's graffiti being done on the walls and the ground free space is a right or make society a festival or let's reclaim life the police begin to hassle us to move on there are a few scuffles a couple of CS rockets go off that don't frighten anyone but they get hold of one comrade and beat him up a bit we leave the square but in the side streets we start to smash up cobblestones and fill our bags with them meanwhile large groups mainly from the outlying ghetto districts make their way to the meeting place

we try to link arms and manage to form into a long snake that's not bad at all we can see the others from our collective they've all come they're in small groups mixed up with the rest the front of the march is heading straight for the cathedral square holding up a banner that says the time for rebellion has come it's a carnival you can see from the confetti and the paper streamers on the ground families have brought children for the outing dressed up as Zorro and Sandokan or the black pirate we go right round the cathedral square and that's when all hell breaks loose because the *carabinieri* attack the back of the march they let off teargas at once the air is impossible to breathe everyone has weeping eyes the families are seized with panic they're chasing after their Zorros and Sandokans and black pirates scattering in the stampede

China and I stay with a group that's throwing broken cobble-stones and next to us we find Cotogno Valeriana and Nocciola we see the *carabinieri* starting out at a run to charge then some comrades move a few cars into the middle of the road a couple of petrol bombs on the cars and the *carabinieri* are lost behind the flames and the clouds of black smoke a hundred yards ahead there's a group that's got it in for a Rolls Royce the bodywork battered with sticks and crowbars stones hailed on the windows and a petrol bomb there too and the boss's car makes a nice bonfire we play hide and seek a little while longer with the *carabinieri* through the streets of the centre finally we scatter and we all meet again at the station

all our eyes are stinging and we keep rubbing them even though it makes it worse and there's also the stinking smell of teargas in our nostrils we wash our eyes at the water fountain Malva turns up she's had a fall she'd come in high heels she hit her nose and it's all grazed Gelso's glasses fell off as usual and in the melee someone smashed them and and he can hardly see now Verbena breathed in a lot of gas she feels sick and she's going to throw up Ortica arrives lifting the skirt of his raincoat to show us a big black truncheon we very nearly brought back something else didn't we Cocco Cocco found a rifle on the ground they'd even lost one of their rifles you should have seen Cocco running along like an ostrich with the rifle in his hand everyone was laughing and clapping but then we threw it away what were we going to do with a rifle

another time one evening in mid-April on television there's the news of a comrade's murder a fascist shot him he was seventeen and there's an immediate spontaneous reaction in the morning we all meet on the train for the city the same faces the same tennis shoes the jackets the shoulder bags the scarves the kerchiefs the gloves the berets the carriages are packed people are standing in the corridors nobody's talking and at each station more get on on the walls of the villages we pass through you can see the fresh graffiti the same words that can be read on the silent faces of the comrades at the last stations in the suburbs a tide of people gets on pressing on the platforms they've got plastic bags with helmets in them and under their jackets spanners bars iron rods in their pockets slings ball-bearings bolts

when we arrive there's a long procession filling the platform and it's moving up the stairs of the metro no one's bothering with tickets and in the carriages there are flags and the long poles for the banners someone has a go at singing but the mood is grim threatening we reach the university in the square in front of the university there's a tide of people but not just students not just young people all ages are there old people too there are workers in overalls with red kerchiefs round their necks the demonstration is already there drawn up ready to go the stewards in front kerchiefs masking half their faces and the heavy sticks with small red flags tied on there's a dull rumbling sound then a shout and a slogan launched murdered comrade you'll be avenged everyone together a roar and the demonstration sets off

in front of the law courts in front of the steps there are ranks of riot police poised for battle with teargas canisters stuck onto the muzzles of their guns and helmet visors down the demonstration comes to a sudden halt and slogans are launched against the police the tension mounts seriously the demonstration moves on again and then stops once more in a square hoisted up on the base of the obelisk that's in the middle of the square I see an old man with a red kerchief at his neck lifting a bugle to his lips and sounding the call for silence and at once there's a fearful silence you can only hear the bugle's high notes when the bugle stops there's a roar a great roar all around thousands of fists are raised all armed with bars and spanners

in the streets we cross all the shops are closed the shutters are all rolled down and then suddenly all the helmets go on I can see row after row an expanse of coloured helmets like a sea of billiard balls coloured red white blue green black the demonstration stops in the avenue at a crossroads there ahead just a few yards past the crossroads is a roadblock cars jeeps super-jeeps lock up vans of the police and *carabinieri* protecting the fascists' headquarters that's a few yards behind the roadblock the front of the march with the stewards is at a halt a few yards away from the roadblock the spanners and the bars are raised threateningly police and *carabinieri* close ranks and take cover behind the shields stones are thrown in a hail that seems never-ending you can hear the thud of the stones as they hit the shields and the policemen's helmets

dozens of petrol bombs fly through the air then come the blasts loud as can be yellow red blue they make a high wall of flames ahead of us some jeeps have caught fire the police break ranks they all turn and run tripping and stumbling in their flight one more volley of petrol bombs and other cars are catching fire a cloud of black smoke you can't see a thing any more then you hear the dull thumps of the teargas canisters that hail down on us by the dozen a downpour of teargas that rains on us from all sides in a single moment the air becomes impossible to breathe the stewards' lines move back and get to the road junction they stop at the junction behind in the avenue the march has crumbled and suddenly from the end of the avenue we hear the piercing sirens of a column of super-jeeps

the sirens get closer louder and louder I hear shouting all around then suddenly everyone's running towards the sides of the avenue towards the pavement and all at once as the crowd parts there appears a huge grey-green super-jeep driven at top speed brushing right past us I'm running on the pavement as well more super-jeeps arrive from the column the sirens really close ear splitting stones and a few petrol bombs are thrown at the super-jeeps whose windows are guarded by iron grilles flames rise up from the side of one so many of them that they seem never-ending from the pavements the comrades are still throwing stones and petrol bombs they're shooting ball-bearings and screw bolts with slings I see a super-jeep zigzagging in the middle of the avenue and then aiming straight for the pavement

people fling themselves against the walls of the houses they scramble up the grilles the shutters of the shops onto the first-floor windowsills the super-jeeps mount the pavement they graze the walls they brush against us I scramble up the grille of a shutter everyone is trying to scramble up but there isn't room for everyone people hang on to one another the super-jeeps come on to the pavement scraping against the walls of the houses brushing against us one two three I hold my breath and close my eyes someone near me is screaming in terror I keep holding on to the grille even when the column has gone by and I can see the last super-jeep that has brushed against us and then kind of jolts and suddenly turns towards the middle of the road I can hear a lot of screaming all coming from the place where the super-jeep turned round

very loud screaming shouting I see a lot of comrades running in that direction I can't see a thing there's smoke and confusion they all have red eyes crying with the teargas I get down from the shutter and head over there running with others we collide with others coming from the opposite direction anguished faces staring eyes some lower their kerchiefs one's running his hands through his hair I can't see what's happened there's a group of comrades standing in a semi-circle some are weeping it's not with the teargas some are sobbing one girl shouts something I don't understand then further on I see the bloody body on the ground I see the long trail of dark blood and further on I see the reddish mass of brains the wheels of the super-jeep have spattered out of it out of the head spattered out

4

Then suddenly a puzzling still image that I couldn't quite make sense of it wasn't a photograph because inside the frame were hints of movement there was the intense glare of a floodlight it must have been filmed at night something shot very close up so close that you could make out nothing in any detail there was no commentary there was only that mute puzzling image I could hear only the rustle of China's fingers rolling the joint then the camera lens zoomed back to focus on a head a man's head the head lay on a stain a broad red stain and there was a red stripe coming out of one ear and running down along the cheek as far as the white collar of the shirt

the camera zoomed back again to show the body of the *carabiniere* shot down beside the yellow column of a petrol pump beside the body you could see a pistol I don't know whether it belonged to him or the person who'd killed him I turned up the volume on the television which was down low the newsreader was saying someone had waited for the *carabiniere* outside his house and killed him with two shots in the head from a nine calibre no one had claimed responsibility yet then there was a review of casualties in the security forces since the beginning of the year pictures of *carabinieri* and policemen killed in the street or through the windows of cars a long list of names and dates

the images of the casualties were intercut with other images there was commentary on mug-shots of fugitives scenes of terrorists being arrested of gun battles with terrorists of killings of terrorists scenes of terrorists on trial lined up in the cages with fists in the air and threatening faces the tone of the commentary was like a war dispatch China who had by now lit the joint passed it to me and took the remote control and cut out the sound now you can see two *carabinieri* in full dress uniform stiff young men carrying a vast wreath of flowers with a big purple ribbon across it with The Government in big gold lettering on it then China changed channels she started changing backwards and forwards from one channel to another at that time I had just stopped working in the dye factory and China and I didn't have a permanent place to live any more we were moving around here and there for a bit with comrades who could let us stay with them we weren't the only ones for sure to live like that not at all at that time we were all more or less compelled to be nomads because of the oppressive atmosphere at the time there were strings of arrests and house searches nearly every day and carried out quite at random on just anybody in the movement on anyone who in some sense was a comrade or had dealings with comrades so it was usual not to stay too long in one place

we tried to spend the nights at the houses of comrades who considered themselves less known less exposed or better still staying with friends who weren't involved at all or staying with friends of friends the demonstrations and festivals in the square were a thing of the past the movement was like a great ghost absent withdrawn sheltering in its ghettoes the stage was now held by the trickle of clandestine armed actions where responsibility was claimed by dozens of signatures of combat organizations in competition the life of the movement was over but for the comrades it wasn't over it wasn't as if they could stand on the sidelines saying let's wait and see because the repression involved everyone there weren't too many distinctions made

and so we were there that evening me and China on that unfamiliar bed strewn with newspapers magazines clothes smoking a joint and watching television which we usually never watched and outside you could hear the police sirens going by nobody went about any more at night even at our centre we would see one another only by day and when we were out we were careful meeting comrades and then there was the business of Scilla and his friends that worried us we were worried about them and worried about how it might reflect on us I remember that we talked about it that evening too while China switched backwards and forwards from channel to channel with the remote control

before that Scilla was the typical steward who in fights with the fascists stood out as a very firm character very violent very aggressive Scilla had always been at the centre of all the fights he'd even fought the fascists alone and this is how he'd gradually turned himself into a myth because there in that small town the fascist presence had been sizeable and there too like anywhere else they didn't let people go about the town centre dressed in a way that marked them out as left-wing carrying a left-wing newspaper so the fascists provoked and attacked people who could be recognized as left-wing or just suspected of being left-wing

later the movement managed to win the upper hand thanks to guys like Scilla but at that time it was the fascists who ruled the roost and the police and judiciary shielded the fascists and through this Scilla and his kind let's say the military branch of the movement built their status by virtue of a necessity acknowledged by all of the left the physical challenge to fascism was recognized as a legitimate necessary function and on this role of antifascist militant Scilla was able to build the status that in days to come placed him above suspicion when he began to play the role of police informer

Scilla always displayed an attitude of physical competitiveness towards everything and everyone even with comrades also because he probably felt unable to compete in other areas so that he was always aggressive sometimes pretending it was just in fun but it wasn't much fun unpleasant yes that's it unpleasant and with those he couldn't draw into this physical competition his demeanour was a rather slimy and forced kind of awe in short he reproduced within the movement the same levels of violence expressed towards the enemy he always felt at war with everything and everybody and in everyone he saw an enemy on whom to take out his violence and he'd hit a comrade in the very same way he'd hit a fascist

and so inside the movement even Scilla's kind had their uses he was an internal policeman he carried out a function that was maybe unpleasant but considered useful Scilla and his kind never took part in the internal debates of the movement in the meetings and mass meetings they were largely silent interested only in where the violence came in they experienced the stage of intensified conflict in merely mechanical and purely military terms of escalating the conflict and using violence against the State as earlier it had been used against the fascists they were always outside the struggles in the local factories and little by little began to mimic clandestine ideals and behaviour the habit of hiding a gun in the cellar and so on

later when things got as far as that meeting that conclusively split up our group and which I'll talk about later after that meeting we heard nothing more about him and those who took the same road we never saw them again we heard nothing more about him Valeriana Cotogno and Gelso except in the leaflets claiming the armed actions that they carried out they carried out a series of armed actions before this *carabiniere* but I only discovered this once I was inside they didn't do killings they did robberies a few woundings until this *carabiniere* but then when I saw it on television that evening with China we didn't think for a second that it could have been them

China presses the remote switch again this time the screen shows a boundless plain the lens zooms in it must be filmed from a helicopter and you can see an ostrich running very fast on a flat barren plain it's running fast in a straight line its head still the body rhythmically trembling the legs are so fast you can't see them sometimes it turns its head and runs even faster a long low shadow comes fast behind it it's catching up the ostrich turns its head the shadow is a few yards away the ostrich is running in zigzags now it gains a few yards but in seconds the shadow's again very close the ostrich runs towards the void with all its strength the shadow rises into the air and in one bound the cheetah's upon it they form a single still shadow the helicopter turns there's just the grey sky and the noise of the blades

5

It happened right after Christmas on Christmas Eve I'd had a telegram from China to tell me she was coming to see me on Monday for a visit this telegram had arrived in the middle of a discussion I was in the dormitory cell with four other comrades discussing how to share the tasks of cooking the Christmas dinner I was making the risotto I was making yellow risotto and I was making the stock with a stock cube on the camping-gas stove a guard called me I turned and saw the little yellow square against the bars I thought it was the lawyer about the trial which was getting close now but then when I saw it was from China I thought I didn't think anything I think I was very pleased because it had been a surprise and I thought that China had given me this surprise of a Christmas visit and I was very pleased

it's funny I thought because all the Christmasses we'd spent together I don't think we ever once celebrated one but now there I was preparing Christmas dinner I thought about China's hair her long hair that when she laughs she throws forward covering her whole face with her long long black hair that when we talked with the glass between us I couldn't even touch but luckily here there was no glass separating visitors now but then I remember how awful it was that we couldn't even hold hands for a moment and this depressed us a lot even though we were happy to see each other but not in that inhuman humiliating depressing way and sometimes I'd get into a furious rage before the visit knowing I'd see her there behind the glass and that we'd have to talk through the glass without being able to touch not even a finger

again I was overcome by that feeling of hatred I'd had other times before the blood rose to my head a violent desire to kill the guards any of them right there and then with my bare hands if I dwell on it it's as if I can still feel it now even after all this time well I wasn't expecting that visit because China had come just the week before it had been a lovely visit we'd talked about so many things made plans because I believed I'd get out soon right after the trial and so I was touched now thinking about that unbelievable journey that she had to make for me every time a thousand kilometres to come and see me and every time another thousand kilometres it was unbelievable but after all that visit wasn't to take place in the end because of all the havoc that was to come

Monday came no it was Sunday it was afternoon exercise time in the morning there'd been a search but oddly unlike the other routine searches this search had been a bit tougher than the rest and the guards had also done a strange thing they'd left because there the symbolic runs right through these things through the searches and such things it's a matter of giving reciprocal signs and so the sign they'd left this time strange to interpret strange for me that is without any inkling of what was going on while the guards probably did have and no mistake because they had a nose for the mood of the moment there was this sign we found it there on the table when we got back up to the cells after the morning exercise they'd left on all the tables in all the cells in all the dormitories they'd left all the objects everything in the form of a box a receptacle a tin a bottle in other words all the containers they'd put them there on the tables from boxes containing detergent to ones containing coffee or sugar to bottles of oil and shampoo all the boxes all the containers the bottles they'd left them there on the tables as if they were hinting at something or other I realized what it was only later to begin with I didn't pay much attention the fact of finding all these things lined up there on the table surprised me and then later when I went for the afternoon exercise it also surprised me to find out that the same thing had been done in all the other cells too

so I remember that the atmosphere of that afternoon exercise was particularly tense there was an atmosphere you could cut with a knife and what I thought in the light of earlier situations I'd been in and experiences I'd had I thought somebody was going to get done in because there was a lot of tension and you could see it in the air you could feel it in so many things in a strange silence that was different from usual and especially from the looks quick rapid looks that passed suddenly between some people as they were walking up and down and then the thing that I surmised and that must have been on their minds a stabbing or at any rate the settling of some score or other and I was expecting it to happen any minute something like what I'd seen other times before like once shortly after they arrested me and it really upset me at the time

that time it happened as we were exercising outside as usual when three or four non-politicals because we exercised along with the non-political prisoners these non-politicals went up close behind another non-political they went up close to somebody exercising there like them and from behind they put a noose round his neck a knotted steel wire they put this noose around his neck from behind and two of them took his arms they held his arms tight to keep him from moving and they pulled the noose it's this system that's used to immobilize someone during a stabbing for it isn't as easy as it seems to stab someone so that the blade can get deep enough into a vital organ but it can happen that the person survives even after twenty or thirty stab wounds

it's not easy to stab somebody it's not as easy as it might seem I mean it's easy to stab him but it isn't easy to kill him because besides he isn't just going to take the stabbing without putting up a struggle he struggles he wriggles he goes wild he thrashes all over the place it's very difficult to hold him still I mean and one of the techniques is precisely to put a noose around his neck first to pull it until he half loses consciousness because he's nearly choking and in the meantime you stab him with the knife pushed up from below because wounds angled down are less effective you have to push the knife up from lower down and most important you have to try to aim for a vital organ maybe just under the sternum here

and so they put this noose around his neck and the others held his arms and the one behind him started pulling the steel wire noose but the steel wire noose broke or it's more likely that the knot was badly tied anyway it snapped or it worked loose or I don't know anyway they didn't succeed in pulling it tight round his neck of course he was terrified because he knew at once what they had in mind trying to get a steel wire round his neck but as for them after a moment's awkwardness they treated it all like a joke all the more because they hadn't brought out the knives yet the knives hadn't appeared yet

so they were making a joke of it they were slapping him on the back saying so we gave you a fright as if it was all a joke but he didn't believe it was any joke he didn't fall for it at all because besides you don't play jokes like this in a prison if someone plays a joke like that on you then you're the one that murders him because these are no jokes then the guy went over to the exercise yard gates and he started to yell to call the guards to let him out and that was when the ones who were after him realized that either they went for him right then or the guards would arrive and it would all become trickier and if he managed to get out in time they'd never get him because then he'd obviously be transferred or shoved into the isolation cells anyway he wouldn't be showing his face there again that's for sure

then just as the guards were running to see what he was yelling about four or five of them jumped on him with knives with blades skewers and they started stabbing him all in a muddle and obviously he put up a fight he didn't just stand there and let himself be stabbed he was kicking trying to shield himself to wriggle free and he took quite a few stab wounds before he fell to the ground and all the while screaming and the guards were rushing about the exercise corridor they could see what was happening but they didn't come into the yard there was a sergeant yelling from behind the gates cut it out cut it out the whole scene lasted a few seconds the others were at the far end of the wall we were all there all at the far end watching without a move the whole scene lasted a few seconds

he was screaming and screaming like a lunatic then he was thrown down on the ground not just thrown he fell on his knees and just then he was stabbed two or three times with a skewer down on his head just like that with the skewer down on his head and just as he turned his head a skewer another stab with the skewer caught him right in the eye a skewer caught him right in the eye a skewer stabbing right into his eye and he was really screaming in an unbelievable way then he fell down on the ground then when he fell down on the ground they kept on stabbing him trying to get him in the heart because they kept on stabbing him in the chest but they were stabbing him in the neck too they were trying to tear his neck open

the blood he was on the ground with the blood gushing out of him from every one of the holes from all the wounds from all the cuts he had from his head from this eye with blood coming out of him all over the place it was a lake of blood it was a pool of blood that must have been ten feet wide really and he wasn't moving any more with that eye that was a red stain with one eye half out and the other gaping and he seemed dead and he wasn't moving any more he seemed dead he wasn't moving even a finger then they stopped and went back to where everyone else was at the far end of the wall of the yard and the guards opened the gate a little because the guy also happened to be only a few feet away from the gate they took him by the feet and they dragged him out

6

But meanwhile time was going by out there and nothing was happening and when the time came to go up because we were exercising in the volleyball court but no one was playing volley-ball they were all walking up and down exchanging those rapid glances and now and then a few muttered words and time was going by and nothing was happening I was expecting somebody to be stabbed but nothing happened and even when the time came for the guards to take people back to the cells people started going back up with no fuss just as usual and so everybody went back up and I went back up lagging behind talking to another comrade and I didn't have the faintest idea that at that very moment a fuck-up like that was happening

I got back to my cell and it was just a few minutes after I got back to my cell when I heard shouts coming from the direction of the rotunda I should explain what the rotunda is the special section of the prison we were in was a small three-storey block ground floor first floor and second floor and each floor was split into two wings at the centre of these wings on every floor there were two gates and in between the two gates there was a space that was the rotunda the same rotunda where the stairs were and from there people dispersed into one wing or the other the right wing one side and the left wing the other side I was in the left wing of the top floor the second floor that is

on the first floor there were all the non-politicals and on the ground floor there were the so-called working prisoners the ones that carry out food distribution duties in the corridors and do the cleaning in the corridors and so on the top floor on the other hand held all the politicals there were sixty of us politicals and incidentally it's worth mentioning that shortly before this there had arrived the overwhelming majority of prisoners both politicals and non-politicals who'd staged a very tough revolt in another special prison and who'd then been transferred it had been a very tough revolt there had been two dead two prisoners with a reputation as bastards had been killed and just about the whole prison had been wrecked and so now in ours the politicals' floor was full there was no room at all to spare there were sixty of us and it was full up

I was at that time in a cell with four other comrades and I heard shouting coming from the rotunda very agitated shouting and I saw the guards who patrolled the corridor of our wing at first I saw them running towards the rotunda at the far end of the wing and everybody in the cells came to look through the bars separating them from the corridors and a moment later the guards came back at a run shouting and they started closing the armoured doors because the cells have a barred gate and in front of it they also have an armoured door and precisely because of the protests there'd been in that prison we'd won the right to keep the armoured doors open all day and have them closed only between eleven at night and seven in the morning

so this was in the afternoon the armoured doors were open and so the guards reacted that way as soon as they realized what was happening was that the guards in the rotunda were being seized by two comrades because at that time we came up the stairs in pairs which was later stopped so when those two comrades got up to the rotunda they brought out the knives they had on them and they seized the guards they seized them and threatened to kill them they got them to open no since the guards had the keys of the gates on them they removed them and themselves opened the two gates that led to the two wings the left wing on one side and the right wing on the other

and so the guards who happened to be in the two wings found the way closed off they found themselves closed in a trap because at one end of the corridor there was the gate to the rotunda with the comrades who had captured the guards and at the other end of the corridor were the big windows at the far end of the corridor and so there the guards were left with no way out they were scared stiff too because they had no idea how things would go so the thing they did instinctively because it's probably what's laid down in their rule-book is that in these cases they have to close the armoured doors and so all that occurred to them to do and all they did was to try and close the doors

and so they managed to get some doors closed no just one door they didn't get any others closed because in their confusion in their fear they didn't manage in time to get any others closed they didn't manage to close them because the comrades who were in the cells immediately stuck brooms broom handles through the bars past the door between the bars and the door stopping the doors from closing you have to picture all this happening in a split second so they really only managed to close just one door there were others they tried to close or forgot about or didn't make it in time to close the fact is that all the guards surrendered at once they all surrendered in wholesale terror

but in the meantime while those two comrades were taking the guards in the rotunda they were taking three or four guards I don't know how many in the meantime it turned out that in the right wing I was in the left in a dormitory cell in the right wing the comrades had sawed through the bars there were eight comrades in that dormitory because then you could leave your cell for the midday meal to cook and eat together this was another thing we'd won with the protests there'd been in the months before in that prison and you could get together in a dormitory cell to eat along with other comrades and so at that time up to eight of us could be together in a dormitory

they'd sawed through the bars of the gate and by the time those two comrades seized the two guards in the rotunda they'd already sawed through them and were waiting for that moment they removed the bars of the dormitory cell and the eight of them went out then there were really ten prisoners who were out the eight from the dormitory and the two in the rotunda and that's how they also got all the guards who were in the second floor corridor obviously I found all this out later because I was locked in my cell I was in the left wing and I saw nothing we just heard loud shouting we heard shouting and we just heard all this uproar the guards trying to close the armoured doors running up and down the shouting but it was all no more than a moment

what happened and what then became known later or at least in part because these stories can't always be told in full was that very quickly the comrades who'd taken the guards came down with the keys they'd taken from the guards they opened the gate leading to the stairs and they went down to the first floor and they seized all the guards down there and in that way they opened the two wings of the first floor and then they began unlocking the cells of the non-politicals and so all the non-politicals came pouring out of the cells and then they too came up to the second floor and started unlocking all our cells as well

they didn't go down to the ground floor because it couldn't be defended like the upper floors and the working prisoners stayed there for the whole duration of the revolt cooped up in their wing between the two floors in revolt and the guards that were outside at this point I saw people wearing masks arriving in my wing they got to my cell and they unlocked every cell in the left wing they unlocked my cell too and then there was enormous confusion and some people told us there's a revolt we've taken the guards we must keep calm put mattresses over the windows because they're likely to fire teargas rockets into the cells and then everyone put mattresses over the windows and then we all poured out into the corridor

just at the same time as I went out of my cell into the corridor I heard a tremendous rumble an incredible bang what had happened was that a comrade who'd stayed on the first floor to keep watch had seen guards reaching the ground floor and trying to come up guards already turned out in full force so he'd thrown a few grams of plastic explosive but loose I mean not packed in a canister but just with the detonator and the fuse he threw this plastic purely to frighten them away in fact I don't even think anyone was injured I'm not certain only in that enclosed space it made a terrific bang then the guards all ran away and from that moment the revolt was under way

7

I remember that when I was transferred to that special prison I was a bit scared just that name special prison scared me and the evening before I left I was up all night talking with my cell mates they realized I was frightened and they stayed awake all night with me to keep me company then there was the whole transfer trip which was very long the whole length of Italy chained up in that armoured van but I'd no sooner arrived at the special when that fear more or less went when I got there I was pretty astounded by the way that prison worked I hadn't had any idea it was like that now that I'm describing it I realize that in fact the atmosphere there was tense to say the least there was enormous tension but on my arrival it looked to me like a big fair

that name special prison I thought when I first got there they could label it as that but it was really a fair and the cells were bazaars you could more or less have anything in your cell all the cells were overflowing with things of every kind you could play musical instruments there were guitars and tamborines bongo drums accordions there was even somebody who had a violin and he played it whenever he wanted you could have every kind and colour of paint you wanted you could have canvases oils tempera pastel crayons charcoal typewriters you could have the books you wanted all the magazines and newspapers you wanted you could have tape-recorders and cassettes football boots and tennis shoes there was no limit to the amount of clothes you could keep in your cell all the shoes all the sweaters all the hats you could keep everything you wanted there in the cells

the association time there as they called it was quite unbelievable considering it was a special there were four hours two in the morning and two in the afternoon there were four exercise hours a day and on top there were two hours twice a week when we could all meet in a big room together and what's more at the time for the midday meal there was the opportunity for the comrades who were in the single cells to go and eat with the comrades who were in the dormitories which meant association time was this you got up at nine you went for exercise at eleven you went back up and it meant an incredible lot of work for the guards at eleven you went back up from exercise and then they had to organize all the shifting around to escort all the people who were moving to go and eat in other cells

all you had to do was apply to go to another cell you did it on the spot on a slip of paper and that was enough they really should have carried out searches but you can't start moving sixty people in less than half an hour and search them as well and so everybody moved around with no fuss from one cell to another to go and eat it wasn't a case of applying a day ahead you did it there on the spot it was a formality for sure they couldn't keep track of the applications they could maybe do it later on and it helped them most of all to figure out how things fitted to work out from the people who spent time together what the political links were between the comrades the groupings the different political tendencies

the guards were really duty-bound to search you when you left your cell in the morning for exercise and they were duty-bound to search you again when you went back up to your cell and to search you again once more when you left your cell to go and eat in another cell but all this had become impossible they'd stopped doing it and so they'd stopped checking altogether there was this constant movement there was this constant cell locking and unlocking there was this huge mass of objects piled up in the cells and when this is the situation when there are all these areas that you take for yourself that you win for yourself then the situation becomes ungovernable what struck me there was the enormous scope there was inside the prison it was a special prison but you could move around there just as you wanted nor were the cell searches properly seen to the more stuff there is in a cell the harder it is to search it all well the difference from the normal prison that I'd just come from was that here they did one search a week where there they did one a month but here the way things were with the guards meant that if a ballpoint pen went missing during a search there was an outbreak of hammering on the bars in every cell so that right away this guy would come back with the pen and apologize and here the way things were with the guards meant that they put up with the worst insults and the worst threats and if you called a guard at midnight to get him to take cigarettes or a newspaper or wine or a plate of pasta to someone in another cell even if it wasn't his job he'd do it right away all the same and in double-quick time this was the way things were with the guards

if one day during a search you told him no don't you lay a hand on me he'd even stop searching you and if while they were searching the cells they found knives they didn't even say a word they didn't even give you a hard time about it any more they'd got used to finding knives in the cells they confiscated them and that was all that was the atmosphere there was there before the revolt there were visits without glass screens the rules said they were to be an hour but they were always two hours to the minute and sometimes even longer if you pushed it and you could have four visits a month plus a special visit that you could have on top and if you didn't have a visit you could make a ten-minute phone call instead

the non-politicals in the specials aren't the non-politicals of the normal prisons they're people who in prison have tried at least once to escape they're all people from the world of big-time crime or important gangs and there you could associate with the non-politicals too you could exercise with them and go and eat with them too all you had to do was apply to go and see them so this amounted to a situation of progressive extension of areas inside the prison there was a state of permanent protest that had its effects on the regulatory structure because the prison is this it's a structure that elaborates the regulation of the body to the maximum and so the fact that this regulation is rearranged corresponds to a shift in the balance of power between prisoners and custody

I soon became aware of the strained and tense atmosphere arising from this situation and underlying the fairground appearance that had been my first impression there'd been a whole series of protests there were protests to stop the guards doing searches every time cells were left for exercise or demands about going to eat in another cell or demands about visits or meetings with lawyers and so on when you mount a protest and for instance when you refuse to be searched there are two outcomes either the administration gives way and as a result you wind up in a much stronger position and that's that or else the administration reacts and then the struggle goes on and the tension rises until there's a confrontation

so there were constant disruptions at exercise people would refuse to go back to the cells and there'd be concerted hammering on the bars of the cell gates and things like that there's always a ceiling when a protest begins if the administration doesn't give in right away you trigger the mechanism of mounting conflict but then there's a ceiling and this ceiling measures the balance of power for example if the prisoners are in the position of power to threaten to take guards hostage then of course the administration yields first because it knows that the prisoners can go as far as taking hostages and the administration usually always yielded there because it was afraid of this that the prisoners would take guards hostage of course you couldn't ask the impossible you couldn't ask them to unlock the cells for you and let you go home but you could push all the time to extend social spaces and the protests succeeded because they were solid everybody joined in right away without even thinking about it by now the guards no longer took any responsibility the guards reacted on every occasion by passing on decisions to their superior who in turn dumped them on his superior and so on up to the prison governor and he'd take it to the minister which meant whatever you did inside the prison you were never confronting the guards but the strength of your position was such that you ended up dealing directly with the minister with every protest you made and since by now what was at stake was by now always the trigger for a sequence of events leading to taking guards hostage perhaps proceeding merely from the fact that you wanted a blue felt tip pen it was their policy to give way over everything

also because the minister's strategy centred as always on the distinction making that special prison a cooling-down prison let's say at the positive end of the special spectrum while at the other end was a maximum security prison the prison regime is entirely based on this strategy of differentiation with its potential to blackmail you with the threat of a worsening of your conditions with its potential to warn you if you protest watch out or I'll send you to a prison worse than the one you're in now and so the comrades' argument was just because we're well off here it doesn't mean we don't have to make demands but we have to make demands just the same here as well so as to break this blackmail situation that threatens us all with ending up in a prison where we're worse off

8

The first time I met China was during the Cantinone occupation that's where I first saw her China had come round there I'm not sure when and she was helping Gelso with the mural that Gelso had decided to do on the biggest wall she had a big brush and she was dipping it in a bucket of white paint but she was dipping it in too much and the paint was spattering all over the place and it was running down on to the floor I saw what a mess it was and I went over to show her how it should be done but also because I thought she was very pretty and I remember that there's where she gave me that scarf it was that time when I first met her because when I went up to her of course I got a good splash here on my front and she made up for it then by putting her red scarf round my neck it was a really long scarf ankle-length and she told me keep it I'm giving it to you it'll hide the stain

to see how little need there was you only had to look at how I dressed in those days the battle-dress shirt with baggy sweater threadbare at the elbows riddled with holes and with loose unravelled ends the jeans frayed at the hem with a safety pin in place of the zip broken months ago one shoe split at the seams that let the water in when it rained the other had no lace but it held with a permanent knot odd socks one black and one grey and most of all the off-white raincoat that's my second skin all scruffy and dirty so many buttons missing that I always leave it open a tear under the armpit holes in the pockets but stuff always ending up in the lining newspapers leaflets felt-tip pens always the same old rags until they fall apart because it's part of the gamble because we're staking everything and how do you think about clothes when you're betting everything you've got

the morning we occupied the Cantinone we'd got there very early we'd got there very early in the morning it was Saturday morning and the night before while Valeriana and Nocciola were keeping an eye on both ends of the street Cotogno Ortica and I used a hand drill to drill through the big padlock from underneath where the lock is we sprang the chambers and the padlock fell open so that by the following morning it would be all ready and we'd only need to undo the chain then all along the ditch on the other side of the road we placed plastic bags hidden in the brushwood with stones ballbearings and cata-pults in them not too much because inside the Cantinone there was all kinds of stuff we could use to defend ourselves in case of immediate attack

in the morning at seven prompt as can be we five met at the station and with Ortica's car we drove round the streets where the groups of comrades who were to do the break-in were to be ready and waiting they were all there as planned all armed to the teeth like for demonstrations where you know trouble might flare up scarves gloves berets and everything we undid the chain and we went inside and right behind us came groups of comrades we made a quick inspection inside it was still nearly pitch dark there was no electricity shining a torch inside we saw piles of timber of every size piles of planks and beams it was so big an area the torchlight couldn't reach the far wall but we thought it was lovely

the Cantinone was one wing of an old castle belonging to the Curia the other bits of the castle were occupied by a nursery school run by nuns and an old people's home also run by nuns the wing we were interested in was used at the time by a construction firm to store materials it was a big rectangular building on the ground floor was a single vast hall that was now full of beams and timber on the upper floor there were rooms on the ground floor two rows of columns ran its whole length supporting two high crossed vaults in the centre there was a big main door between two rows of big windows running right along the facade protected by grilles but with no glass and no frames

since everything had gone according to plan one comrade
went out to go and give the signal to another group waiting
outside that went off to put up posters and hand out the leaflets
we'd done to announce the occupation while we inside started
forming a chain to clear the Cantinone of the building lumber
we carried out everything through the door leading to the yard
and we heaped it up there outside the nuns and the old people
from the home started looking out of the windows more and
more of them they were looking at us in amazement and disbe-
lief perhaps at first they thought we were building workers but
they must have doubted it for they saw that there were girls at
work there too

nearly an hour goes by then those on guard outside sound the
alarm that they're on their way and we all rush out into the
street the *carabinieri* are driving up in their two minibuses in no
hurry at all and once they pull up opposite the door they stop
and get out there would have been ten or so in no hurry and
empty-handed the *maresciallo* comes towards us he looks
puzzled and Valeriana takes a few steps towards him and tells
him it's an occupation and she gives him the leaflet and tells
him it's all explained here the *maresciallo* glances at it quickly
but then he says he wants to come in and see and he points to
the door and makes a move in that direction but at once all the
comrades who'd gone outside spontaneously form a tight
human barrier we form a wall between him and the main door
of the Cantinone

the *maresciallo* looks at us in astonishment more than anything else
then he says but you know what you're doing is illegal Cotogno
answers yes but there's a lot of us doing it and we're not the only
ones occupying round here the *maresciallo* shakes his head and asks
and who's in charge here and we answer all of us all of us are in
charge here rather abashed the *maresciallo* waves his men away but
we don't budge we stay there waiting for them to leave in earnest

they all get back on their minibuses they go into reverse and pull away slowly but when they get to the junction one of the two minibuses stays there while the other vanishes then we go back inside and Scilla gets busy setting up a defence team it's sickening what we need is petrol bombs because those guys can come back any moment now and there'd be a slaughter

all this time new people were starting to turn up they came in groups the students who knew all about it already and then the first ones to come out of curiosity workers and unemployed people came who'd seen our posters and the leaflets word had got round and people turned up came in and hung about the place taking a good look round we were explaining why we'd occupied what we wanted to do now and people were talking asking questions more and more people were turning up people I'd never seen before there were children running about the hall and going into the rooms upstairs it was total chaos everywhere then standing to one side we notice three well-dressed guys we hadn't seen coming in grim-faced looking around anxiously and keeping their voices down the word gets round at once the mayor's here

the three come towards us the mayor in the lead a big tall heavy man with a long camel coat nearly down to his ankles and when the mayor opens his mouth the deafening racket stops only the children go on running about the room he comes straight out and asks abruptly who's in charge here you know what you're doing is illegal immediately we all burst out laughing they look around at a loss to understand then the vice-mayor a thin old man with a red face who's also the party secretary lays into us you're provocateurs you've done this tomfoolery to undermine the new left administration this is a provocation there's a whole crowd of people who're not from round here who've come from outside it's a deliberate provocation I've been in politics for forty years and I know provocateurs when I see them but the mayor takes over again listen kids we've come here to tell you that charges have already been filed against you and legal proceedings are already under way to have you forcibly evicted we promise you we'll withdraw the charge but you must clear out right now and put everything back just as it was and we guarantee that there won't be any legal consequences everybody's jeering and Nocciola steps forward turning to the three of them look there's no question of us leaving here not for a minute the only thing we want here is to go on with this occupation and to achieve what we set out to do which is something you aren't even bothering to find out I don't know if you've got the point the mayor makes a gesture of annoyance he turns round and leaves followed by his retinue

then I don't remember what else happened in the afternoon we also had a visit from the extra-parliamentarians who'd just founded their own party and so had stopped wearing their jeans and anoraks they turned up with the party newspaper sticking out of the pockets of their grey lodens they came up to Cotogno and me their leader got straight to the point what you need to do right away is call a mass meeting to discuss what's to be done this spontaneous movement has to have political leadership first of all we'll have a closed meeting between us and the occupation leaders to decide on the programme we'll get the mass meeting to approve and so on finally they left none too happy but their leader threatened us all mass struggles are doomed if there's no vanguard to lead them you've got no political line and you're dragging the masses to defeat and blablabla and blablabla

9

Well right at the start of the revolt there was pandemonium in the sense that the first word going round was that there are nineteen guards taken hostage and this provoked outright amazement there was incredulity fear and amazement but then at once the general mood rapidly became a mood of great excitement probably because what everyone felt most of all at that moment was the fact of being in control of this space the fact of freedom of movement all over this space and just the simple fact of free movement in a space bigger than the cell you were confined to released this whole general excitement

then what happened was that those prisoners who'd planned the whole thing who'd organized it immediately set in motion all the organizational functions of the revolt these comrades assigned themselves roles precise tasks which involved guarding and surveying the most likely points where a break-in could be made from outside because the guards could always try a break-in even if the hostages we were holding meant it wasn't so simple and then somebody had to attend to guarding the hostages and all this took place in great haste the whole organizational machine was quickly set in motion despite the great amount of confusion because obviously it had all been decided in advance and these roles had all been assigned well ahead

there were comrades with a weapon made from those coffee-makers they were moka coffee-makers later on in fact they were banned from being used in cells the fuse came out of the coffee-maker there was the detonator and inside was the explosive and these coffee-makers functioned as grenades the explosive had been hidden in the cells and it was this the guards were looking for when they'd carried out that peculiar search they'd searched in all the boxes and bottles because that's where people hide explosives they hadn't found any but they'd left them all on the tables to make it clear that they knew there were explosives in the prison that they'd got wind that something was going to happen

the guards were all put in a dormitory cell and there began the whole ritual of the search and so on the guards weren't molested nobody harmed them only some comrades began to mimic though without any malice very ironically it looked like the kind of thing the indians* did in '77 they started mimicking the whole ritual of the guard towards the prisoner and then they were all searched like that exactly the way they searched the prisoners every day they were made to stand there with their legs slightly apart their arms raised and then they were searched in the routine way as they did to us day in day out whenever we went out and whenever we returned to our cells

first the head was searched fingers through the hair under the hair then down the back of the head on the neck down on to the shoulders and under the armpits and then going right down the back under the bum the legs the backs of the legs and down the legs to the feet and then back up again up the legs the thighs the inner thighs the stomach and then all the way up the trunk back to the neck and then making them undo their trousers pull down the zip feeling the waistband feeling the balls and then making them take off their shoes hand them over and turn them upside down to look inside them all this with the guards there waiting one after the other like our routine with arms raised legs slightly apart

but what we all confirmed after these searches carried out on all the guards was that among the nineteen guards taken hostage

---

* The 'metropolitan indians': a term used to describe groups of young people who staged a form of anarcho-theatre through disruptive public happenings, mainly in Bologna and Rome during the period of violent demonstrations in the spring of 1977.

there wasn't even one non-commissioned officer just some poor wretch of a lance-corporal who obviously just happened to be there and this fact that there wasn't even one non-commissioned officer there made us all think that the non-commissioned officers had got wind of something going on they had a good idea what was going to happen because it had never ever come about that there wasn't at least one non-commissioned officer on the floor there wasn't a single non-commissioned officer not even a sergeant and just by a complete coincidence on the whole floor no on both floors the first and second floor in every wing there wasn't a single sergeant

then later they made them take off their uniforms too they stripped them and they brought them clothes the prisoners wore and they made them put on these clothes because they were hostages and so if they were wearing their uniforms if there was a break-in they would immediately be identifiable by whoever was breaking in police *carabinieri* or guards themselves to free them so that they could carry out on-the-spot reprisals against the prisoners without running the risk of endangering the lives of their guards if instead they were dressed like the prisoners it would all be more difficult

but there was no violence directed at the guards everyone I remember was concerned about this and they kept on saying that in any case nothing should be done to the guards because that was our insurance that things would turn out all right the hostage guards were all put in a big cell and watched from outside they were always well treated they even ate the same as us what we ate during the revolt was spaghetti which there was plenty of in the cells there were comrades who cooked spaghetti for all the rest of us and they came to take orders three *alla matriciana* four *alla carbonara* five with tomato sauce everywhere spaghetti was being cooked on the camping-gas rings and the hostage guards got their spaghetti too and the rest of the prisoners the ones that weren't involved in starting the revolt right away they got themselves organized too to deal with taking on the guards in the likely event of an attack so a whole machinery was set in motion with everyone very involved basically people started arming themselves they started pulling down the window frames to make blades bars and things like that out of them they started making skewers by sharpening the points of the metal fittings of the camping-gas rings they started breaking off table-legs to make clubs and things like that then the armoured doors were pulled off their hinges and placed against the big windows at the end of the corridors because from outside they could fire in at us and so on

in the process of taking over the entire prison people had also got hold of some tools and machinery too for instance they'd taken an electric grindstone and used it to cut through the iron slats of the beds and so with those slats blades could be made they could be made in quantity and there was also an electric welding machine that was used to weld the gates of the rotunda and so block the possibility of a break-in from below and also a break-in from above because from the second floor there was a spiral stair leading up to the roof and then we were also able to make use of the guard-post telephone on the second floor and on this telephone we communicated with the prison administration and this was the medium of communication for negotiations

and then there was the television because another peculiar thing was that when there's a revolt they usually cut off all the electricity and this time instead they hadn't cut off the electricity and they'd left the television working as if to let us stay in touch with the news from outside they could easily have pulled the plug on the lot but instead they left the electricity on they left the telephone working they left the television working and on the television we got news about the negotiations all the televisions in the cells were on all the time with the sound turned right up especially when the news was on and the news of the revolt was always the lead item

inside the cells weren't damaged in any way everything was turned into a huge bivouac in the sense that all people did was go up and down the whole length of the corridors which would be about fifty or sixty yards everyone was walking up and down the whole time some disguised with just a scarf or a handker- chief around their faces while others were unrecognizable hooded in a pillow-case with two holes for their eyes a blanket like a poncho over their shoulders and these were obviously non-politicals because the non-politicals had their own way of doing things in a revolt so that they wouldn't be recognized as you always see in photographs of a rooftop revolt they always have their faces hidden so they won't be recognized so as to avoid any bad consequences

and everywhere people did nothing but move about they all did nothing but walk up and down the corridors inside and outside the cells they truly seemed to be measuring a larger physical space a bigger space for manoeuvre that they'd won and they kept on walking they went on up and down the corri- dors in and out of the cells all of them open that lined the corridors and everyone was shifting around all the time from one cell to another to such an extent that the cells looked quite different there was a continual movement of people and things shifted around carried from one cell to another a continual movement of objects of clothes of things it had all become a great bivouac a party

the atmosphere there was euphoric there was a festive atmos- phere I can remember this great euphoria this excitement this festivity and what everyone was saying over and over again and what they were convinced of was that there could never ever be a military intervention by the guards by the *carabinieri* by the police by the forces of repression and this all because of there being nineteen guards held hostage and this made a break-in nearly impossible because it would have been very dangerous for the guards held hostage I can remember that there were no worries I can remember there was no anxiety whatsoever I can remember there was euphoria and excitement there was this mechanism triggered in everybody's head to see this situation as holding no danger and making everybody feel they were at a party

10

Things were hectically busy at the Cantinone there was somebody doing electrical work and they'd run in an electric cable attached to the outside wiring of the old people's home there was somebody doing plumbing and they'd fixed the pipes and so we had water too there were some doing building work they'd gone and got their tools and they'd started filling up the holes in the floor and fixing the tiles there were some doing carpentry and building wooden frames for the windows and then covering them with plastic sheets and at the far end of the big room with the planks and beams we'd found there we were building a big stage for the concerts and performances we wanted to put on the opening concert had already been announced with a poster and leaflets the comrades were giving out wherever they went

three or four old men from the home next door had also turned up and were recalling the days when the Cantinone had been an *osteria* and had had huge casks tables and benches running the whole length of it because that was where the peasants met to drink wine and play cards and we promised them that we'd put back the casks and the benches and the wine like there used to be then a bunch of comrades who'd gone out to advertise the concert arrive back with the cars full of stuff to eat we think they've stolen it and we get mad but instead it had been some shopkeepers who'd given us packs of drinks and pasta and then some Neapolitan guys turn up who worked in a *pizzerìa* they arrived with a pile of pizzas so there was food for everybody

at the same time the first working groups had been formed and had moved into the rooms on the first floor Valeriana and a group of women were meeting to set up a collectively run clinic others were planning a counterinformation service on soft and hard drugs others were discussing food and the counterculture others music film theatre there's a decision to get in touch with the youth circles in other towns that we've heard from to exchange news and experiences and to set up a resource centre with their newspapers and their documents and in another room on the first floor a press office was already in full-time operation with typewriters and duplicators parcels of leaflets of press releases announcements documents were piling up on the tables of the press office waiting to go out

the evening of the concert arrives and the bands arrive from the different surrounding villages the sound system is set up the lights are ready the lights cast bright-coloured stains on the whitewashed walls of the big hall and the bands begin turning up they play all at the same time and the intermingled sounds pour out into the street and fill the air people are arriving loads of people young people are arriving from all over and not so young too the street outside is transformed into a car park with all the cars jammed into it there's a sea of heads everyone sitting on the benches and on the ground tapping their feet and all this echoing out as the bright-coloured lights turn faster and faster I look about to see where China is and I see her against the wall with Gelso whose head's shaking with laughter his hair hanging right over his face when he lifts it he sees me and waves for me to go over there too

the party was at its height there was such euphoria such great excitement people coming in and out in and out indescribable confusion they all really liked the place we should stay there they said we should stay there whatever it took we'd do terrific things in the Cantinone the music was blaring out loud as can be in the thick of the crowd I meet Scilla carrying a 15-inch spanner saying there are too many phoneys here I spot one he gets his stuffing knocked out Scilla was the only glum face in the entire place they were all looking at the stage where somebody was singing I love to play pound out my music all day but I don't earn my wages that way for I play like a mule I'm a wild boy I wanna win I'm kinda rough but believe me I'm cool and I went to be with China right under the stage and I stayed right there holding her close while the music blared out loud as can be

suddenly the music stops Scilla has gone up on to the stage and over the microphone he says the cultural *assessore** is here outside with a message from the mayor and the council people roared with laughter saying bring him in here to us and we'll eat him up the cultural *assessore* is young small and nervous with a little moustache and a white raincoat and he'd been a 68'er he waits patiently until the voices quieten down to let him speak and then he says I must tell you that the situation is urgent we've just had a telephone call from the chief constable telling us that you'll be cleared out of here within twenty-four hours by order in the name of the council and the mayor I'm appealing once again to reasonableness and good sense evacuate the Cantinone

---

* The municipal or provincial council member with chief responsibility for a particular department.

and we promise you room in the new multi-purpose centre as soon as the work on it is finished

uproar and shouting come from every part of the hall then Nocciola begins speaking you're conning us first you go and say that we're provocateurs and fascists then that you want to find somewhere just for us the truth is that you're shit-scared about your council majority because if it was up to you you'd be the first to call the police but we know very well that this story of the multi-purpose centre is a fairytale you only have to look at how little you've cared about our problems in the past no no the *assessore* bravely interrupts him I want to point out that this is a slander the problems of young people are problems of great concern to us in the next budget we've allowed for considerable expenditure on youth and culture but there are timetables that have to be respected however I assure you that a satisfactory solution will be found for your problems too

you should have talked to us about it first he says in a conciliatory tone you should have trusted us and together we'd have found a satisfactory solution I think the needs underlying what you've done here are valid what isn't valid however is the way you imagine you're going to satisfy them together we must find another way but meanwhile the Cantinone needs to be cleared before any irreparable damage is done people have had enough out out everyone's shouting I'm waiting for an answer I'll only leave here when I've got your answer whether it's negative or affirmative he manages to add then from the stage Valeriana gets some silence and she says the decision is up to the floor and we must all discuss it but not while he's here and if he wants he can wait outside and we'll give him our decision later

Scilla escorts him outside and before leaving the stage he raises his arm holding up the spanner thunderous applause breaks out everyone's shouting we in the collective don't really know

what to do we confer briefly then Cotogno takes the microphone comrades we can't leave here under the threat of police
intervention if we clear out of here voluntarily now letting
ourselves be blackmailed by the mayor and the parties then
we've lost we must decide what's the best thing to do whether
to stay here and defend the occupation which means confrontation or not I think that for the time being confrontation isn't
in our interest I think it would split the movement whether we
win or lose in military terms because whatever happens we'll
lose politically and even if we win in military terms we'll be up
against an unmanageable situation

we must decide what's in our best interest for the growth and
strengthening of this movement and so the most pressing problem for us is not to preserve the Cantinone at any price the
problem is that we must preserve this strength that we've built
and that's why we must say no to the voluntary evacuation
they're suggesting but we must also say no to confrontation
maybe just at the last moment but we must decide for ourselves
autonomously when and how to evacuate if we evacuate as the
result of our own autonomous decision we keep our political
strength intact and tomorrow we'll be able to carry on the
renewed struggles of this movement for the conquest of a social
space we'll be able to carry on with other occupations and other
struggles if instead we go for confrontation here today we risk
everything I believe we lose everything

there were a lot of disgruntled faces even if the majority were in
agreement with Cotogno but in that general euphoria it was like
throwing cold water on a fire our position is agreed in the discussion and so we send word to the mayor that the mass meeting
has decided to go on with the occupation to the bitter end but
then we decide that we can't just all hang on waiting for the
break-in there must be 400 people there for us all to stay there
and then all leave together at the last moment is impossible it's

better for just a few to do it because then it's easier to leave it takes time to persuade everybody nobody wanted to leave nobody wanted to admit the party was all over but at last they went they dismantled and took away everything that didn't have to be left behind and in the end only those of us in the collective were left about sixty in all

in the big hall candles are lit and the main lights are switched off the atmosphere of earlier evenings returns with sleeping bags being unrolled and people lying down only this time no one wants to talk or sing to tell stories and make plans to roll joints and make love this evening everyone has a stick or a bar besides their sleeping bag I see Valeriana sitting against a pillar smoking her eyes fixed on the angled shadows on the cross vaults I go up to her with China and I see her eyes are glistening what's wrong Valeriana shit all this work for fuck all I liked this place we'll never find a place as nice as this maybe if we occupy some broken-down hut right out in the wilds maybe then they could let us have it but a place like this that they don't even know what to do with no way are those bastards going to let us have it

from time to time someone who's on guard comes back inside for the changeover it's bitterly cold outside it's not too warm inside either any more we put the sleeping bag down and I slip inside just as I am the floor is hard but I'm tired and it feels comfortable enough all the same China takes off her man's tweed jacket she rolls it up and puts it under my head we'll be more comfortable like that she says and she slips in too China isn't sleepy and she sings to herself I'm a wild boy hear what I say ain't nobody better groovin' tonight don't you ever stand in my way or you'll be in trouble alright eyes closed I say they're already standing in our way we'll be lucky now if we don't get into trouble but China goes on sometimes it's rough on me if I misbehave like you see but even in jail I could fight and I liked to go out on the town every night

II

After that first retaliatory sally was driven off with that charge of plastic explosive on the ground floor the guards outside the prison didn't make another move also because there was a moment when a comrade at a high window displayed a lovely bright orange ball something like two kilos of plastic and that bright orange ball up there was enough to bring down the entire prison and so they understood that that first explosion was just a warning that a lot worse could happen if they persisted and then from time to time one of the captured guards was also displayed at the big corridor windows with a knife at his throat as proof that they were alive and to tell those down below not to try anything

the captured guards had been split into small groups and every half hour they were moved into different new cells there were precise shifts a whole system of half-hourly moves had been worked out in advance so that from outside no one could ever tell which cell there were guards in so that there was no chance of trying anything to free them the ones in charge of the negotiations kept us up to date minute by minute about how things were going they said that taking part in the negotiations on the other end of the 'phone as well as the prison administration and the guards' commanding officers there were also politicians representing the ministry of justice and the government and that they seemed to be stymied by the seriousness of the situation they were taking time but they also seemed willing to negotiate

when it started getting dark shifts were set up to maintain a watch on what was happening outside to keep an eye on what was happening around the prison from the big windows with the armour-clad defences particularly the guards who were patrol-ling along the periphery walls that were only twenty or thirty yards from the prison or even closer the prison was all brightly illuminated in the yellow glare of the searchlights and from the second floor where we were you could see on the other side of the periphery wall a large number of jeeps cars armoured cars vans the cars with blue lights on their roofs going round and the jeeps with their headlights on going round the prison and in the shadows now and then confused movements groups of people in uniform shifting about here and there in the shadows around the prison lit up by the searchlights

nobody slept that night because there was massive tension over what had happened I remember there was this to-ing and fro-ing of people inside the cells the corridors a great procession of people there was an indescribable racket with the radios and televisions on all the time at top volume there were very heated discussions not everyone was in agreement there were comrades who maintained that this revolt would spell disaster for the pris-oners' movement but there was nothing they could do but accept the situation like everyone else because they were inside there was nothing for it they were inside in this situation too even if they made no bones that being in it went sorely against the grain and while the others maintained instead that it amounted to a great victory

but it turned out that while they were taking the guards hostage there was one who'd gone and got injured I mean this lance-corporal the only non-commissioned officer who was in the cell-wings who was a lance-corporal and who'd been injured stabbed with a skewer and this injured lance-corporal provoked a lot of anxieties he was kind of the flaw in the whole affair the only flaw everybody was aware that a death in those circum-stances would change everything what had happened was that as they took the guards hostage this lance-corporal tried to resist and a comrade who was involved in the kidnap stuck a skewer in his side a skewer made out of the usual metal fittings of a camping-gas stove this lance-corporal was clearly pretending to be worse than he really was well the comrades running the revolt had tried several times to release this wounded hostage two or three times they'd taken him down to the gates that were the start of the no-man's-land that was in fact the ground floor rotunda to let him go saying we'll open the gates and we'll let him out to you but nobody caught on the fact was they didn't want him they'd say no no keep him because all you want is to take the ground floor you want to open the gates to get the ground floor too this was the reason they gave nobody realized that it was a clue to what was going to happen

there were even others who suggested sawing the bars off a window and lowering down this lance-corporal in a sling because nobody wanted him there nobody wanted to run the risk of him dying there because it would have ruined the whole thing because everything up to then had really gone smoothly for instance it hadn't occurred to anybody to wreck the prison nothing had been touched nothing had been destroyed whereas in the revolt there'd been a short time before in that other special prison the prison had been completely wrecked there they'd literally demolished the lot they'd destroyed the electrics they'd destroyed the plumbing they'd pulled down the walls they'd made the prison totally inoperable

later on I went back to my cell there was no one there there was a heap of sweaters shirts trousers scattered on the bunk the little wardrobe had gone I flung the lot on the floor and I flung myself down on the bunk the television was turned on but the transmission had finished there was a blizzard of dots there was this guy playing the violin in the next cell he always played the same tune I thought of China and that I certainly wouldn't see her tomorrow with all this crazy business I must write to her tomorrow as soon as I can I must my cell-mate looked in what are you doing there what's wrong are you sick have you heard the news there's news about the negotiations and maybe we've won maybe now we'll win here

but look I told him I don't know why but I sounded annoyed but you know I really can't stand any more I really mean it that we're still stuck here with this bullshit still with this bullshit about winning or losing and it seems to me that it's always really been our big misfortune that every time we've thought the thing that mattered was basically just winning or losing when instead the things we've really done have never had anything to do with winning and losing because after all if it's just a question of winning or losing it's clear that here we've already lost everything and not just in the last five minutes but the fact is that I think and a lot like me think so too that deep down we've never had not only have we never had any notion or desire to win but not even any notion that there was anything to be won anywhere and then you know if I really think about it now to me the word winning seems exactly the same as dying

that injured lance-corporal stayed there through the whole revolt because they didn't want him they didn't want us to hand him over to them this poor wretch no way did they want us to hand him over to them we did everything we could to hand him over but they didn't want him no way at all he stayed there lying on the floor the whole night moaning pretending to be worse than he was the night went by and we were at a loss as to what to do and then in the morning came tiredness and the fear that in the long run things wouldn't work out gradually as time passed you could hear in more voices the tiredness that was starting to get to us people were very tense and everyone was saying that a solution to the problem had to be found as soon as possible

let's stop dwelling on this stuff so long as we've got this positive feeling between us so long as there's a chance of things turning out all right the thing is the prison here is still standing we haven't wrecked it the guards haven't been touched there's no real damage been done we've done something really big but there hasn't even been one casualty there's one injured with a stab wound and we have to hand him over before he dies these were the things being said this was the kind of tension then towards evening the latest news of the negotiations got around one of the comrades conducting the negotiations came out of the guard post and announced that things were going well that things were in motion for dismantling the revolt that shortly preparations would begin for the release of the kidnapped guards and that in other words we'd won

after this news there was momentary relief there was momentary relaxation there was momentary fatigue but also relaxation everyone was asking but what will they do to us now will they beat us up maybe not comparisons were made with how other revolts had ended and there were some packing their kitbags because they thought there'd be immediate transfers and at the same time the surveillance of what was going on outside had slackened nobody bothered any more to keep a watch from the big windows the comrades were assuring the guards that it was all over that soon they'd release them there was this atmosphere of relaxation and fatigue when at five in the afternoon when by now this was the prevailing mood there was a deafening noise

12

After something like two or three hours we're woken by Nocciola's voice they've seen the *carabinieri* drive up in the second bus blocking off the road and they've got out of both the buses they're all carrying machine-guns and pistols they've closed the road off at both ends I struggle out of the sleeping bag it's five o'clock it's still pitch dark China says take it easy please let's sleep a little longer I stand up I'm shivering all over with cold and when I move I ache with stiffness I get dressed quickly gently I shake China who's sleeping with her face buried in her hair and I tell her to hurry and join me downstairs because they're coming I dash downstairs putting on my torn black leather gloves and winding the red scarf twice round my neck

down in the big hall among the remains of the party the comrades are hurrying to get ready the floor is now a sea of bottles beer cans paper wrappings there's nothing left on the stage on the wall behind the stage you can now see the murals Gelso did that nobody could see last night in the dazzle of all those lights it was a tropical landscape with palms and monkeys in the trees and in the background a huge erupting volcano with red lava running down towards a kind of New York skyscraper scene we hear people running down the stairs Scilla arrives clearing the steps four at a time followed by the others who've been taking turns at watching the barracks I've been round the back he says gasping for breath there's now a line of lorries that goes on for ever they're in the barracks square but the line goes on right out to the street

then we get moving we barricade the doors we all barricade the doors we shove the benches against them we shove the stage up against them too against the big main door and we turn on all the lights in the big room then the first of us start climbing up to the attic where there's a trapdoor that gives access to the roof in the attic someone stumbles and the candle goes out pitch darkness and time is wasted finding it and lighting it again Scilla is swearing and insulting everybody fucking idiots move your tails he's like a sergeant-major drilling his platoon into shape we can hear the lorries arriving then stopping with the engines still running Nocciola gives a push to China who's in front of him and he too vanishes up through the trapdoor Scilla asks where are the petrol bombs don't worry they're already on the roof we climb up last and Cotogno closes the trapdoor and we're all on the roof

on the roof they can't see us because the street-lamps aren't lit because we threw stones to smash them I can make out the line of comrades heading across the roof voices reach us from below curt orders mingled with the noise of the engines that are still running I can see Scilla stretched belly down on the tiles crawling to the edge of the roof he supports his hands on the gutter and leans his head out I and some others reach him and we look down just then they cut out the engines they're all lined up in three rows with their shields and their helmets their visors lowered the front row with rifles with CS cartridges stuck on the end the other two rows carrying long truncheons there's a small group of non-commissioned officers and plain-clothes men talking quietly at the end of the street

the big windows shed their light on the front row motionless with the rifles and CS cartridges pointed upwards we expect them to give an order through a megaphone for us to clear out because they're sure we're all inside instead nobody goes near the building a non-commissioned officer leaves the group at the end of the street he signals and the front row lower their rifles aiming at the windows muffled shots are fired almost all simultaneously we can hear the cartridges puncturing the plastic sheeting on the windows four petrol bombs and we'll get the lot of them says Scilla we should throw them now now that they're all bunched together but Cotogno puts a hand on his shoulder they'd deserve it those bastards but we decided that the petrol bombs would only be used to stop them if we didn't all get out in time

we'd be better off getting out of here says Valeriana we can see the smoke below coming out of the windows and it rises slowly thickly we start to smell the teargas and we climb back up the roof diagonally stooping forward I cast a final glance down the police are still lined up in the same formation maybe they're waiting for us to open the door and come out we hurry on to the rooftop Ortica and someone else are carrying the heavy sackload of bottles that are knocking about as if they're going to smash we go on to the little terrace and from there we climb down into the park everything's quiet there you can't hear a sound we run across the park we get to the railings and we climb over them there across the road are the cars the others have already left we've arranged to meet at the centre

Ortica is already waiting to put the sackload of bottles in the open boot of a car we hope we don't get stopped with the bottles in the car they'll put us all away yes it's better not to take them in the car they'll put us all away if they find us with this stuff and then it would come in handy for them to heap shit on the occupation it's better if we leave them here no it's better if we empty them for if they find them here later it's the same thing yes but not here over there behind the hedge Ortica carries the sack over we take the bottles out of the sack but the stoppers are well and truly stuck and I can't get them out so we break the bottles with stones after taking off the cap with the sellotape still stuck to our fingers frozen with the cold then we throw the shards a long way away the stink of petrol fills our nostrils and clings to us even when we're in the car

we take a road through the fields everything is quiet we make a long detour and we get to the centre there are no police around inside the light's on and all the comrades are already there we decide we'll all go home and meet there again this evening but somebody has to go and see what's happening at the Cantinone we decide that a group is to go and see in a couple of hours' time four or five are all that's needed the comrades mill about in little groups talking quietly Gelso goes home to get his camera we stay there talking to keep ourselves awake for if we stop talking we'll fall asleep except China who falls asleep right away it starts getting light we get back in the car we go to the bar in the station for a cappuccino

a bit later Gelso turns up with the camera we get into the car and we get to the road junction there they are the two minibuses and the car from police headquarters the line of lorries is gone and on the corner across from the Cantinone there's no one to be seen and I tell Cotogno to drive round the block so we can stop there and take photos we drive round and we stop at the beginning of the street that runs past the Cantinone China and Valeriana stay in the back seat of the car Cotogno Gelso and I get out and go behind the car so that we aren't seen Gelso leans the camera on the roof of the car and starts taking photos in front of the main door I can see building workers laying cement over a wall of bricks across the main door they're walling up the Cantinone there are *carabinieri* there watching with their hands in their pockets

we can see the plastic sheeting on the ground floor windows ripped and scorched from the cartridges we're so absorbed that we don't notice one of the police cars has left gone round the block and comes up behind us I hear Valeriana speak she's seen them coming she says look out the car brakes with its tyres screeching two people come dashing out of the back the car stays there in the middle of the road with the engine running and the doors open the two are beside us one is gripping the butt of his pistol Gelso hasn't even time to try and hide the camera one of them wrenches it from his hand and says what are you taking photos of the other opens the car door and says you two out right now get out the policeman who was driving came over too and they ask us all for an identity check

while one policeman takes our documents over to their car another searches Valeriana's handbag while the other one keeps us at gun-point a moment later the one who's gone to the car waves me over I don't understand right away and the other one prods me with the barrel of the pistol I walk over and stop by the front window hunched up in the back seat there's a guy with a light-coloured raincoat who's turning off the radio receiver he's holding the identity cards mine on top of the others he lifts his head he looks at me through square glasses haven't you caused enough trouble in your school he says but it's not aggressive it sounds like a reprimand to a disobedient little boy I say mildly we were only taking photos I don't think there's a law against it

he says nothing then it occurs to me that this is Dottor Donnola the head of the political squad at headquarters the one who's outside the school whenever there's any commotion always there in his car some distance away talking into the transmitter one of the policemen now brings him the camera but he doesn't even touch it he nods and then the policeman opens it and pulls out the roll of film then he closes it and thrusts it at me I take the camera and keep it in my hand one by one Donnola flips through the identity cards again then he slaps them on the edge of the window and hands them to me I take them and he looks straight at me from behind his square glasses and as if he was sighing he bids me goodbye

Part Two

13

This is something I'll always remember a truly deafening noise a noise coming from high above an all-enveloping noise getting louder and louder more and more deafening we realized almost at once that it was the sound of helicopters and these helicopters were making a thunderous noise it wasn't just one helicopter there must have been lots of helicopters everybody froze for a moment everybody was very confused because they were all convinced there was no possibility of a military intervention at this point in the situation just when the negotiations had got this far and then there was the matter of the nineteen guards nobody thought they'd risk the lives of the nineteen hostage guards with a military intervention

and there they were you could hear this deafening noise of helicopters everything was shaking the walls were shaking and it felt as if everything was shaking and everyone's reactions then were different to me it was total mayhem it was a situation I'd been through other times before when the police charge into a demonstration and there are no stewards to take on a police charge and protect people in the demonstration to keep things calm so that they can retreat and get away calmly that's it that was the situation a state of general panic but despite this panic everyone was still sure it was a bluff that these guys were bluffing that they really weren't coming in and even when the first blasts were heard the thought was that it was only meant as a warning

so this is how the military action unfolded what happened was that these guys arrived in the helicopters the scene I witnessed was these huge helicopters coming in making this deafening noise and through a window in the corridor I quite clearly saw these guys in black uniforms every one of them armed to the teeth with these all-in-one helmets completely covering their heads I saw them on the helicopters and climbing down from them getting ready to climb down with little rope ladders and cables I don't know what anyway they were landing on the roof they were landing from the helicopters on the flat roof above us and there was this deafening noise these explosions the helicopters were coming in waves these guys were climbing down and more were arriving right behind them and so on

these guys arrived on the roof they climbed down on to the roof and they started throwing grenades they got on to the roof and on the roof there was a trapdoor they blew open this trapdoor with grenades this trapdoor led to a spiral staircase this spiral staircase led to a metal gate that led to the second floor rotunda and that we'd welded so right away they blew open this trapdoor on the roof that led to the spiral staircase and no sooner had they opened this trapdoor on their way down than they started throwing down a series of small plastic explosives I mean they were actually throwing bombs down the staircase and as the bombs reached the rotunda there were these really deafening blasts these explosions

at this point everyone realized that these guys were really coming in that it wasn't a bluff at all and what's more it wasn't only above us that you could hear the explosions but you could now hear them below us as well because they were also

64

attacking from below then there was widespread panic and just then what happened was that everyone made their own decision about what they should do there was no coherent response to the thing there it is there was no collective coherent response and even the ones who'd made organized preparations failed to react in a disciplined organized way not even those who'd reckoned with a break-in who thought that could happen there was no organization at all when we saw that these guys were starting to throw bombs in earnest

there was well a structure along military lines and so on had been organized that was armed I mean there were these guys who had there were comrades who had bombs all ready who had this plastic stuff inside the coffee machines but there was no coherent response I found myself caught up in total confusion I was caught up in total confusion everyone responded instinctively they responded with what they thought was the best response in circumstances like these but individually meaning that there was no sign then of any coherent response nobody took anybody else into account they reckoned only with themselves and their own instincts

people began taking to their heels running running backwards and forwards backwards and forwards inside this restricted space running backwards and forwards up this corridor going in and out of the cells all in a shambolic and chaotic way those endless minutes with no idea of what to do searching for somebody else and not finding him going in and out of the cells in fact the classic situation of flight from an oncoming police charge when you've made no defences but the difference is that when you take to your heels from an oncoming police charge you have ahead of you an infinite space here instead they were all rushing around like mice in a cage because they all knew instinctively that there was nowhere to go you were inside a blocked space and these guys were coming at you throwing bombs and there was this deafening sound of non-stop explosions that were ear-splitting

well I remember that I just had time to confer with my cellmate about what to do I saw him there in the corridor and I said listen what do we do and he said I think we should go down to the first floor because these guys are dropping down on us they're coming down on us from the roof in a few minutes they'll be here and so it's better to go down to the first floor and I remember saying to him but look they're coming up from the ground floor as well which makes it exactly the same thing and the problem right now isn't whether we stay here or go down to the first floor the problem is what to do do we surrender or do we do something and what do we do if something can be done but he said no I'm going down to the first floor

so what happened was that instinctively everyone made a spontaneous choice about what was the best thing to do in this situation and there was this division between the ones that stayed and the ones that went below and the ones that stayed up there wound up as a mixture of those who were against resisting because it wasn't possible to resist because anyway there was nothing to be done and it would be enough if we got out of it alive and then those who believed instead that we could put up some resistance even if they had no idea no notion how to do it it wasn't a case of these ones staying up there and the rest going down below but they ended up all mixed up together everybody in a muddle

on the second floor I heard someone shouting that we should all gather together in the big dormitory so about thirty comrades went into this big dormitory and then there were some awful moments because they'd cut off the electricity by now it was dark you could hear the most terrifying explosions all of us were there in a row against the wall the back wall of this big dormitory cell all crouching close together in the certainty that they'd kill us all because from the moment they'd appeared they hadn't stopped throwing bombs and you could see masonry and bits of the stone floor being blasted away this is the last thing I saw before they cut off the electricity holes in the floor from the bombs they were throwing down from the roof

some of the hostage guards were taken down to the first floor with knives at their throats other guards stayed up on the second floor in the big dormitory with us and the guards were scared stiff when the cells they were in were unlocked and they were hauled out into the middle of all that uproar going on in the middle of that infernal noise and confusion with people running in all directions with the non-stop explosions of the bombs going off all the time they were hauled out of the cells and they thought they were sure they'd have their throats cut and be thrown downstairs one at a time they thought they'd be murdered and thrown downstairs to stop those guys coming in

the guards didn't say a word their eyes stared wide open there was one of them who kept fainting with fear he was white as a sheet his legs gave way and he'd keep fainting then a comrade would slap him to stop him from fainting then a bucket of water was thrown in his face and the ones holding him up by the arms would tell him to calm down they weren't going to kill him the guards who were in the second floor dormitory cell had no one restraining them no one threatening them they were shouting themselves hoarse from the windows don't come in don't come in or they'll kill us all and then a comrade told them it's your own people who'll do the killing not us

besides the guards didn't have uniforms any more they wore ordinary clothes like us and so they were as exposed as we were to those guys coming in shooting and throwing bombs they looked no different from all of us and at the same time nobody was threatening them nobody was doing anything to them they were there with us crouching like us shaking with fear like us and just then there was an instant of solidarity between us all because we were all in the same situation because our lives were at stake and the guards were perfectly aware that the *carabinieri* were putting their lives at risk too the *carabinieri* didn't give a damn about their lives and by coming in they'd doubled the risk of them being killed in the first place by us and then by themselves at that moment there was clear solidarity between us and the guards

14

The elections of the *decreti delegati** came along when things were really hotting up early in the morning as arranged about a hundred of us met in front of the school gates it's Sunday and there's lukewarm sunshine we've all got jackets scarves woolly berets gloves banners we're all gathered together very aggressively putting on a tough show of being ready to take on all comers Malva is furious she disagrees she keeps on saying so she quarrels with everybody she says we need to get rid of all that pseudo-military paraphernalia that we ought to concentrate completely on discussion and not on threats but nobody takes any notice of her and Scilla who has brought along a bunch of

---

* the principle of the *decreti delegati*, giving a representative group including parents and students some say in the administration of individual schools, was introduced in 1974. In many cases elections were opposed and boycotted on the grounds that it amounted to a paltry and inadequate reform.

pickaxe handles with strips of red rag tied round them yells at her fuck off you piece of shit go and join the rest of them on the election list of candidates and give us a break

the gates are opened by the janitors who're not wearing uniform and are paid overtime for this weekend work we form four ranks that block the entrance right away two police squad cars show up two *carabinieri* vehicles and a lockup van there's the usual light-coloured police surveillance car giving orders over a radio transmitter presently an NCO comes up to us and asks us to make way for people going through but we don't move the atmosphere is really tense the police get into formation in ranks like us but they haven't got any clubs or helmets or shields they're empty-handed and they're a bit cowed by our banners

the *carabinieri* are standing to one side watching the police have formed tight ranks and advance on us and come so close they're nearly touching us we stare at one another insultingly and we start pushing body to body for the moment we don't push with our hands we just press with our bodies against theirs at the front of our formation we hold the poles of the banners horizontally and we push with the poles to stop the police from getting nearer then the police catch hold of the banners too and they push them against us there's pushing from both direc-tions and the horizontal line of the banners is what divides our bodies from theirs it looks like a game a tug-of-war the wrong way round and there's even some fun being had with this game that goes on for a good while

as we're pushing we shout one two three-ee while the police push without saying a word the mass heaves backwards and forwards one section loses a yard but then regains it and a few minutes go by like this I'm right in the middle and I feel myself flattened like a sardine squeezed from every direction overheated I feel as if I'm suffocating then finally we manage to throw them back because there are more of us and there are also lots of people pushing from behind the last push we give them is very violent the police ranks can't hold against it one or two police end up on the ground with their legs in the air and hurry to their feet again picking up their hats and swearing in a rage and so we succeed in occupying the whole area in front of the gates

the same NCO as before comes forward again and starts bargaining he says all they're interested in is keeping the entrance clear that they're there to guarantee this for people to go in and out freely and that if we don't give way they'll get their clubs and charge us then Canforo mediates and we reach an agreement to line ourselves up sideways leaving the entrance free because we're not there to stop people from going in to vote but to put arguments to them but in fact we do fuck all talking some small groups of students who show up there to vote see how things are and do an about-turn but the vast majority don't even turn up only some bewildered parents are left standing they don't know what's going on but there's too much tension for talking as for us we don't even feel like it

all our concentration is now on the police we sense that the real clash is with them meanwhile they've formed their ranks again they've formed ranks parallel with ours leaving clear a corridor a couple of yards wide and about ten yards long right up to the gate finally there are a couple of brave parents Communists for sure who start out along the corridor left clear in front of the entrance and then at once we advance suddenly all together and immediately the police ranks advance too and so we wind up in the same situation as before face to face with the parents caught in the middle like a sandwich beside me there's Scilla we're linking arms I can feel his arm tensely gripping mine

then suddenly Scilla's arm wriggles free of mine quick as a flash and all at once I see the bloodied nose of the policeman opposite him it's taken an instant no one has seen his fist fly and now it's back under my arm the policeman's arms open limply and he sinks backwards with his hair falling on his face at the same time the two groupings have divided again and everyone's back in their original spot the policeman on the ground is carried away without any clear idea of what really happened to him a bit later a little group of Catholics turns up and they stop a few yards away talking in hushed voices among themselves and then they come forward in single file straight into the corridor

the interplay of battle formations starts all over again we all thrust ourselves forward once more and the little group of would-be electors rushes back after having taken a bit of shoving and spitting a bit later the head boy turns up he's in the FGCI* he turns up along with a dozen other nicely dressed kids with nice clean faces just like his obviously all militants in their phantom organization for a bit they make a point of stopping the few students that turn up to persuade them not to go away then they have some hushed words with the policemen and some hushed words with the little group of Catholics Valeriana's the first one to yell out there it is the historic compromise† then the slogans start united we agree but against the DC

the police make a surprise dash forward they gain a few yards the outlines of the two groupings get frayed in the scramble kicks and punches get delivered by both sides a few students manage to pass through taking advantage of the mêlée hardly anyone is unscathed Cocco gets the purple lining ripped out of his coat Gelso gets a little finger broken I get hit on the arm I feel a shooting pain I look round but there's such confusion

---

* *Federazione Giovanile Comunista Italiana* the Italian Communist Party's offical youth organization.

† The pact between the Italian Communist Party and the ruling parties of the right after the 1976 election.

that I can't tell who did it the police are pissed off because we have the banners and they know that we'll start using them meanwhile the PCI* militants turn up in droves more and more of them all the time and they get behind the police and egg them on to clear us off

one of the PCI people a big tall guy with a bully's face comes up and grabs Pepe by the collar and shouts fascist at him Pepe wriggles and manages to land him a kick on the shins a really hard kick with the tip of his heavy boot hard enough to break his leg but the guy doesn't budge and he doesn't loosen hold of his collar then Ortica who's there beside him raises the banner and with both hands brings it down on the brute's arm a howl of pain and he lets go it's chaos blows lashed out from all directions by now it's a free-for-all the banners shoot into the air screaming swearing insults I feel someone grabbing me by the hair but then it's let go of at once I see Scilla hitting out like a madman with the banner as a cudgel against the police who are trying to pick up the banners dropped on the ground so that they can use them too

ambulances arrive with sirens going the brawl suddenly peters out and we split once more into the two groupings going back to the initial positions suddenly I hear shouting that they've got Canforo and I'm just in time to see Canforo with his arm held being pushed into the lockup van by four police we all rush at the lockup van and surround it more shoving more punching between us and the police but the lockup van can't leave because it would flatten somebody then we start shaking the lockup van rocking it with all of us pushing together that's when the police promise to release Canforo in exchange for handing over the banners we accept we leave the poles there on the ground and Canforo is let out of the lockup van

---

* *Partito Comunista Italiano* the Italian Communist Party.

it's midday we've been there for four hours the polling stations close in the evening and we don't want to leave but we can't keep on fighting it out until the evening this is what we decide to have a reduced picket until the afternoon anyway by now we've achieved our aim traffic to the polling booths has been next to nothing we decide to call a truce with the police and I go with Canforo to talk with the NCO who's there across the road leaning on a squad car talking to a plain-clothes man in a cream double-breasted raincoat the tension has slackened completely someone is sitting on the pavement eating rolls a young policeman is taking out his pocket transistor to listen to the football match and he speaks to us what's all this then it's Sunday why aren't you out in the country with some girls instead of hanging round here creating all this bother

15

The time they arrested me we'd just got in on the train from the village I was walking with China and two other comrades along the road from the station towards the centre there was a meeting at the centre about the radio station we were setting up it was Gelso and Ortica doing it and the broadcasts were to cover the whole province one of their fucking local squad cars goes past we often saw them lately parked outside the centre but we don't take that much notice just snooping as usual we think but then they skid to a stop right alongside the pavement just yards ahead of us they skid to a stop and suddenly get out they rush out towards us with guns in their hands towards me it takes me by surprise for these guys knew us all right and there was no way they needed to put on this act to check our papers as they'd already done a load of times before the three plain-clothes guys don't bother much with the comrades who're with me but they surround me they point their guns right at me and they tell me to keep still don't move they shout and who's moving I say they close in and one of them puts the comrades against the wall and China too with their hands up then they search them a bit but halfheartedly while the others take me by the arms and push me towards the car they push me inside the car and I wind up squashed in between two guys holding guns that they stick into my sides they were quite edgy and they didn't say a word and so nor did I say a word only by turning my head a little can I glimpse China on the pavement running towards the car which speeds off just at that moment

all this happened all very fast once he saw I'd got into the car the one that was left outside released the comrades he was holding against the wall at gun-point he ran to the car and got into the front seat and he took off with the tyres zigzagging then he looked in the rear-view mirror and said did you search him no goes the one on my left still shoving the gun in my ribs the one who's driving gets mad how come you didn't search him then bloody idiots you were supposed to search him and he brakes and makes to draw up by the kerb but the same one on my left says don't stop now the one driving accelerates again and says at least put the handcuffs on him then eh and then he asks me menacingly are you armed

no I say the one on the right brings out the handcuffs and the one driving tells him put them on with his hands behind his back then the one on my left takes hold of my hair with one hand and says lean forward put your hands behind you I obey but I move very slowly because I can feel the butt of the gun pressing into my side the one on the left pulls me by the hair again until my face is resting on the front seat while the other one puts the handcuffs round my wrists but he makes slow work of it because there's so little room and like this finally I'm handcuffed the one on the left lets go of my hair now I'm handcuffed and very uncomfortable with my arms pinioned behind my back and the two beside me who are still pressing the guns between my ribs but I choose to keep my mouth shut and ask no questions

the road to the police station is a short one but I have time to think a thousand thoughts I think that these guys are going in for some serious intimidation I don't understand why but they're serious about it for sure and seeing the way these things go as soon as we get to the station they'll beat me up and I think of how I'm handcuffed and that that makes it easy to hit me without me even being able to defend myself and so I get really scared about being beaten up I can't even give any thought to why they can have detained me I can only think about the beating they're going to give me and when we get to the main entrance they shove me out still with the guns in their hands they shove me up the stairs and keep shoving me even when there's no need they shove me if I go slowly and if I hurry they say where do you think you're going and pull me back by the handcuffs

well we go up two flights like this with these guys shoving me and pulling me all the time then they take me into a room and make me sit down on a chair the moment I sit down still with the handcuffs behind me I think this is it they'll start now and instead the one who'd handcuffed me brings a tiny key out of his pocket and takes them off I breathed a sigh because I thought that if they were going to hit me it would have been easier to do it when I was handcuffed I rub my wrists a bit for they're red and they hurt then the one who was driving tells me brusquely strip come on be quick about it I don't raise any objections I take off my jacket my scarf then I take off my sweater my shirt and vest come on be quick about it the trousers too I take off my shoes slip out of my trousers and then I look at them

75

but he still keeps on at me bad temperedly I said the lot you have to strip right off the lot have you got it and he flicks my back with the tip of his taut outstretched fingers and with contempt on his face I see this contemptuous expression of his and my immediate reaction is to look straight at him and I see this contemptuous expression in his eyes and I feel a surging burst of hatred and rage you're a piece of shit I tell him with my eyes I'm not brave enough to say it to him because I can see him there all poised and ready to let me have it if I make the slightest move and so I take off my socks and underpants and I stand there naked I'm cold but I don't move it's like a revelation for me and I think to myself this is the way they are this is what they're like but why do I find it so staggering how many times have we told ourselves that this is how they are

the three of them start searching the clothes they turn out the pockets of the jacket the pockets of the trousers they empty out their contents onto the table then one by one they finger all these things the usual sort of things the cigarettes the lighter the coins pieces of paper the keys the usual things there always are in pockets they look at them and look again they shift them from hand to hand two or three times they turn them round fingering them then they pass them on to one another the lighter the keys the pieces of paper they read them studiously they look at them against the light they put them delicately down again then they take the cigarettes out of the packet they take out the silver foil as well they study it carefully on one side and the other but what are they looking for I ask myself what do they think they'll find

then they hand round the clothes they feel the collar of the jacket the seams they pull away the lining and each of them feels inside it they feel the collar of the shirt they turn it back they inspect the seams they turn the trousers and the sweater inside out they inspect every inch with the same measured calm you can tell that for them these are routine mechanical actions then they pick up the underpants they feel these too then they get to the shoes slip their hands inside they lift the tongue they hold them in the light to look edgeways inside them they inspect the sole they bend it back then throw them on the ground finally the red scarf and the socks their hands never relaxing they lift them they feel them they turn them over and over about three or four times they hand them back and forth then when they've finished one of them leaves the room

I gather up my things scattered all over the floor I do it all so slowly I still don't understand what they're after I think that now they could at least tell me something but I avoid asking questions I take my time getting dressed again and then I sit down on a chair I look out of the window even though there was nothing to see because it was the second floor and there was just a grey sky outside the window I was looking out into the grey sky so as not to look at those guys who appeared relaxed now too and weren't bothering much with me any more one had sat down on the desk and was dangling his legs backwards and forwards while he fiddled with the things that had been in my pockets and now formed a little heap on the desk

I had the shit behind me I couldn't see him but I was sure he'd placed himself there deliberately to make me insecure for I couldn't take my mind off the thought that I was about to be struck until a few minutes later the one who'd gone out reappears and they ask him if the chief's arrived just imagine I think to myself they really do call him the chief and the guy answers he's on his way in I know who he is this chief I've already seen him every time we've had a demonstration he was always there in the cream double-breasted raincoat behind the window of an unmarked car holding the radio transmitter up to his mouth and giving orders to his boys because that's just what he calls them my boys and they call him the chief what kind of people are these cops they really do act and talk like the cops you see in the movies

16

There was a long long moment of silence after these guys stopped throwing bombs down from the roof until they began climbing down the spiral staircase climbing down the spiral staircase from the roof to the second floor rotunda crossing the length of the corridor and entering this dormitory cell where we all were is ordinarily a matter of seconds but they took a full minute to do it and get there because they were coming down very cautiously they were coming down all kitted out in their bullet-proof vests in their all-in-one helmets and when they finally got down into the rotunda first thing they started spraying sub-machine gun fire randomly into the corridors they were firing like madmen pointing the sub-machine guns round in every direction and all of us were shouting we surrender we surrender don't fire

the scene I saw was that I saw one of these guys all kitted out coming in but in no hurry he stepped inside the dormitory cell he saw everyone at the back crouched on the ground and the first thing he did was blast a volley from his sub-machine gun at the ceiling then he threw a grenade inside inside the dormitory a non-explosive grenade a grenade of the type meant to blind you the type used by those commandos what the hell are they called and the fact is it stuns you because it produces an incredible blaze of light a tremendous bang that deafens you and at the same time a blaze I mean a blaze that really does blind you and what happens is that you close your eyes but then afterwards you've got this light still in your eyes it's still there even if you close your eyes it stays for several seconds and you're dazed you're left utterly stunned

they hurled one of these grenades into the dormitory where we were and then the sensation I felt was that one of the guards had got himself under my legs and was gripping me tightly as he clung to me because by now we'd all lost control of our reactions we were all sitting with our backs against the wall and then these guys at the door started firing submachine-gun volleys less than two feet above our heads then of course everyone's instinct was to lie flat on the ground as low as possible because these guys were firing and screaming abuse bastards we'll murder the lot of you and that kind of thing and they went on firing just above people's heads then they started making us all turn over kicking us down with our faces flat against the ground

everybody got the point at once and they all turned face down on their own even without too many invitations even the hostage guards who were there who'd taken a few kicks in the face even the ones who'd tried to say they were guards we all had our faces pressing on the ground so that you couldn't see a thing any more then they started taking out the people in the dormitory one at a time they started taking them out into the corridor I couldn't see a thing any more but I could hear the sub-machine gun volleys they kept firing at the walls the screams the abuse the sound of kicks being delivered to the ones who were being taken outside they were screaming red swine scum bastards we'll murder the lot of you at the same time down below you could hear terrible explosions because at the same time they'd also burst in below and some coffee machines had been thrown

they were taking people out of the dormitory one at a time I was the last since everyone was in a row along the wall and they started at the other end from mine I was the last the very last and I could only hear sounds for I couldn't see a thing any more I had my face to the ground I could see hardly anything all I could hear the gunfire and abuse from these guys they were high on amphetamines they were shouting really as if they were crazy they were firing non-stop then they were taking people out into the corridor I could hear the beatings they were giving them as they took them outside they took them out into the corridor and then I heard there were no more volleys just single shots they were saying get on your knees I could hear them saying get on the ground kneel put your hands on your head and then I'd hear two single shots being fired

there and then I said these guys are killing them they're killing all of them I swear to you now it's some time ago I swear to you I was perfectly convinced they were killing everyone that they were taking us out one at a time to kill us all one at a time in the corridor and all of us there were convinced of this we would hear those isolated shots out there in the corridor and then they would come in again to take out someone else I don't know how long this went on there I was with my face down I hadn't a clue how many were left before me I expected it to be my turn any minute I was convinced they were really killing us all also because it was that kind of situation I told myself if they come in like this it's because they're going to kill you if they throw bombs like that it means they've come here to kill us all

and the guards too suffered the same treatment because these guys couldn't sort out the hostage guards from the convicts they were shouting we're the guards we're the guards but these guys took no notice of them they gave them the same treatment just the same for them as well they hit them they kicked them too as they dragged them outside they took them out into the corridor as well and they too were absolutely sure they'd be killed as well they were convinced like the rest of us they took them into the corridor they made them kneel and they fired over their heads and left it to another time to identify them because after they took the ground floor as well a commandant of the guards who did know them came upstairs but before that they suffered just the same treatment

anyway the strangest thing to my mind was the way time went on and on it was endless for I was the last then and I could hear everyone being taken away one at a time before me and I was saying to myself they're going to kill me right now the weird thing was I was really convinced that they were going to kill me so I was telling myself it's all over it's all over any time now they're going to kill me like all the others but the weird thing was I was utterly calm about this I didn't lose control and then I saw that none of the other comrades had lost control either they'd all been quite calm as they waited their turn to be taken outside I don't know maybe because all of them had come round to accepting this as inevitable I don't know

then when they got to me they grabbed me by the hair a few kicks some verbal abuse a bit of a beating that I didn't even feel just think whether you feel a beating at a time like that the beating was something you didn't feel at all because all you had on your mind was the fact they were going to kill you but even then I was perfectly calm and when I got to the corridor they struck me a blow with what I don't know a blow as if with the butt-end of the sub-machine gun I think they threw me on the ground and then I had time to see that everyone was there on the ground in a heap there bleeding but they were all alive they hadn't killed anyone they were all injured bleeding but every one of them was moving as they lay there on the ground faces to the ground

and then at that moment I saw one of these guys in their commando outfits lifting up grabbing a comrade by the hair he lifted his head and asked him what's your name and the guy told him his name then the other one struck him a terrible blow here with a pistol butt I mean a really hard hard blow right here between the eyes and it smashed him all up here and all the blood was pouring down and then one by one they started with torches they started pulling them up by the hair and asking them with torches asking them their names because by now it was dark and among the shadows you could see these huge looming figures moving about for incidentally they were all huge very big and their bulk was exaggerated by those outfits

maybe also exaggerated by this psychological situation you found yourself in with these huge great shoes these camouflage fatigues these bullet-proof vests with these grotesque outfits with these heavy boots kicking everybody screaming abuse as if they were demented and then picking you out with a torch there was one with a great big torch he pulled you up by the hair he lifted your face and shone the torch dazzling in your eyes and he asked you your name he asked me my name and he put the gun he put the gun in my mouth and he asked me I told him and this guy said to me are you scared I nodded yes I nodded yes that I was scared but I swear to you that at that moment I realized he wouldn't fire I was sure he wouldn't fire

17

The door opens and Dottor Donnola enters the room he comes towards me his manner thoughtful his expression concerned but relaxed he asks the others if they've searched me and then he tells them to leave because he wants to have a few words with me the shit asks him if he should handcuff me oh no goes Donnola and then he looks at me and says we've already met and the others hurry out of the room leaving the door ajar the chief moves round the desk and sits down on the other side with the tips of his fingers he brushes aside my things that are still there he seems in no hurry then at last he gets started his manner paternal and confiding listen I know you're a good lad you're the kind that speaks at public meetings and goes on demonstrations but I know you're not the kind that shoots I wait for him to go on and say something else instead he stops and I'm left with him staring straight at me from behind his square glasses without another word

so it's my turn to talk I don't really know what to say and the only thing I can think to say is why have you brought me here no no this isn't an interrogation says Donnala at once I can't do that the law doesn't allow it don't you see that we're here just the two of us and that I'm not writing anything down I only want to have a few words with you if there's something you want to tell me I was bewildered and I chip in but what am I supposed to tell you you're the ones who should be telling me you're the ones who've brought me here it's not as if I came here myself did I in short you've got nothing to tell me goes Donnola nothing about what I ask why about your friends about where you live no this guy was really doing it the slow way he was playing cat and mouse which friends how do you mean where I live I go and Donnola smiles ironically how do I mean I mean your home I mean the house you live in

but for a while now I haven't had anywhere permanent to live I reply at once I live in different places here and there I get friends to let me stay with them sometimes I stay the night with my family Donnola's still smiling but aren't you the tenant of the place in such and such a street isn't the tenancy in your name yes I am why and Donnola sighs and says all of a sudden staring

83

straight at me we've searched your place and we've discovered arms I didn't believe him I swear I didn't believe him this guy's bluffing I thought and not bluffing that seriously either and then I shot him a smile listen Dottor Donnola I told him listen that's not on but Donnola remained thoughtful too thoughtful there was a pause then Donnola starts all over again then you've got nothing to tell me nothing at all no I say if you've got questions to ask me I want a lawyer saying this because I didn't really know what to say

all right says Donnola then after a pause you've got nothing to tell me at all a pity and he's still sitting there not moving watching me waiting but I don't move either and I don't speak until Donnola gets up he calls the other three who were there outside waiting in the corridor and he tells them go to his parents' house and then he turns to me and he says look there's a warrant now we have to make a search of your family's house then we're taking you before the judge who has to question you I said all right but my only concern was to call a lawyer and I told Donnola all right but now I have to call the lawyer let me call him from here and Donnola without turning a hair no you're not calling him from here later from your place if you want

then they put the handcuffs back on me this time though they put them on in front and when I went down the stairs they didn't push me at all we got downstairs and there were two unmarked cars already waiting sitting in one of them were four plain-clothes men they gave me the once over and I was put in the other one in the back between two of the ones that arrested me but the shit was left outside in the front seats there were two new ones I hadn't seen before and we set off for the village I was very worried about how my father and mother would take it there was no doubt they'd be frightened and I went on thinking about what to do so as not to frighten them to calm them down the police were calm enough and the only sound you could hear was the crackling of the radio in contact with the station

they stayed in contact and every so often they indicated their position they indicated their whereabouts as they drove through each of the villages they hadn't pulled out the guns to point them at me and the one who was in front and who I hadn't seen before at one point turned round and asked me if I want a cigarette I'm dying for a smoke but I tell him no it's instinctive to say no though I'd like to say yes then after a bit more driving round we get to my house the cars stop in front of the gate without the slightest hesitation clearly everything had already been under surveillance and the one who offered me the cigarette must have been the sergeant in charge of the raid because he gave orders for my handcuffs to be removed and he asked me straight out if I had any arms in the house of course not I answered

the two drivers stayed in the cars and all the others went up the stairs into the courtyard I went in first and I spoke at once to my father and mother who'd come out to meet me surprised at all those strange people I told them keep calm don't worry these are police who have to carry out a search it's nothing serious nothing has happened now I'm calling the lawyer the sergeant interrupts me in a pleasant enough manner he says no look there's no need to put the lawyer to any bother we'll only be a minute not even that if you've got any arms in the house tell us right now and that way we'll all avoid wasting time my mother turns pale when she hears the word arms I say no there are no arms of any kind here but I do want to call the lawyer all the same nah go all the cops in a languid chorus

in the end the sergeant asks me where the lawyer lives and I say nearby here in the village nearby I'd just thought of the name of a lawyer I knew defended the local low life I didn't know him but I'd heard of him from someone I look up his name in the telephone directory and I find the number the lawyer's there but he makes excuses it's supper time and he says he'd prefer not to come but I insist I tell him that he really must come and so we all settle down to wait for the lawyer in silence the police follow every move I make and they don't take their eyes off me I'm only worried that my mother doesn't suddenly get the idea of offering the police something to drink out of politeness my father is clearly upset hunched in his chair he stares at me wide-eyed

time is going by and the lawyer hasn't turned up the police start complaining because it's getting late and they're doing overtime we meet half-way I tell them they can start the search while we're waiting for the lawyer but one room at a time and in my presence I don't want them to spread out through the rooms so that I can't make sure they don't plant something that wasn't there before I wasn't worried about the search because I knew there was nothing incriminating in the house the only thing that could interest them was in the cellar my records of the move-ment all the newspapers the magazines the leaflets of these past years I was jealous of my archive I'd spent hours organizing it but it was all perfectly legal and so I wasn't at all worried about keeping it in the house

the lawyer arrived shortly before the police went down to search the cellar a fine lawyer I'd picked myself a real mafioso pimp to start with hearty handshakes with the police with whom he was clearly on intimate terms and when he found out it was political he said straight away that he never handled that kind of thing it took some effort to persuade him to stay a bit longer now that the whole thing was nearly done with he did it reluctantly but the whole time he didn't stop talking and joking with the police and then down in the cellar when they opened the cupboard the sergeant wiped his brow dejectedly and now what do we do it would take us two days to go through it all no what we'll do is we'll confiscate the lot and then the magistrates can put their minds to it

and so they started the gradual removal from the cupboard to the boots of the cars I was wretched I knew I'd never see my archive again it would rot in the cellars of some police station or court house it would vanish just as in years to come all the comrades' archives would vanish deliberately destroyed by them all the newspapers all the magazines all the leaflets all the documents all the posters all the publications of the movement destroyed vanished all bundled in cardboard boxes and plastic rubbish bags and burned or thrown on rubbish tips tons of printed matter the written history of the movement its memory dumped among refuse consigned to the flames through the fear of repression a fear well justified because all it took then was a leaflet found in a search to put you in prison for a year or two

the police load my entire archive on to the cars and when they've finished they tell me okay now we're going into town to the judge as if they were sorry about it they were sorry about it for themselves because they kept going on about how long it would take about when they'd get back the lawyer says he can't go into town and I don't even insist better not to bother with that bastard my father and mother start asking the police anxious questions but where are you taking him when will he be back and so on they're vague with their answers they don't really say I'm under arrest and I reassure them too saying it's likely I won't be back for the night but not to worry and to pack a bag for me with a pair of underpants a vest toothpaste a toothbrush just like for my brother when he left for military service I joked with my mother

then we go downstairs and when I turn and see them pale-faced at the top of the steps I feel guilty it occurs to me that they won't get any sleep tonight I'm still thinking about this as the cars are driving through the village and I was thinking that later it would be even worse for I was sure that this time I'd end up inside that this time I'd really end up in gaol we've driven through more villages by the time we reach the motorway I looked out of the window at the houses the cars going by the people walking and riding bicycles people going about their lives that flow of people there in the streets so unexceptional that you never take any heed of it but at that moment I saw it as something beautiful I began to feel sad then on the motorway I saw the mountains in the distance the sun was going down I could see the mountains and the whiteness of the villages below further down as I'd always seen them and as maybe I'd not see them again for christ knows how long and I felt I was saying goodbye to them for ever

18

The village where I lived was a shit-hole and the people in it were shitty people too I didn't like this village and I didn't like these people but this village and these people were the same everywhere round here they were all villages like this all villages just like this one and all people just like these round here if you don't know these villages if you don't live in one of them you can get confused you can easily mistake one village for another they're all alike in the middle there's the square which always happens to be the church square and they've invariably got the same main street running through the village with a few shops and one or two bars the school and the munic-ipal offices all built more or less identically and the main street crossing the square going in one direction to the cemetery and in the other to the little railway station that links up all the little villages to one another the railway is old and runs at a loss the carriages are dilapidated and look like something out of a western and in these carriages people travel between one or other of these villages all villages of two or three thousand inhabitants though some were even smaller people born here from families here are even fewer they're half the population the other half are people who've come from elsewhere who came here in successive waves first people from the Veneto that came before my time then the *terroni* as they still call them here who settled here like flies whole families of them whole villages from the South I remember them coming here these people who look so different different with their darker complexions with a language different from our dialect but also different from Italian and almost impossible to understand and dressed differently too

they came here and they found room to stay in the old half-ruined houses the big houses with the courtyards where the peasants used to live and that were now falling down and they moved into them all together in large numbers into small damp tumbledown rooms and they lived on top of one another there was the village priest who made an effort to find places for them and they queued up outside the priest's door while the local people refused to accept them shunned them they looked too different from them they seemed by comparison bad mannered dirty but the men immediately found work in the numerous small factories that were sprouting up everywhere in the surrounding area they did the shittiest jobs of course and when they could they brought back homework for their families to do on the side

and the whole family would get down to work in the kitchen and the bedroom and they would all work the children the aunts and uncles and the eighty-year-old grannies dressed in black all worked there together as a production line assembling toys *topo gigio* toys hairbands plastic spectacles electric torches and that kind of stuff the *terroni* lived on the margins of village life the village people didn't want them they didn't want them in the few village bars and there were the famous words spoken by an old woman who owned one of the bars when a southern boy came in and ordered a drink she'd told him I'll give you a drink now and I won't charge you for it you can have a drink free on the house but after that you're not to come back ever again and so these words were quoted as if people were quoting the words of a heroine there you are that's the way to do it in other words

now and then fights broke out between locals and southerners but not so much among us younger ones because we went to school together and what we heard said in our families about the *terroni* was modified by the fact of living and playing together of being at school together for so much of the time and then at the church hall in the afternoon where we played together because here in this village the church ran everything the cinema where people queued up on Sunday afternoons belonged to the church and in order to go to the cinema we children had to go to the oratory and go to mass and there they stamped your little card that you had to show to the ticket seller who otherwise wouldn't give you a ticket even the football ground the tennis court the basketball the volleyball court the gym all belong to the oratory and the library too and half the bars

there the priest was very powerful and not much different from the local administration of the village who'd never been anything but Christian Democrats they were the powerful families of the village who'd always been wealthy first from the land and then in the economic boom of the sixties with the area's proliferation of hundreds of small factories where people were working thir-teen fourteen sometimes fifteen hours a day with overtime my father also worked in one of these small factories and did those long hours too and in our family too we did home-work like the *terroni* and we'd always done it like everyone in the village I grew up surrounded by big cardboard boxes containing parts of table lamps and moped ignitions to be assembled it was quite usual for a family to do this work they all did it all hours of the day and my parents did it all night too in the kitchen

after supper the boxes would be brought out from under the kitchen table the hand-press would be assembled on the edge of the table it was a kind of rudimentary hand operated rivet-ting-gun and we'd start to assemble the parts we had a kind of production line somebody assembling and somebody else rivetting with the hand-press fitting the parts together with the aluminium screws the rivets so tiny that they always slipped out of your fingers and with the rivets you attached the switches for the light and the horn to the chromium-plated cover this work went on for hours and hours this idiotic work always the same thing had been done every day for years on end this work that was paid at a fraction of a lira for each piece but with all of us working together we could make thousands of pieces and then what you ended up with was the thousand lire that boosted the family income

the assembly materials passed through various hands before they reached the families there were middlemen who were usually the factory foremen who put out the work to the families and who made money out of this simple transaction and who were also regarded as benefactors and then there could be other transactions because everyone was free to redistribute in turn to whomsoever they wished so that they could meet the delivery dates my father too passed on work to the southerners' families and they came to our house to collect it he wasn't a racist which is not to say he was fond of the southerners but he didn't despise them either although the southerners were regarded as people who did the work badly and didn't meet the delivery dates and so he guaranteed the deliveries for them and answered for the work even if of course he gained something by that transaction obviously in the small factories that manufactured the pieces it suited them to put them out for assembly it suited them to have the assembly done as homework because that way it worked out an awful lot cheaper and the whole economy of the village and of the surrounding villages was organized accordingly between work in the small factories and sweated homework the one home-working hardest was of course my mother who'd being doing it for years who did it all day as soon as she'd finished her chores and her cooking then she got down to it at once and she was there for hours adjusting the screws fast with that dry clicking that you could hear in our house all the time at all hours and that nobody noticed any more

in our family we all worked including my brother who'd left after primary school and gone to work too as a mechanic I was the only one who didn't work because my folks got it into their heads from the time I was very young that I should study not study this or that to become this or that but simply that I should study followed by the old chestnut that it means you won't have to work as hard as us and by dint of hearing this over and over again not even my brother got pissed off if he saw I was doing nothing while he worked hard I did nothing because I was destined to study and even if I was reading a comic book I was studying it was a big deal there for families like mine to have one of their children staying on at school it bred a kind of pride

people lived there in this atmosphere resigned without even thinking that anything could be different only education it was perhaps the only thing that could change anyone's life and in fact in the last few years something important had started changing from when more and more young people started going to the nearby town to study in the upper secondary schools it meant every morning getting on the train packed with people with

students workers commuters it meant that half-hour journey
where you met so many different people and it meant the city
which though it wasn't a big city seemed vast to us compared
with the village the city with its traffic the busy centre the shops
the offices and it also meant the school which was new and
different with so many new people who came from backgrounds
different from mine

the city people were very different from the village people they
were better I thought they were better because they weren't
always watching you spying on you like in the village in the city
what you did didn't at once become common knowledge it
didn't at once reach your parents' ears your neighbours everybody you didn't have to account to everybody for everything
you did while in the village that's just how it is everyone knows
everyone they all know one another and the least thing you do
at once becomes a subject for gossip and when you walk along
the street you're aware all eyes are on you everybody watching
you and talking about you as soon as you've gone by I didn't like
the people in the village I didn't like them because they were all
sanctimonious bigots all priest-loving hypocrites and rotten all
rotten inside

after a year of going to the city I felt detached from this nonsense
I didn't give a damn any more and I was even less tolerant of the
people in the village I couldn't stand them at all any more and so
I started taking the train into the city it took only half an hour to
get there I'd go in the afternoon too when school was over and
in the city I made friends with people of my own age with young
people of fifteen or sixteen like me who lived in the city and I
couldn't have cared less about being in the village I was never
there any more or I was there as little as possible of course there
was a problem in the evening after supper when I couldn't go to
the city because there were no trains to get back and then I sank
back into that village bar atmosphere into that void that I and

also other young people of my age couldn't stand any longer after we'd got to know the city because everything was different everything was better in the city

19

Meanwhile what had happened on the first floor was different altogether because instead of all getting into a big cell and doing what we'd done on the second floor some of the comrades put up a fight they tried to stop them from coming in and they flung the coffee machines at them that's what they told us afterwards and then the *carabinieri* who came in up from the ground floor started firing non-stop I mean they were firing at random they were coming into the corridors they were firing inside the cells they fired inside all the cells and they started wounding people they wounded a guard who had obviously got free in that chaos nobody was holding him any more and he started yelling I'm a guard I'm a guard

he got a spray of machine-gun fire that sliced him in two but he wasn't dead and then another guy who was a non-political and he got two bullets in the femur he's lame now he's lame for the rest of his life and you can still see the bullet marks on the armoured sheeting you can see how many bullets they fired and at what height they fired them you can see from the holes left in the metal even though the newspapers later said they'd fired rubber bullets like hell those guys started throwing grenades right there in the corridors and going berserk shooting and then the situation was that instead of all gathering together in one big cell there the people split up between different cells each group taking a guard as hostage but even with the guard as hostage clearly everybody realized that given the stage things had got to the guard as hostage was no longer enough of a guarantee that they wouldn't kill you on the spot then the *carabinieri* came along firing from cell to cell and saying either you come out right now or we'll throw in a grenade and they came out but the strange thing was that the real carnage was carried out upstairs even though upstairs there was no resistance because in reality downstairs they didn't touch anybody they didn't beat anybody up whereas upstairs they pulverized them they beat everybody up they acted out all those mock dramas they fired they took aim at people they pressed the butt of the machine gun here against the temple then they fired that's the kind of play-acting they did

after this I thought that the worst that could happen had passed I naively thought that the worst was over they made us all put our hands up and since we were on the second floor they started making us go downstairs everyone in single file down the stairs of course it wasn't a case of walking down they kicked you down kicking you hitting you in the back with the guns and you reeled down each flight of stairs caught in the thick of the beatings they came at you from every direction but the fact is that I personally didn't feel those blows much I felt nothing as I reeled down the stairs lit by flashlight we could see nothing we were knocking into everything I felt nothing probably because the only reaction I had was the thought that they hadn't killed me

they didn't kill me now I thought they didn't kill any of us only I didn't understand where they were taking us what they were doing what are these guys doing now what are they going to do now now that it's all over now what are they doing where are they taking us I couldn't make out what they were doing where they would take us and then when I finally reeled to the bottom in the ground floor rotunda at the end of the stairs and I went through the gate leading to the ground floor rotunda there the scene was very brightly lit there was plenty of light while where we'd come from upstairs was all in darkness there were only the bulbs of the flashlights while there when we arrived downstairs all the lights were on it was all dazzlingly bright

and there but in a flash a split second the time it took to cross the rotunda in all that light there I glimpsed a lot of people in uniform and plain clothes there were the guards' commanding officers sergeants and warrant-officers there were people who'd come in from outside and there they kicked me shoved me struck me and punched me in the direction of the open corridor leading to the exercise yards I saw they were herding us into the yards only the problem was as soon as I started down the three steps into this open corridor I realized I saw that that was where the punishment was because there lined up on both sides were all the guards masked in balaclavas they were there in two rows in these big overcoats and with clubs and iron bars in their hands

well since these guys were making us run down the open corridor with our hands behind our heads and you couldn't shield yourself then clearly we were glad enough to have to keep our hands on our heads because the blows were being struck mainly at the head they were terrible blows these guys were striking with all their strength with the clubs and with the iron bars I'd hardly got down the first two steps when there was a guard trying to trip me up to make me fall right away because the thing there was to make you fall down and then hit you while you were on the ground but they didn't manage to make me fall this corridor was very brightly lit on one side it was bounded by the dividing wall and on the other side there was a big wire mesh fence enclosing the exercise yards

and then I saw ahead of me there was a comrade and I saw him take a terrible blow with an iron bar he took a terrible blow on his side and he doubled up and two or three guards jumped on him to give him a savage beating I managed to get clear of them to go forward still with my hands on my head with the blows coming from every direction it came into my mind that we had to go along the whole length of the corridor that would have been about thirty or forty yards it came to me that there was this whole long way to go where these two ranks of guards were lined up hitting out and I went all the way along running the gauntlet of the blows but without falling thinking if I get right to the end it'll be over

and I managed to get as far as the end without falling taking blows from every direction because the main thing was not to fall for I realized that if you fell it was all over because if you fell it was clear they would pulverize you they could hit you any way they wanted and so I took the blows but I kept going and I got there to the end but the awful thing was that when I got to the end I realized then that that wasn't where I had to go because I saw that they were making people go into the first yard which meant I'd done half a corridor's length for nothing then I turned round and had to go back the same way and for a second time go through the blows I went back the same way and I got as far as the exercise gate where we had to go in because I saw that there was a masked guard opening the gate

however the gates leading to the exercise yards precisely for fear of kidnappings this gate never opens out at right-angles it doesn't open like an ordinary door on the ground there's fixed on the ground there's a peg that ensures the door only opens at an angle of forty-five degrees in other words it opens very little so that only one person at a time can get through and sideways at that the one opening the gate was an NCO and it was up to him to judge whether someone had taken enough of a beating or not and he judged by whether the guy could still stand up or not which meant if he saw that someone could still stand up and wasn't dragging himself along on his knees then when you reached the gate he closed it in your face

well I remember that I reached the gate and I managed to get myself inside this gate but since the gate opened in the way I've mentioned it only just opened it meant I didn't manage to get right inside while these guys on the outside kept on hitting me and so they managed to pull me back out from the gate to pull me away from the gate as I was going through and hit me even more and the last thing I remember about this beating was as one of them was pulling me by the hair and then there was a piece of luck because I had a very long scarf of very thick red wool that China had given me and I always wore it and when the *carabinieri* had arrived up there I couldn't decide whether to keep it on or take it off

it was a very long scarf it could have been a noose and I started thinking they're going to strangle me now right here with this scarf it was the first thought I had I thought of taking it off but then I said no I'm not taking it off and instead of taking it off I wrapped it right round my neck and so then when this guy grabbed me by the hair while at the same time another one was pulling at my jacket the thing I remember is that I got hit really hard I'm not sure if it was with a truncheon or an iron bar a terrible blow on the neck here on the neck and the result was that I fainted only that by good luck there was this layer of wool scarf that softened the blow in fact later there was no sign of it only at the time I fainted but since I was already half-way inside the gate someone inside pulled me through into the exercise yard at last

20

Once we're in the city the car turns on the siren it goes through a red light the driver is enjoying himself going fast you can see that in the city he enjoys accelerating sharply suddenly putting on the brakes overtaking all the other cars then suddenly after a mass of bends that seem to me like one long bend that goes on forever it comes to a halt in front of a big doorway in a building all ablaze with yellow lights with squad cars going in and out of it with the blue light turning on the roof and I can read Police Headquarters on a plaque opposite me on the wall the police officers at the door wave our car in and the guy goes through the doorway with the usual sharp acceleration and then stops with the brakes screeching among a row of blue and white squad cars

before getting out I ask but weren't we supposed to go to the courthouse for questioning the one who's in front who's the one in charge tells me that at this hour the courthouse has been closed for a while and that I'll be questioned there at police headquarters that the magistrates are already there waiting for me we get out and they take me through a small door off the courtyard leading to a stair so very narrow that it can only be climbed in single file and we start going up these stairs me in front and all the others following the stair twists after every ten or fifteen steps I can hear the shuffling tread of our feet echoing in that narrow space and we keep on climbing the stairs endless stairs and landings I get out of breath every so often I stop on a landing but the one behind me always says get a move on

we reach what's clearly the top floor because there are no more stairs and at the end of a short corridor we come out into a little room with two small armchairs and a small sofa upholstered in rather grimy green plastic they motion me to sit down the NCO goes out of another door and comes back right away and tells me to go through I go into another small room that's full of people all in plain clothes most of them young wearing jeans and duffle jackets beards and even long hair I'd never seen police disguised as comrades before and I was a bit astonished by it all I didn't understand why all these people were there waiting for me then I realized that it was the culmination of a police operation in which they'd obviously taken part and which ended with me

behind the long narrow desk there's a long thin guy who gives me a single stern look as soon as I come in and then goes back to reading from a pile of papers he has in front of him they sit me down on a broken-down wooden chair that looks as if it's going to collapse at any moment and that creaks with my slightest movement I'm sitting in front of the long thin guy whose head is still bent over the papers and I recognize that face because I've seen it before in the newspapers that guy is Judge Lince the others are all standing leaning against the wall there's very little space between them and the desk and when somebody new has to come in there's a general movement to make way for him and they all press back against the wall

one door of the room is open and outside it there are more people walking backwards and forwards they put the handcuffs back on me with my hands in front of me and the NCO who'd brought me there says that they're leaving that they're going home that they've done their report and they've put it in that there's a pile of material they've confiscated and that they've left it downstairs the judge looks up briefly and nods approval and says goodbye then suddenly he turns to me looking me straight in the face and he asks me if I've got myself a lawyer I say no he says it's late and that at that hour it's virtually impossible to find a lawyer willing to come there but that all the same they already have one they've notified there and if I accept him as a lawyer appointed by the Court then tomorrow I can name another of my choosing at once the lawyer appears through the open door he's so much like the rest of the people there that I think he must surely be a policeman too and that they're playing a dirty trick on me but when Lince has my particulars typed up by a fat uniformed guy behind a massive ancient typewriter and he dictates first my particulars and then the lawyer's which I can't even remember any more and he names him lawyer so and so I'm somewhat reassured and I look at the lawyer in the hope of some shared understanding he looks at me impassively sitting there on his creaking chair fiddling with a big bunch of keys and getting on my nerves with the noise he's making Judge Lince then starts speaking to me his tone of voice is hard hostile and aggressive and he uses the formal *lei*

do you intend to answer you can choose not to answer if you prefer no I say I intend to answer and I try to be as steady as I can and I'm thinking that that atmosphere is worse than all the question and answer situations I've ever been in in my life all the teachers from primary school and secondary school and so on you're aware what you're charged with aren't you no not exactly but was nothing said to you when you were arrested no nothing clear-cut Dottor Donnola only referred to weapons that were supposed to have been found in a house that I rented three years ago and all the while the guy behind the big typewriter is typing with a diabolical racket that interferes with the words I'm speaking and gets on my nerves so when he stops from fear of not having been understood I repeat everything from scratch

then I get very anxious thinking that I must be even more careful about everything I say and I realize that I'm not prepared for this business that I don't know the procedure that just a single word out of place can land me in a mess but I'm thinking that I have to keep answering because I'm sure I can cope with it explaining how things are even if I feel that I'm there alone against all those around me and who I can't see and who are listening to me in silence and my thoughts turn again to beatings I think of how they can beat me up and instinctively I look at my lawyer to make sure that he at least is on my side but I realize at once that I'm fooling myself that this guy couldn't care less he isn't even looking at me his only concern is with cleaning his nails with the point of a key

precisely goes Lince you admit to it then admit to what I say that the house was rented by me yes I admit to it there's even a contract no what I meant by my question was if you admit that the arms found there are yours no what do you mean arms I know nothing at all about these arms I don't know who could have brought them there what do you mean you don't know there were arms in your house no no wait I don't live in my house any more that house I mean I've never said I live in that house and while this is happening I'm looking anxiously at the guy who's bashing it out at the rate of machine gun fire without pausing to look up for a second Lince notices and he tells me not to worry because afterwards he'll have me read the statement and if I don't agree with it I don't have to sign it but that everything that's said has to be written down

at any rate I start talking again and I say it's more than two months since I stopped living in that house and that I sublet it and right away Lince asks who to as if that was just what he'd been waiting for and he jerks forward staring right at me and I feel shitty and I'm thinking what a mess what do I do now I can hardly come out with the name but as if reading my mind Lince starts right back at me and says if you're not going to answer you know you can always refuse to answer the questions it's up to you I'm standing there still with my mouth shut like an idiot with no idea what to say then Lince smiling ironically says very well you don't answer we'll have it recorded that you don't answer and before I can say a thing but what could I say I don't know anyway that guy sets off his diabolical racket and a split second later he's stopped it

shit I thought I've had it now he's got it down in writing and that's how it'll stay but Lince breaks the silence again however I'll tell you the name myself the names rather because we've arrested your comrades all four of them and he mentions Gelso's name and three others I've never heard of it occurs to me it isn't true that the names are to make me talk it's a trick and if it turns out they haven't arrested them and they've only found the arms if even that you know these people don't you no I don't know them to be precise I know one of them there's one I know Gelso but I've never even heard of the other three and would it be this Gelso you sublet the house to damn we're back there again he's come in on a different tack I couldn't say I don't know Gelso but there's no way I could tell him I let the house to him what a mess I say nothing more and the truth is I feel quite muddled

so that's it you don't want to answer this question we've already got it in the statement but look you can be sure there's time to think again there's no problem at all in desperation I look at the lawyer say something for christ sake help me out but he was looking at me with an expression that said what the hell are you stalling for and Lince comes straight back at me very well you don't want to say let's continue the three you say you don't know have refused to speak and they've declared themselves political prisoners while this Gelso you've admitted to knowing has also given me this story about the sublet therefore you lose nothing by admitting it even if I have to tell you frankly I don't believe it I'm sure you've agreed your stories between you in advance but be assured that inquiries will prove you knew one another and that you too were well aware of the existence of those arms in your house

and he goes on raising his voice threateningly but you know that what amounts to a real arsenal was found in your house who do you expect to convince that you knew nothing about it listen for your own good I advise you to tell everything you know if you don't want to run into worse trouble so if you want we'll do the statement all over again we'll tear this one up and you'll tell me how things really are all you have to tell me is the truth but the real truth not what you and your friends concocted if you tell me the truth your crime could be altered from armed conspiracy and possession of weapons to aiding and abetting I can promise you I'll argue for this before the investigating judge otherwise I'll insist on the heaviest charges and you must know that with these charges you'll face years and years in prison

21

After the secondary school certificate exams I'd made up my mind to leave home to stop living with my family to leave the village for good and move elsewhere to rent a house and live there with China and the other comrades who made up our affinity group that's what we called it affinity group precisely because we were all in affinity about our way of living there was a natural understanding between us about how to take things about how to live them there was a great stress on doing things together in living together the whole time there were five of us and for all five the movement was our interest and our first commitment there were two girls and three guys and we'd decided to live together as a natural result of our involvement with one another as a small group

all five of us were fed up to the teeth with family life with going through the motions of being part of the family that really came down to just mealtimes and sleeping mealtimes where there was nothing to say to one another round the table there was no communication there was no interest or involvement and apart from these estranged empty times we spent with our families we spent all the rest of the time on the move like strays at the centre in the movement's haunts with comrades and that's where there was interest involvement communication there were things happening experimentation research the movement was my family with its dozens of open houses hospitable available that was where I had hundreds of siblings to talk to and do things with

the two main problems were money and living space the space had to be big enough to provide everyone with a room of their own as for money there was a bit of a problem because only two of us had a job and a regular wage me and the others who didn't have work would have to look for it however Cotogno and Gelso said not to worry because they could guarantee the rent for a little while and the living expenses too and food would be a shared kitty you put money in whenever you had it and that was all then maybe we'd take turns at going to work the ones who were working now would stop for a bit and the others would work and so on so really the money problem was a problem that could be solved

we started going round inquiring at the agencies but there was nothing to be found and what we did find was at prices we couldn't possibly afford then one day going round the outskirts Cotogno saw a house a little two-storey villa with a small garden in front it was clear no one had lived in it for years there were weeds even trailing up the walls yet there was no to let or for sale sign we rang a few doorbells nearby until we found out that the owner of that empty house for the past six years was a solicitor in the city called Spinone we looked in the phone book and we found the address of Spinone the solicitor and we made up our minds to go there and rent the house for ourselves

we'd decided three of us would go to the solicitor Cotogno me
and China and since we had to deal with a solicitor we thought
we ought to be well dressed Cotogno even put on one of his
father's ties for the occasion that was a hideous sight to behold
with a huge knot against a white shirt that hadn't been ironed
what's more he'd given his unruly beard a trim and pulled back
his long hair that was always sticking out untidily and put on
lacquer to keep it flat only he'd put on too much and his hair was
so flattened that his great big flapping ears stuck out though he
hadn't removed the earring that was his pride and joy and to
complete the picture and give himself a serious air he'd put on a
pair of glasses with tortoise-shell frames that made him see all
fuzzy when we saw him we didn't recognize him and all we did
was laugh the whole time we had to wait in Spinone the solicitor's waiting room

when it's our turn Cotogno jumps to his feet and says peremderpto-
rily let me do the talking he goes into the office with the two of
us behind him and Spinone the solicitor was sunk back in his
brown leather armchair behind a huge desk all fancy and
polished without a speck of dust he started when he saw Cotogno
directly in front of him he just glanced quickly at us two and
went back to staring at Cotogno visibly disturbed by the sight of
him but given that we were clients he forced a smile and a question about how he could help us and Cotogno got right to the
point at once listen my cousin here and his fiancee are getting
married in a few weeks and they're looking for a house you see
and the solicitor nodded with a smile

by good luck we found out that you have a house vacant in such
and such a street and we'd like to rent it blurted Cotogno smiling back at him but the solicitor at once became serious even
irritated and he replied no look I've got no intention of letting
that house as you've seen there's no sign up I'm sorry good day
to you and he gets up ah you don't want to let it to us says

Cotogno no replies Spinone getting impatient it's not that I don't want to let it to you it's that that house isn't to let as I've just told you Cotogno gets up too and says fine if that's how it is we'll see you again no look why do you have to see me again there's no reason to see me again but Cotogno insists good day see you again soon and he makes for the door with us two in tow quite baffled

when we're outside Cotogno explains his plan to us first of all to find out more through a comrade who works in the land-office and it turns out that Spinone is the owner of two other houses and five flats all vacant and then to ask a score of comrades to give us a hand naturally they're more than willing and so a week later we reappear at the solicitor's office of course without warning we leave the comrades down in the street and the same three of us go up this time Cotogno is dressed normally but he still makes quite a startling impression no sooner does the solicitor's secretary set eyes on us than she stiffens and tells us at the door the solicitor's out today but Cotogno brushes past her oblivious and heads straight for the door of the office

as soon as Spinone sees us coming in he goes bananas well how dare you but Cotogno doesn't let him speak listen sweetie you are now going to let the house to us and none of that nonsense about it he threatens to call the police if we don't leave at once then Cotogno says that he'd better not because otherwise it'll come out that he has eight vacant houses that he's moreover not even paying taxes on Spinone gets madder and madder he looks as if he's going to explode any minute and he erupts hurling himself with a scream at China who looking as if the whole thing had nothing to do with her had casually lifted a gold fountain pen from the desk and was unscrewing the cap with a scream Spinone hurls himself at her and grabs the fountain pen from her hand and puts it back in its place

Cotogno has gone to the window come over here instead of yelling and the guy goes towards him at a loss to understand but so as to keep his distance from Cotogno he opens the window next to his and looks down into the street below all the comrades were standing there looking up at the open windows and as is the way of it the passers-by had also stopped to look up within a few minutes there was a small crowd looking up without any idea what was going on at that point one comrade unrolls a big sheet of paper which has written on it Spinone do the decent thing give us the house Spinone turns back inside his face pale and whispers through his teeth mafiosi criminals Cotogno goes up to him and staring him in the face says it's you that's the criminal it's you that's the stinking speculator we'll pay for your house we want a fair rent give us a contract otherwise we'll call the police and report you do you want me to call them right now I mean it I'll call the police says Cotogno with his hand on the telephone receiver

reeling Spinone goes back to his desk he drops into the armchair and sits in silence for a minute or two biting his lips while through the open windows you could hear the chorus of comrades Spinone give us the house Spinone give us the house Spinone's goose was cooked now he made a try at saying all right but I have to think it over come back in a few days it takes time to draw up a contract no way said Cotogno adamant sitting down on the desk you're going to do us the contract now at once otherwise we're not leaving and we'll even get our friends downstairs to come up and so in the end seeing as there was no other way Spinone gave in and so we got that house that became however the source of all my troubles

22

I'd fainted then the first thing I felt was that a comrade took me
and dragged me right outside at that moment there was complete
darkness in this courtyard and there were still only a few
comrades there and I remember that this comrade who was able
to stand up because he must have come off a bit lighter in the
guards' brutality session that was still in progress I could still
hear the screams and the blows the guards' insults this comrade
carried me to the fountain there was a tap he splashed some
water on my face until I began to come to then I remember that
I hurt all over everything crushed but I managed to stand up to
walk everything hurting but I could still manage to walk

and at the same time all this is continuing and from there outside
the gate of the fence I could see that the comrades were still
going past the bloodbath was still in progress they went on beating people up I remember that there inside it was dark you
couldn't see what was there in the yard I found myself in but I
remember seeing one comrade who was sitting on this concrete
bench there leaning with his back against the wall he was on this
bench not moving and his face was completely covered in blood
my first thought was that this comrade's face had been smashed
up he was no longer recognizable I recognized him by his clothes
you could no longer see his face it was a mask of blood then I
took a handkerchief and we started to wipe his face a bit

the ghastly thing was this what was absurd was having to stand
by powerless and witness this massacre that was going on right
in front of your eyes behind this wire fence and you could see
the whole spectacle you could see this ghastly spectacle and
the ghastly thing was not only that you felt powerless because
you were mangled up but doubly powerless because not only
could you do nothing about what was happening but if you
even gave any sign of retaliation maybe even verbal retaliation

because what else could you do these guys would have come in and you were absolutely in no state to make the slightest resistance after having taken all those beatings and it would only have been worse

now this brought you down quite unbelievably it brought you down worse than the beatings you could only stand by powerless instinct told you to keep quiet but how could you manage to keep quiet in front of that spectacle and then you were forced to watch how these guys beat up your comrades and they were dishing out different kinds of beatings because they weren't giving them all the same treatment there were some comrades they were really taking it out on and they were clearly the comrades they hated most because with them there'd been rows set-tos threats and so on and also because there were the ones who in the internal scheme of prison relationships were thought to be the leaders but through the whole thing the guards were like fiends out of hell and really determined to beat the life out of us all

an incredible degree of hatred was being unleashed and the proceedings were noisy there was a dreadful noise it was noisy because of the blows you could hear being struck it was noisy because of the moans but it was noisy most of all because of the screams of hatred because of the abuse scum bastard and when a comrade they particularly hated came along a whole lot of them would throw themselves on him screaming abuse and dealing him terrible blows there was one of these comrades who was greatly hated by the guards he was barely five feet tall they really pulverized him because they hated him and you watched this scene powerless and you thought to yourself there's no way this guy's going to stay alive with the beating they're giving him it was a pounding that went on too long to be just a pounding they were hitting out with truncheons with sticks with iron bars and this comrade who was small they really pulverized him then another scene I watched was a guy they took by the hair after having trampled him to the ground they dragged him up by the hair and stuck him up against the wall and then one of them hit him in the face with an iron bar just like this a blow with the iron bar like this across the face and they smashed his nose and his forehead and then there was another horrible scene with another comrade that they hit in the mouth with an iron bar while he was lying on the ground and they smashed all his teeth here at the front these were the things to be seen while we were there in the dark powerless behind the wire fence

they forced another one to put his hands against the wall they took his hands and they held them fixed there on the wall and they hit him on the hands with the bars they hit him an awful lot on the fingers and they smashed all his fingers here here here and here they smashed his hands and then his fingers here his fingers here and his fingers here and now when this comrade eats he loses hold of his spoon he drops his spoon because he can't keep it in his hand afterwards when this guy used a plastic spoon to eat with in prison he always dropped the spoon because his fingers could no longer keep hold of anything he could no longer feel a grip on anything and his hands were broken for ever

the guards mainly took it out on the ones they'd had aggravation from this fury this hatred this thing of theirs was mainly centred on all those earlier goings on in the prison things that had happened there before the revolt but also because they were convinced that one of them had died because they were convinced that in all the chaos there'd been during the revolt someone had got killed we'd killed some guards the news they'd had was that there'd been some guards injured but they'd mistakenly believed that they'd been injured by the prisoners and were now in danger of death while in fact they'd been injured by the *carabinieri* by the machine-gun fire of the *carabinieri* so these guys were saying you knifed the guards and now we're going to murder you they'd got it into their heads to kill us in earnest I mean to kill some of us with their bare hands and the absurd thing was that while the *carabinieri* were shooting and they'd been shooting like lunatics and I'd thought as I heard the shots they were firing I was thinking they're going to kill us all the absurd thing now was that it wasn't the *carabinieri* here it was the guards beating the life out of you not the *carabinieri* when they fired their machine guns and threw their grenades and now behind the wire you saw they were killing someone in earnest they were beating him to death you said Jesus Christ they're murdering that guy they won't stop hitting him he's been on the ground for I don't know how long and there are still ten of them on top of him laying into him the guy's going to die no mistake

then some guys came in who were in a terrible state they were all mangled up covered in blood all smashed up they had broken legs they had broken arms you saw them with their broken arms their broken legs they were screaming there in our yard there must have been thirty of us we counted ourselves in the end there were thirty of us but there were only three of us standing I mean standing meant just able to stand up not to run around but to manage just to stand up without falling there were three of us and it was by pure chance that we three weren't also in a state like all the rest who were there lying on the ground the rest were all on the ground with their bones broken with their bones really broken with broken legs with broken arms with broken faces with broken heads with blood all over the place

23

While I was listening to that threatening tirade from Judge Lince I tried desperately to concentrate my thoughts on what I should do I thought that if what he'd told me was true then Gelso had tried to put me in the clear by saying that I'd sublet the house but if it was a trap I couldn't see how I'd manage to extricate myself it was a real shambles and I realized how naive I'd been to think up to now that I'd be able to explain under questioning that I'd be able to explain that I had fuck all to do with that business and that they'd understand and let me go so I put my mind at rest that in any case they'd persist whatever I said the questioning was just another thing to screw you with and so it was better to put a stop to it at once because however it went on it would only make things worse

when Lince finished he paused then since I was silent he decided to go on with more detachment and in a more self-congratulatory tone I should tell you moreover that I've also taken evidence from Spinone the solicitor the owner of the house rented by you who states that he was quite clearly threatened physically among other things by you and other individuals to persuade him to draw up the contract what do you have to say about that then without me even thinking about it the words came out almost of their own accord I reserve the right to clarify these matters the next time I'm questioned and so the questioning came to an end I didn't give a fuck if Lince took those words as an admission of what he'd said I didn't give a fuck because it was obvious that in any case he was only there to put me in prison whatever happened

Lince had no objections he got me to read the statement and he got me to sign it the lawyer signed it too he wished everyone good evening and without even glancing in my direction he rushed off by this time the prison was closed they took no admissions at that time of night and so Lince told the police officers to take me down to the security cells inside headquarters I picked up my bag with the toothbrush and underpants in it for they'd taken off my handcuffs that were clearly only meant to stop me from strangling the judge everyone left and they made me go back the same way I'd come down the narrow stairs but when we got to the ground floor we kept on going further and further down

we go down between the damp walls lit by dirty light bulbs hanging from frayed electric wires when we got to the bottom they took me into a tiny room a lumber room where there was a young cop with a pistol in the holster under his armpit and this guy took my fingerprints every finger first one hand then the other hand he pressed them on a big pad of black ink and then pressed them on the page of a register and then underneath he wrote down my particulars he looked very fed up you could see he wasn't at all happy at having that work to do then he held out a filthy rag for me to clean my hands on but it was useless none of it came off and after persevering for a bit I gave up and made do with black hands

I lifted my bag again dangling it from two fingers we came out of there and went along the corridor a bit turning corners all the time then one of the cops escorting me knocks at a big wooden door all worm-eaten with peeling varnish no one comes to open it then he knocks louder and calls out officer open the door and there appears a giant of a man with a great beard as black as ink a mouth the width of an oven door and a pair of red eyes who was holding a big bunch of keys with which he closes the door noisily behind me and I find myself in a big room dimly lit by one light bulb hanging in the middle no windows the floor and walls filthy the walls flaking away with the dampness

the giant takes us in and we go up to a long table up against the wall the guy curses in a fit of temper for some reason from one of the corridors there comes confused shouting mingled with moans and howls then a louder scream and the giant swearing in a rage and uttering broken phrases in a southern dialect I don't understand rushes towards the corridor where there's a row of heavy grey doors he opens the spy-holes one after the other yelling threats and slamming them violently shut then he comes back to the table and yells at the two who brought me there pointing at me with the bunch of keys and what about him they explain that I have to spend the night there the giant takes them back to the door opens it and shuts it again then he hooks the bunch of keys on his belt again and comes back towards me still standing there with my bag dangling from my fingers

he rips the bag from my hand and throws it on the table then he yells at me aggressively to strip I don't even attempt to tell him that I've already been searched because I can tell from his face that he's only waiting for the slightest excuse to lift his hand to me his face is all sweaty and his uniform soiled and greasy with big dark stains all over it and so there's a complete re-run of the search routine only this time more violently because it's as if the guy wants to rip off my clothes by the avid way he handles them cursing all the time in a foul temper rolling his red eyes finally he makes me turn around naked two or three times he runs his filthy big hands two or three times through my hair which was on the long side and at last he tells me to take my stuff the clothes the bag and the stuff that was in it all scattered across the table and to follow him

I don't know whether I'm supposed to get dressed again first but I don't ask *him* he's at it again shouting and cursing I notice now that in that big smokey room there are three more of his kind hanging about obviously his subordinates and he's shouting things at them through that gaping oven of a mouth he's got and so naked as I am I tuck all my stuff under my arm and I follow him into the corridor past the row of grey doors from where there's still shouting and moaning he opens a door and pushes me into the darkness with a great shove at my back that nearly throws me to the ground then he slams the door shut with a clang I feel very cold and suddenly it occurs to me that there might be someone else there too who I can't see but who's seen me when the door opened I'm shivering with the cold but with fear too thinking that someone can jump on me at any minute somebody vile and monstrous because nobody there could be anything else but vile

I stay there for a few moments in a state of paralysis the fact that I'm naked makes me feel somehow the impossibility of protecting myself I stay there motionless waiting for the monster to jump on me unable to lift a finger it seems bound to happen until I hear the curses getting close again and without warning the spy-hole is opened I can see his head silhouetted against the light and a weak beam of light briefly illuminates the depths of the cell and I can see it's empty at the back there's only a kind of raised concrete platform I grope in the darkness I climb on to it until my hands can reach the back wall which is damp and cold taking my time I manage to get dressed again I roll up my jacket then I stretch out on the concrete and rest my head on it

I close my eyes my ears are filled with the muffled voices coming from the other cells the moaning the shouting the cursing I try to stop my ears but it's pointless but I'm tired out I'm exhausted the muscles in my legs hurt as if I'd been running all day and I fall asleep straight away but it isn't an undisturbed sleep every so often I'd wake up with the shouting and the slamming of doors and then I'd be plunged into sleep again and then again I'd wake up once I heard a woman singing in a loud voice everyone sleeps at night but I never sleep she was drunk then when they made her stop she started to cry even louder I fell asleep and woke up repeatedly and that's how the entire night went by

I realized it was morning when the fire eater opened my cell door and ordered me in his incomprehensible dialect to get outside at the double he was even dirtier greasier and sweatier and he was scratching his great black beard with both hands he took me up to the table against the wall where he gave me back my bag and handed me over to three new policemen who'd come for me two young ones and an older guy in plain clothes with white shirts and ties freshly shaved glossy hair all three with the same smell of aftershave they put the handcuffs on me behind my back one of them took my bag after looking inside it and feeling about a bit we went back up the stairs and when we got to the ground floor I had to screw up my eyes with the sunlight

24

Suddenly we're bathed in a strong bright light they'd brought in two big engine-generators a deafening hum started up and they set about shining giant searchlights onto the yards they were in shadow and you were totally exposed to the light surrounded by this scene of blood everywhere of people with their heads split open everything broken and moaning to themselves and these guys still masked in the shadow started hitting the wire fence with metal bars and clubs and shouting bastards queers we'll make you all pay for it on your knees beg for mercy cocksuckers motherfuckers this is only the start and this really scared us stiff fuck if these guys really come inside and just deal out a few more beatings to these guys lying here mangled on the ground that's it it's over for them they did all this crap stuff and at the same time it happened that there was a comrade in my yard sitting there not moving I didn't speak to him because since I was able to stand up I was helping the ones that were more badly beaten and since I'd seen he was sitting up not moving and had no sign of blood or anything I thought he must be in a state of shock with it all but nothing really wrong then when the more serious cases the injured and the ones covered in blood pulled themselves together a bit people got themselves into a sitting position against the wall it was something anyway if not much and I said to him hey how are you he spoke slowly I feel something broken inside and the fact was that he had all his ribs broken later he was taken to the hospital during the night because he couldn't be left there he couldn't make the slightest movement without screaming from the pain of all his broken ribs

I was waiting for my cell-mate who I'd got separated from in the confusion when the *carabinieri* made their entrance I was very worried because he'd gone down to the first floor and I thought that downstairs there'd been a disaster that people had been killed because as the comrades were gradually turning up I was asking them all has somebody been killed then and somebody had answered I think more than one and so I was waiting for this cell-mate of mine then I saw him go by and I saw what a beating they'd given him they'd really given him a bad one then he came into the same exercise yard as me he walked in still hopping about without taking his hands away from the back of his head he was wearing woollen gloves and I asked him how are you and he told me OK but I must have all my fingers broken then I took off his gloves as gently as I could one finger at a time with him blaspheming every madonna you can think of but he hadn't broken them all just one or two

after the guards threatened to come back into the exercise yards they went away a fearful silence descended nobody was speaking to anyone else any more and this was something that struck me again later because at that point I believe everyone thought it was futile to speak to say anything at all there was a moment when everyone froze just as they were petrified like statues under the brilliant light of the generators and you could only hear the noise of the generators then the din started up again the guards had gone upstairs and they were breaking everything up they wrecked everything they destroyed everything smashing everything wrecking everything everything to be found there they were screaming like damned souls and they were taking it out on your stuff that was in the cells

they took the television sets and hurled them to the ground they took all the objects all the boxes all the bottles and smashed them to smithereens and trampled them underfoot they broke up stools and tables they broke up everything they tore the books to shreds they took the clothes and pulled them apart and threw them on the ground and pissed on them they yanked out the radiators and the water flooded out over the entire floor they wrecked the entire prison they made it unusable they were the ones who wrecked it not us for half an hour they took it out on our belongings on the prison shouting screaming they were in a frenzy then they calmed down also because probably some news had reached them the kidnapped guards had talked about how things had been that they hadn't been injured by the prisoners that it had been the *carabinieri* who'd injured them

while those guys were demolishing the prison people had calmed down a bit because as long as they were destroying things it meant they were leaving us alone then it was clear that the worst was over when the guards came back down and they weren't masked any more they weren't wearing the balaclavas any more and that was when we realized they wouldn't be beating people up any more because their faces were uncovered and the sergeants started saying if anyone's sick we'll take him to hospital but nobody wanted to leave the yards because they didn't trust them not even the worst cases not even the ones who were really in a bad way and had broken bones and the sergeants started giving reassurances no we won't do a thing to you we'll take you to hospital and we'll take the ones who're not so bad into the infirmary here

well there was a comrade who was in a particularly bad way because they'd hit him in the throat and he couldn't breathe this guy kept fainting he was wheezing as if he was going to suffocate so we'd had to take turns at putting a finger in his mouth because this guy's tongue kept twisting backwards and into his throat he wasn't breathing and he was going blue in the face he was close to suffocating so we had to keep him sitting up with his back against the wall and put our fingers in his mouth me and another comrade took turns at it we took turns at putting our fingers in his throat we held his tongue with our fingers trying to flatten his tongue to keep it still so that some air could get into his throat but it was hard because the guy wouldn't keep his head still

it went on like this for an hour and whenever we managed to get him breathing a bit easier the guy would say his voice really faint I don't want to go to the hospital because I heard a guard who was beating me up say that they want to kill me then we had to reassure him because the way he was he was really in danger of dying meanwhile other comrades started going out to be taken to hospital then there was a stream of people all through the night going to hospital or to the infirmary and the ones with broken bones had plaster-casts put on the ones with cuts had them sewn up had stitches and so on but this guy who couldn't breathe was still there half the night not wanting to go out and we thought he was dying then around four or five in the morning we made up our minds and we took him to the gate because he really couldn't stay there like that any longer

from that point when they started taking people to hospital and
to the infirmary the guards no longer made threats and they
stopped being violent this freezing cold night passed maybe it
was Christmas night I don't remember now just imagine if it
mattered at all to anyone there that it was Christmas the temper-
ature was below zero and we didn't have a thing at dawn the
guards turned up with milk we couldn't believe it with bread
and hot milk and blankets people were still there in a lot of pain
but with plaster-casts on now fear had subsided and so there was
the first sound of voices people started to talk to one another
inside each of the yards and then there was the first sound of
voices resounding from yard to yard because there were walls
between them and you couldn't see either side how's x how's y
we were glad that no one had died and then the main thing was
that they weren't beating us any more

for the whole day we all lay there stretched out on the blankets
on the ground because all the pains the bruises the blows were
coming out now at noon they brought us sausages cooked food
bread as well then the darkness came down again and that night
was splendid because the sky was clear as can be and there were
oh so many stars the air was extremely cold and then very slowly
one by one they started taking us out of the yard and they took
us into the ground floor cells they'd taken everything away and
they'd only left the beds the ground floor hadn't been involved
in the revolt they couldn't put us upstairs because everything
had been wrecked and so they'd taken the working prisoners and
they'd put them somewhere else for the time being

they'd taken everything away from inside the cells they'd taken
away the little wardrobes the tables the stools anything there
was nothing left in the cells there were only the bed frames
attached to the floor and the usual foam rubber mattresses which
were plain blocks of foam rubber and nothing more and they
started taking us out one at a time and they put us in groups in

these cells they put me in a small dormitory cell with five beds there were ten of us and by the time we'd all stretched out there was no room to walk about and we were there like that ten of us with no belongings with blankets with the clothes we'd been wearing because there was no way we could change our things were upstairs on the floor that was wrecked we still had on the same torn dirty bloodstained clothes and we stayed there in these conditions for three weeks

25

It was a lovely day and the weather was mild in the courtyard at police headquarters there was a great to-ing and fro-ing of people in uniform and in plain clothes blue and white cars driving in and out very fast they made me get into an unmarked car me in the back seat with the guy carrying my bag next to me the other young one was driving and in the passenger seat the oldest guy with the fatherly look about him we drove off and as soon as we were outside I looked at myself in the rearview mirror my face looked dreadful my eyes red and swollen my hair dishevelled and lank my hands so blackened that I couldn't even touch myself but more than anything I felt as if I had a layer of filthy slippery grease all over me on my skin on my clothes on my hair like the guards in that sewer down there I'd just come from

now I'm going to prison I wonder what prison is like I have no clear idea I ransack my memory for whatever I've read in the movement literature or the stories I've heard from those who'd been there but nothing much came back to me to help me imagine what was in store we came up to a red light the driver brakes through the window I can see a girl on a bicycle alongside the car one foot on a pedal the other resting on the ground I'd like to be riding around on a bicycle now too if I'd thought about it yesterday I wouldn't have cared less I'd have thought that riding a bicycle isn't that much fun in fact it's extra work for nothing whereas now I was thinking it's a lovely thing to do

then the light changes to green and the car drives straight on while the girl is still there stationary with one foot on a pedal and the other resting on the ground I'd have liked to turn round but I don't I'm stuck between two policemen and my role is to be someone who's going to gaol I can hardly turn to look at girls riding bicycles the oldest guy turns and asks me in a fatherly tone of voice if it's the first time I'm going inside yes I tell him and he makes an apologetic face and asks me how old I am you're young it's a nasty thing to go through and shakes his head they're always like that the older ones the younger ones are hard tight-lipped they don't say a word to you if they talk to you at all it's to give you orders you can sense the hatred and contempt but the old ones too they're all the same thing they're all the same at heart they all do the same things the same job

my role is to be someone who's going to gaol now I was thinking about the comrades and this consoled me because I was thinking that now they would all be rallying round busy making efforts on my behalf they wouldn't leave me to fend for myself and I was proud of the fact that I had all these comrades this big family that was taking responsibility for my situation and my problems that would think of everything a lawyer money all the other things that for now I couldn't imagine I felt that I wasn't on my own I was part of a collective strength and this made me feel very strong I would bravely bear everything that lay ahead of me and I was thinking that now I had to behave as if the comrades could see me I wasn't on my own they were with me always there whatever happened we reach the prison for a bit the car drives round the outer wall with the guard towers then it stops in front of a big gateway that's closed in front of it there's a stationary squad car and round it are four policemen in uniform with submachine guns under their arms and bullet-proof vests on they're looking about anxiously and they're looking inside the cars that go by slowly the gateway inches open and a grey uniform leans halfway out also wearing a bullet-proof vest and carrying a sub-machine gun with the barrel pointing up a bit the oldest guy in my escort gets out of the car goes up to him speaks to him and hands him some sheets of paper the grey uniform takes them studies them for a moment then goes back inside the gateway and the gate is closed again

after a while the gateway opens again just enough to let our car through it comes to a halt in front of a second gateway just as the first gate is being shut inside it's dark in the entrance yard there's only the light from two dim bulbs on the right there's a guard-room with bullet-proof glass its door closed and more armed grey uniforms inside the police escort gets out of the car and they hand over their pistols then they get back in meanwhile I stay put in the back seat the second gate is opened and the car slowly drives on thirty or forty yards along an asphalt path and stops again we all get out and another grey figure opens a gate for us that leads to a long narrow corridor then on the left a door with the notice registration office

we go into a big room full of shelves stacked higgledy-piggledy with registers and big tables in cracked green formica and grey uniforms that look as if they're working as clerks among the papers that are scattered about there's a high counter dividing the whole length of the room in two the escort trio take off my handcuffs they have a hurried word with the one that looks like the office supervisor there they hand him some papers and my bag and they leave without even a look at me the office supervisor motions me to sit down on a bench and goes back to the work he was doing when we came in he takes a pile of papers from one table and moves them on to another table then he takes another pile of papers from another table and moves it on to the first table but he doesn't seem satisfied and shaking his head he shifts it all back the way it was before

after a while he waves me forward to the counter he brings out a big register and an inking pad and he takes my fingerprints all over again my hands get even dirtier from the ink by now they're quite black by now I know how it's done and I try to impress my fingers on the sheet all by myself for I don't want that guy to take hold of my hands but he does it just the same obviously because he's used to doing it then he takes down my particulars too he writes them down underneath the fingerprints and he adds the charge and I can read subversive association armed band and possession of arms then he measures my height with a rickety old ruler like the ones they use in a military-service medical and he writes that in the register too and puts it away

finally he makes me hand over my wallet with my money and my identity card and he makes me hand over my watch and my belt and everything I had in my pocket my lighter and my keys and he puts them on the counter beside my bag he summons two guards and says take him to the cells he's in judicial isolation they don't call you by your name here among themselves the guards always call you him and I go with the two guards we go through an awful lot of gates always with a guard at each one to open and shut it in the corridors we meet other guards who go past singly or in groups or escorting prisoners then eventually we reach a small door that a guard opens for us and we go down the stairs that lead underground to the isolation cells

at the bottom of the stairs there's another small door that's opened for us from inside there's a wide corridor thirty or forty yards long and on each side of the corridor every two or three yards there's a locked grey metal door with a closed spy-hole and at the end of the corridor there's a wall with no windows and a small locked door everything is lit with fluorescent strip-lights the two guards accompanying me go up to one of the guards in the corridor addressing him as sergeant of the guard the sergeant has a big bunch of keys attached to his belt he takes one of them and opens the armoured door of cell number twenty-seven then with the same key he opens a gate that's behind the armoured door

before taking me inside one of the guards escorting me pins a card with my name and number on the wall beside the door a five-figure number then they wave me in I go inside they come in behind me and they tell me to undress naked one more time I undress naked one more time and they go through a whole new search looking thoroughly through all my clothes where by now there's nothing left at all then they go out and the sergeant closes the gate he turns the key in the lock then takes two steps back and pushes the door and the door closes with a dull thud I can hear the key turning and I'm left standing there naked with my hands all black in isolation cell number twenty-seven

Part Three

26

And now here I've lost track of where I left off with this whole story also because there are loads of things I can't remember that I've no clear memory of how they happened and there are also loads of things that can't be remembered but can only be forgotten it's not as if I want to tell the whole story of my life nor do I want to tell everything that happened during this time when so many different contradictory things of all kinds happened that to put them all together and try to make sense of them seems to me quite impossible but what concerns me right now is just to speak about those things that happened to me but from my point of view of course just because maybe now it's worthwhile speaking about it

at school what happened was that after we'd got him on the run the headmaster Mastino left and the teachers had had to adjust their power had crumbled we'd won the right to mass meetings we'd got everything no more oral tests no more registers suspensions excuses and so on the school had erupted in a short time it had become an open school people of all kinds came friends and students from other schools workers who weren't at work unemployed people came instead of hanging around the bars and assorted marginals came instead of just wandering about we called all these people non-residents and so the school became a fair a bazaar where we played chess and we played cards and we brought things to drink and joints and the teachers stood by powerless without daring to lift a finger as everything went to rack and ruin

one of these non-residents was Nocciola who by now was coming to our school every day Nocciola got by with a bit of shoplifting in the supermarkets and the shops he thieved all kinds of things even stuff he didn't need because then he'd resell it the school had kind of become his market in fact there were people who'd order things from him in advance moccassin shoes or a record player and then us too because we didn't have any money and now we were fed up with asking for it at home luckily Nocciola was there teaching us a thousand and one ways to get by with not much money and how to find it we did a bit of mass shoplifting in the bookshops and then we sold the books to stall-holders we forged canteen vouchers Nocciola knew how to get telephone coin boxes open and he always went round with tons of tokens in his pockets he paid for everything with telephone tokens he went to the cinema and paid with telephone tokens

bit by bit we started selling off the school we started taking it apart really taking it apart and selling the stuff piece by piece light-fittings typewriters chairs stools encyclopaedias from the library materials from the chemistry and physics laboratory the glass cases and the cupboards there was nothing left in the school then they bought everything brand new again but we sold it all all over again and so they gave up the teachers didn't even leave their cars in the car park otherwise the tyres would disappear on them the school had now become an empty space quite void of interest too nothing to do with us at all at a certain point we realized we had to leave and go and clean somewhere else out and so we didn't go there any more and we started living at the centre when we took over the centre what happened was that we'd gone to the centre of a Marxist-Leninist group to ask if there was any chance of using it for our meetings it was a very big centre five or six rooms it was on the ground floor of an old building in the centre of town it was very well kept the parquet floor was polished everything was very neat and tidy with red curtains but at the same time it was very gloomy those big empty rooms and the smell of a locked-up church there were huge Chinese posters framed under glass posters with Chinese workers and peasants very muscular and always smiling with fists raised and great big banners hanging the whole length of the walls long live the heroic victory of the Cambodian people there was one room turned into a cultural centre the Antonio Gramsci Cultural Centre it said on a polished plate on the door

when we rang the bell there was only one comrade there arranging the library books nearly all Chinese editions of the works of Mao and Stalin and other things like that and he announced us to the comrade secretary who was in his office behind a polished desk with a telephone on it the secretary was a diminutive individual with a big belly very earnest all the time with a big grey overcoat that was never taken off we told him what we wanted but he started talking about political lines giving us a long tirade about the political line of his party he was looking for a bit of political confrontation but we couldn't have cared less about political confrontation at that time there were loads of struggles going on and it was the first we'd ever seen of this lot and now here he was asking us to take up a position on the political line of their party

we couldn't have cared less but we had to listen to the whole of his triumphalist tirade about his party we kept looking at the telephone hoping it would ring and interrupt him it never rang though but then he tells us that in that particular conjuncture however the party presence in town had been weakened by the expulsion of some militants for right-wing or left-wing deviationism though they did have three workers functioning as a party cell inside two factories and one student but lately this student had been going around with a bad crowd people who hung about at the station and they even suspected him of being on drugs and in the end the comrade secretary let himself go and said that they didn't have any more money to pay the rent and even the telephone had been cut off and the three workers had it up to here with taking a cut out of their wages every month to pay for the centre so we reached an agreement that they would transfer all the rooms but one to us and that was that

three or four of them put up a partition to separate their room from the others and they made a separate entrance but after all this work we never saw or heard from them again until we realized that they'd stopped coming and then we pulled down the partition and we used their room too immediately within just a few days there was a great convergence of people all the dispersed people of the movement began to pour in all kinds turned up workers students unemployed people women dropouts old people comrades from the extra-parliamentary groups anarchists it was a different place from the usual sort of centre the groups had it was a movement centre and since it was big there was plenty of room there for all these differences

we'd inherited all the MLs' furnishings their chairs their bookshelves their cupboards though the comrade secretary had taken away the telephone we'd inherited the big framed Chinese posters with Mao strolling around the middle of the countryside smiling followed by squads of peasants holding sickles or pitchforks or rifles and we left them as they were the centre was always open we made a show of closing it in the evening shutting the door but the fact was that there were no keys there were people coming and going all the time there were meetings of

workers of students of casual workers of hospital workers of
women but also groups that turned up there with guitars flutes
and so on to play to smoke joints to fix up dates for the evening
it had become everybody's regular drop-in place

of course the comrades also used the centre as a place for working out the various systems for not paying electricity bills gas
bills telephone bills systems for not paying for transport for
sabotaging the ticket machines on the buses for forging train
tickets for sabotaging the electricity meters and so on they were
things that started spontaneously with individuals or small
groups and that by word of mouth would then lead to the organization of real mass struggles around these things for instance
we'd started going to the cinema on Sundays for free fifty or
sixty of us would push our way in or at a pinch if it was clear that
they'd call the police we'd throw down a derisory sum that was
no more than token

the same thing went for the fancy shops in the centre of town
for thirty or forty of us to go into a really smart shop was in
itself already pretty intimidating and even without having to
hurry much it was really easy to make off with a stereo deck a
leather jacket a camera and so on the same thing went for the
transport struggles we'd travel in large groups and we'd say we
weren't paying then we'd give out leaflets to the rest of the
passengers to encourage them to do the same thing until it
became routine and the conductor didn't even ask the
comrades for tickets not even when they were on their own in
the early days the bus company had the idea of putting guards
on the buses but then it had to give this up because along with
this it had to budget for the cost of wrecked bus stations and
even a pair of buses that went up in smoke one night our centre
was right in the middle of town and the whole surrounding
area was in fact occupied by us movement people came and
went groups of comrades would hang out all day sitting outside

on benches in the small park about two hundred yards away there was a big department store that was visited daily by groups of comrades at one point the management of the department store decided to tackle these brazen daily raids and they installed a large number of security guards one day they started chasing some comrades who'd stolen some food they ran after them even once they were outside the store and then the comrades started running in the direction of our centre and they started shouting and in no time there was a general alert everyone outside with the banners which were just pickaxe handles with a strip of red cloth attached

the security guards weren't expecting this they stopped short a few yards away from the first banners about-turn and away they went but they knew one of our comrades by name and they reported her to the police and for fear of some retaliation by us they asked for two cars full of cops to be stationed in front of the entrance then the women comrades came up with a nice move and twenty or thirty of them went into the department store and once inside they started making the rounds of the fashion department with razor blades and that was that jackets sweaters skirts trousers raincoats dresses overcoats a real disaster damage to the tune of millions of lire and then they just left calm as you please nobody noticed a thing the police cars stayed on guard for another two weeks and meanwhile people went and did their thieving in another supermarket then they went back there and started all over again

in the early days the centre was used by the movement as a whole mainly for activities like these some even used the centre as a temporary lodging those who'd maybe left home the day before it became their berth for the night they'd pull their sleeping bags out of the cupboard then in the morning they'd roll them up again and store them back in the cupboard there were washing facilities and there was heating and in one room we'd even come up with a bar the gathering point for everybody was the general meeting that was held in the biggest room roughly once a week all packed together in there we'd discuss all the things that the different collectives planned to do or had done during the week and we'd tackle the problem of how to use the strength that we'd built so as to generalize the offensive to the factories to the schools to the hospitals to the local districts to the squares and we'd get leaflets ready

to generalize the offensive means to radicalize disaffection with whichever hierarchy you choose to exercise our destructive creativity against the society of the spectacle to sabotage the machines and goods that sabotage our lives to promote indefinite wildcat general strikes always to have mass meetings in all the separate factories to elect delegates who can be recalled by the base to keep continuous links between all the places of struggle to overlook no useful technical means of free communication to give a direct use value to everything that has an exchange value to occupy permanently the factories and the public buildings to organize self-defence of the conquered territories and on with the music

27

The isolation cell was six feet by nine an iron bedstead fixed to the floor a foam rubber mattress a foam rubber pillow two sheets a pillow-slip a brown blanket a dirty white ceramic washbasin and that was all and on the far wall across from the door there was a barred window some wire netting behind the window which looks on to a passageway that's hardly wide enough for one person to go through it but judging by the accumulation of dust dirt and cobwebs it must have been a long time since anyone had gone through it the cell is lit by a very bright light that comes from a bulb that's out of sight but which must be in the corridor above the door and the light filters in through an iron grating about a foot square

the floor is poured concrete furrowed with cracks of assorted sizes the cracks are full of dust dirty cigarette ends bits of plaster the walls that once must have been white are a dirty yellow colour and here and there all over the place bits of plaster are coming away after having first formed bubbles on account of the damp the bubbles swell up then they break then the bits of plaster start to come away and fall on the floor they are also coming off the low uneven ceiling and falling in the middle of the cell on the walls all kinds of writing dug into the plaster with fingernails or burned in with cigarettes the writing is prolific intricate with some things written over others half crossed out so that it's all muddled up

low down on the left at floor level a small iron door about a foot high not quite closed I open it there's a small opening and inside there's a metal bucket covered in rust which gives off a nauseating stink inside it there are still traces of shit and piss cockroaches foul insects I close the door with a kick I'll never have a shit in there no way right now I don't need to shit but I need to piss I go and piss in the washbasin even that's pretty foul all scummy and full of cracks it's ready to split right open I run the water for a long time there's a stink coming from the little door that almost makes me vomit but maybe the stink was there before and I didn't notice it it's the stink of that subterranean place

a nauseating stink of piss of shit of vomit of enclosure I try to hold my breath for a few seconds but it's just the same it changes nothing in fact when I breathe out again it's worse I look around but there's nothing to look at I sit down on the bed and I listen I can hear only the slow dragging tread of a guard up and down the corridor unlike the cell at police headquarters there's silence here but maybe the silence is worse I look at my hands black with ink I try to wash them with water from the washbasin but there isn't even a scrap of soap and the water runs off the impermeable ink then I think of scraping it off with one of the bits of plaster that's coming off the walls but it's futile I give up and I sit down again on the bed what do I do now I wonder and now what do I do

what do you do in here to pass the time and then it occurs to me that I don't even know how much time I'll have to spend here I don't even know what to wait for no that's it the lawyer I have to wait for the lawyer I'll leave the cell to see the lawyer but then I'll have to come back again and I'm gripped by an oppressive sensation as if something was squeezing my lungs my heart my stomach everything inside everything closed compressed a painful lump I look at my black hands I have to be careful where I put them so that I don't leave marks all over the place my clothes the sheets but I've nothing to keep my hands occupied they've left me nothing only half a pack of cigarettes but no lighter what good are cigarettes to me if I've nothing to light them with

I hear the sound of the key in the door two turns of the lock the door opens the sergeant of the guard appears with two guards beside him and he tells me that I have to go and see the doctor I go out without asking why because I guess that it's routine we go down to the end of the corridor and we reach the last cell that's been converted into an infirmary if you can call it that containing a small bed covered with a transparent plastic sheet a desk and a plastic cabinet with a few medicines in it the doctor is young an unpleasant peevish expression on his face he hardly glances at me then he writes my details on a card and starts to ask me about childhood and adolescent illnesses

measles mumps chicken pox all that sort of thing he reads them off a list rattling away like an express train he doesn't even wait for me to answer he ticks off each line on the list and only looks up with a question about whether I've got any infectious illnesses I answer no and then he's finished he scribbles something at the bottom of the card and signals to the guards to say that we can leave the whole thing has lasted a minute I'm back in my cell again the gate and the metal door slam behind me I stand there for a bit then I decide to make the bed I do it all very slowly I take twice or three times as long as I'd usually take so as to fill up the longest possible time

when I get to the blanket I realize it can't have been washed for months if I move it at all it sends up clouds of dust it's so full of dust it weighs double it's more or less covered in patches of dried stuff it's really disgusting but it's cold and I can't do without the blanket and I spread it out evenly over the sheets I stretch out on the bed and I start reading the things written on the walls trying to concentrate on one bit of writing after the other trying to read that whole muddle of stains and dirt it seems as if the stench is stronger when I'm lying down I get up I lie down again three or four times until I'm sure it's just the same or that at least there isn't much difference

I go back to looking at the writing there are dates and signatures dates going back two even three years before signatures with greetings insults to guards insults to other names and the word bastard recurs often bastard this bastard that bastard prison then women's names with hearts words of love poems drawings of pricks and cunts the odd hammer and sickle the odd fasces political slogans of left and right a few five-pointed stars signed BR*

---

* Brigate Rosse, the Red Brigades.

drawings and writings altered distorted and then everywhere dirty stains splatters stripes and marks in a brownish colour it occurs to me I could write something too the ones who made those marks did it because like me they had nothing to do to pass the time but I can think of nothing I'd like to write on those walls

time passes I'm not aware of the speed of time passing I can't keep an eye on it because they've taken away my watch and you can't see daylight at one point the spy-hole is opened a new face appears he nods for me to go over and he hands me a plastic plate and a plastic glass he asks me if I want soup I try to look out through the spy-hole to see what soup he means outside there's an iron trolley with a huge pan on it a huge ladle sitting in a thin reddish broth I say I don't want any and then he hands me a plastic bag containing a scrap of dry cheese two shrivelled green apples and a piece of bread that at least is fresh

the spy-hole is closed again I hear the sound of the trolley going further away I put my lunch on my jacket because the blanket disgusts me I wash the apples under the tap but I'm not hungry despite not having eaten since yesterday morning however I eat just the same I eat slowly chewing the food over and over I think that even with eating it's better to make things last as long as possible but I also think that it can't be any later than noon since they've brought me food that only a few hours have gone by I'm cold the dampness is getting into my bones I can feel shivers down my back I put my jacket on again its lining all torn from the searches I move about a bit to warm up I try to measure the number of steps I can take in the cell four steps the length of it four and a half steps the width of it and about turn too few for passing the time and so I lie down again

28

The demonstration sets off with our group at the head of it along with Talpa the trade unionist from the occupied factory there are drums and cow bells that make an infernal din first we go through the village everybody's outside watching in the roadway on the pavement at the windows there has never been a demonstration before in this village we start chanting a few fairly tough slogans and all the workers men and women take them up right away and they have a good time shouting out production methods like you've never seen when you stick the boss in the pressing machine prices get higher every day we'll help ourselves but we won't pay we go through the whole village a mini-bus full of *carabinieri* follows at a distance once we've left the centre of the village we head towards the small factories some are shut having heard about the demonstration and the plans to stir things up that were going round the bars the night before and a lot of workers didn't turn up for work

the same thing happens with three or four small factories then Pepe who's a bit sceptical goes right round the fourth factory he sees that the cars are parked at the back that they've kept the cars out of sight the gates are closed to give the impression that the factory was closed Pepe tells the people at the very front of the march and in no time word gets right to the back we turn around and we reach the factory gate everybody is shouting scabs out gutless scum a hell of an uproar with drums and cow bells but not a sound from inside Cotogno with Ortica Valeriana and the others go round the back they climb up the gate and throw a few stones at the cars everybody has an idea what's going to happen and Talpa makes a dash for the back but some workers restrain him and tell him not to bother for those guys are shitbags the workers who were inside come out on to the forecourt one at a time first surveying the lie of the land from the half-open iron gateway the oldest guy comes up to the gate with everybody yelling at him he talks to the trade-union man who he seems to know he says he didn't know there was a strike otherwise he'd have joined it he comes to an agreement with the trade-union man they'll all come out and we'll stay there to make sure the scabs get into their cars while everybody outside the gate lines up on both sides they've no option but to go dead slow and you can see the fear on their faces their windows rolled up and the safety catches down spit hits the windows the odd kick on the sides of the cars it's the women who are most enraged they stop a few cars standing in front of them and shaking their fists

they leave and we get on with the demonstration another small factory and here too people working but here they're not even bothered about hiding their cars they're doing it quite openly tempers rise but no sooner do they hear the uproar than they come out at once they invariably have the same excuse saying they didn't know about the strike we go on like this one small factory after another some are genuinely shut down in others the workers come out before we get there and one guy is actually waiting for the march and he joins it we get to a small rotor factory one of those where they've taken over the work from the occupied factory that the demonstration's for the gates open some of us flood inside on to the shop floor marching round in a muddle because there isn't room for us all

you can hear bumps and thuds the plastic material they're working with ends up on the ground Lauro gets into a fight with a scab he doesn't want to come out they're separated almost at once then the scab comes out pressing a handkerchief to his nose with blood pouring out of it we don't get there in time to clear out the little block where the offices are because the office workers have already all taken to their heels and we go on with the demonstration towards another factory this one is a bit bigger than the others there must be about thirty workers but not all of them are at work there too the cars get kicked and thumped one car window gets shattered Talpa runs backwards and forwards trying to cool down tempers and this time Cotogno gets pissed off and tells him to cut out playing at being a fireman

the gates are closed there's an uproar to get them opened from the entrance the two owners emerge looking pissed off and making a show of confidence they open the gate and start talking to Talpa however the people behind him push and break through the two owners take to their heels and stop in front of the big glass door shielding it with their bodies behind it you can see the scabs who've now stopped working and are peering outside the two owners go back to their argument with Talpa who's telling them flat today nobody's working everybody out I've already been here to talk about this problem if people are working here they're breaking our struggle to keep our jobs because with the overtime that you're doing here you're doing our work from our factory that we've occupied and you're breaking our struggle

the two owners aren't impressed one of them looks at the bus with the *carabinieri* that's stopped about thirty yards away and says now I'm calling the *carabinieri* Talpa answers the *carabinieri* can see perfectly well what we're doing and they're not interfering because I've talked to them too and I've told them that I'm taking responsibility for there being no trouble but you've got to bring the workers out the two owners aren't impressed and they say we've got no right to do what we're doing further back the workers are beginning to get impatient somebody starts shoving that's enough that's enough let's go inside Talpa goes on arguing with all the workers yelling behind him the first stones fly you can hear the shed windows breaking the two owners get even more irate Talpa acts as if nothing has happened and he goes on arguing I'm right behind him beside Cotogno and Ortica I'm holding a flag with a big pole the workers behind me keep shoving I hear the window panes breaking and without even thinking about it I thrust the pole forward against the glass door there's pandemonium the whole door collapses there and then a shard of plate glass comes away from up above and falls smack on Talpa's head fragments bounce off me and others who are nearby a cut opens on the trade-union man's bald head and instantly turns red shit I had no idea it was so fragile maybe it was badly built

one of the two owners the one that wanted to call the *carabinieri* thinks it was Cotogno who broke the glass door and he lands him a punch on the nose Ortica reacts with an instant reflex with both hands he lifts the banner and brings it straight down on to his head I hear the blow I see his eyes rolling then his legs giving way and he falls in a heap the other owner is petrified because Ortica has already raised the banner again over his head but he doesn't bring it down Talpa takes his hands away from his head and looks at his fingers messy with blood he's a bit stunned there's a moment of silence of general dumbfoundment the owner lifts his partner under the armpits and drags him towards the wall

from behind us there's shoving and everyone goes inside all the scabs run away leaving by the side doors but no one runs after them we take it out on things like in the earlier factory only more so all the plastic material ends up on the ground scattered everywhere all the window panes are broken this shit hole of a factory is where I work Verbena tells me the angriest the ones who do the most damage are the young ones and the women but the others think they're quite right they say nothing they don't try to stop them when we go outside the *carabinieri*'s bus is still there it hasn't moved they haven't even got out the two owners have disappeared the march re-forms and other small factories are cleared out but there are no more incidents the cut on Talpa's head isn't as deep as it looked at first but he's pissed off with us because he knows it was us behind him when the glass door collapsed but he doesn't say anything to us he just acts pissed off without blaming us we go back to the canteen in the occupied factory and there's a decision to do a leaflet to be handed out in the village so as to explain what has happened we write it and we pass round the text which is approved unanimously other clear-outs are threatened if in the next few days we get to know of overtime still going on in the small factories then groups of us go to hand out the leaflet in the streets and the shops and the bars in the village

29

The light above the door is bright and it hurts my eyes I'll have to lie on my stomach to sleep or put the pillow over my face but I wasn't sleepy and so I started thinking about the comrades who by this time will all have mobilized around my arrest they'll all be having discussions at the centre they'll be doing things to get me out of here they'll be talking to the lawyer I can imagine how the news got round fast immediately after my arrest telephone calls appointments meetings by this time the whole movement will already know about my arrest and now they'll all be organizing for everything that has to be done when I think about the comrades I feel a bit better as soon as I'm able to write I'll bring them right up to date it's years since I've written a letter I try to think of everyone I must write to there are too many better to write collective letters it comes into my mind that I'll also have to write to my parents I think of them there at home anxious worried by this business that's come so unexpectedly it was unexpected for me too even if it crossed my mind occasionally but though possible it seemed so remote and in any case it wasn't worth dwelling on it so this too is why I'm now so stunned and dumbfounded and most of all so unprepared now that it's happened but my parents couldn't even imagine that I could get mixed up with the law as far as they were concerned I was a being from another planet a crackpot a dreamer but harmless incapable of hurting anybody I hoped the comrades had gone to see them to calm them down to give them a bit of reassurance I really haven't a clue how to write I had no idea how to communicate with them

the spy-hole is opened again it's the sergeant of the guard who stares at me in silence without a word after a moment or two I jerk my head as if to enquire what's wrong he remains silent a bit longer then he asks me you wouldn't be the one who killed our warrant-officer two months ago I answer that I've never killed anyone that I'm there through a mistake that soon it will all be cleared up the sergeant gives me a surprised look and says that all the ones like me he's ever come across so far never say they've nothing to do with it and that they've done nothing they only say they're proud to be communists struggling against the state whereas it's the non-politicals who always say they're innocent even when they've been caught red-handed

I'm put out by this I wouldn't like to have made a blunder I feel as if I've broken some kind of protocol that must exist among comrades in prison meanwhile the sergeant starts telling me that the murdered warrant-officer was a decent fellow who had children and a family that what the people who murdered him put on the leaflet wasn't true at all that he didn't have a gang that beat people up that he'd never beaten anybody up or had anybody beaten up that he was a good humane fellow and so on and he goes on to explain that they're all decent fellows that it's wrong to hold anything against them that you have to understand that they're doing that job just to get by because they have to feed their families

that it's not their fault if there's unemployment that they're the first to want to get out of there if they get a chance of anything else that they've come from the south where there's no work and they've had no education and this is why those are the only jobs they can get but they do the job with respect for others and that it's not them we should hold things against because they're only carrying out orders and they're compelled to carry them out that it's the politicians we should have it in for and not them they're in agreement that things as they are are disgusting and that they need to be changed because they too realize that things can't go on like this but we shouldn't go shooting at them but at who's really in charge who's really to blame for the situation the sergeant goes on like this and there's no end to it

while he was going on like this it sounded to me just like the same reasoning the same things that the blacklegs doing overtime were saying when we went to picket in front of the factories to stop them from going in but here on top there was the naivety with which he said those things which made it evident that they weren't his own ideas they were ideas he'd picked up talking to comrades they were crude basic propaganda clichés and all this became his justification but the point was his reason for telling me all this this was the point and clearly he was doing it because he was afraid of ending up like that colleague of his who'd been killed and he wanted to keep on the good side of anybody who directly or indirectly could be a threat to him

and the way things were at that moment I had a kind of advantage over him I knew nothing at all about prison then but I was beginning to guess that it was a different world with different rules and a different logic that I had to learn as quickly as possible because in there along with the air that smelled of shit of piss and of vomit you also got a whiff of constant fear of threat of danger so it was better to be cautious to be careful better an excess of caution than a mistake that could have consequences I couldn't even imagine I felt the danger instinctively even in what the sergeant said maybe he'd been sent there to sound me out to see what sort of guy I was and how I saw things and so the best thing to do was not to give myself away to be vague about things but then even if I'd wanted to what could I have said in reply to that speech of the sergeant

so all I did was look at him until he stopped talking because a guard was calling him I hoped I wouldn't see him come back but he'd left the spy-hole open and in fact a minute later he was back looking through it but before letting him get started again I asked him if he could give me some matches because they'd left me my cigarettes but without matches I couldn't light any then the sergeant of the guard tells me that the rules forbid those in isolation from having matches because there's already been a case of someone going crazy and setting light to the mattress which is foam rubber and burns in minutes and gives off smoke that suffocates you in no time and if this happens at night when the keys to the cells are up in the rotunda there's the risk of a fire that would burn everyone inside the cells

when you want a light call the guards knock on the spy-hole and they'll give you a light seeing that the sergeant was so ready to give me information I also ask him how long I have to stay there in isolation he's astonished by the question he didn't know how long I had to stay in isolation he only knew I was in judicial isolation pending interrogation and that until then I could have no contact with anyone neither inside nor outside the prison I couldn't go out into the sun nor go into the exercise yard with anyone else not even with anyone else in isolation like me and I

couldn't talk to my lawyer or my parents until I'd been questioned and since I was a political isolation was even more severe
these were the orders he'd received from his superiors who in
their turn had received them from the magistrates

and by way of going back to the earlier conversation he gives me
a wink you see it's not us who've put you in these conditions
we're not the ones who make these decisions do you see who's
making them I ask him how long it usually is before the interrogation with the judge and he tells me that it can take up to
forty days from the day of arrest I think to myself that it hasn't
even been half a day and I'm already in this state I can't even
imagine forty days the sergeant of the guard gives me a light and
then to show him that I don't want to talk any more I turn my
back on him and I go towards the bed then he closes the spy-
hole and goes away I stretch out and slowly smoke the cigarette
savouring every puff and I fall asleep without even noticing

I wake up again with the spy-hole suddenly being opened a
fattish face taps on the door with a biro and twice says the word
shopping the guard is holding a clipboard with a list of foodstuffs
and other things on it I ask him what I can order and rather
impatiently he says how should I know I think of cigarettes and
mineral water and order that he's holding a form with my name
and my registration number and he writes down cigarettes and
mineral water and then shuts the door again saying he'll bring
me the stuff the next day I lie down on the bed again for a bit but
I can't get back to sleep then I get up and I beat on the door with
the palm of my hand no one comes then I shout guard guard two
or three times the spy-hole opens and a guard gives me a light
with a lighter and then closes it again

when the spy-hole opens it seems for a moment that I'm not
locked in that hole and for a moment it makes me feel better in
the evening the prisoner who brings the food comes back some

overcooked pasta with a sour red sauce one forkful with the plastic fork and I leave it all on the plate and go back to sleep now and then in the night you can hear screams from the adjoining cells you can hear people calling the guard who doesn't come the light is left on and if I'm lying on my back the glare's straight in my eyes and while I'm awake during one of the regular cell-check patrols when they open the spy-hole I ask the guard to put out the light but he says he can't that the rules say it has to stay on

a night of fitful sleep with that bright light on all the time then it's morning the first cell-check patrol comes around early and then the working prisoner with the watered down white coffee and a piece of bread half an hour later they open my door for exercise the guards outside in the corridor each carry a long truncheon and one of them uses it to point to the small door at the end of the corridor before I go outside he asks me if I want to empty the bucket but I say no the idea of lifting that stinking pail disgusts me I go through the little door followed by the guards with their truncheons we enter a kind of narrow tunnel and at the end it leads out to the open air into a kind of narrow corridor between two high walls where there's only room for one person at a time at the end it opens out into a small courtyard with an area no bigger than a few square yards surrounded by high walls

they open the last gate at the end on the left and then they lock it on me again above it there's an iron grating and through it I can see a part of one wing of the prison with the windows screened by vents broom handles with television aerials tied on to them stick out through some of the vents I think how those are the cells where I'll go after isolation I'm not clear what difference there is but at any rate there's television I don't know how many years it is since I've watched television but now I have a great desire to watch television to see anything at all with images and sounds anything at all that comes from outside anything at all with faces colours words

30

A lot of girls came to the centre too young women and not so young students workers housewives who'd come to the demonstrations who'd met during the occupations and in the centre they'd taken a room of their own and on the door they put a notice women's room and woe betide anyone who goes in there without their permission especially when they're having their meetings and then outside they distribute alternative information on sexuality on health on reproductive rights on wages for housework they do loads of things they make demands to the council to set up a self-managed clinic they slog up and down streets and squares with the campaign for free abortion on demand and one evening they burst into a cinema during the screening of a pornographic film and they take polaroid pictures of the audience with a flash then they go up to the projection cabin and seize the reels of film

another evening a group of them is in the street waiting for a criminal type who was involved in a rape attempt just recently and about twenty of them jump him with sticks they kick him and hit him with the sticks a bunch of his friends comes out of a nearby bar and they follow the scene hooting with laughter we males get ourselves down there too for when we knew what was going to happen we'd stationed ourselves not too far away just in case of retaliation but the women wave the sticks angrily at the gangsters and at us and they tell us to get going for they've no

need of us to defend them and the next day they proclaim their
action with a notice pinned to the walls which says let's take
back our right to the night

the women at the centre talk more and more among themselves
and if they're talking about the men it's clear that they're not
talking about them in the way that we talk about them typically
male when you come down to it even there at the centre the
women are always regarded as women in other words differently and the women who come to the centre are still given
ratings sized up and gossiped about the usual stuff that men do
everywhere and as time goes on the women emphasize their
separate meeting times and separate conversations and if one of
us goes up to them while they're talking they chase him away
after a bit we get pissed off because we can't make it out we start
teasing them and they turn aggressive they withdraw among
themselves they go around in a group they leave in their cars
without us they have private discussions and they give us dirty
looks so what the hell has happened

one evening they don't turn up at all and for the whole evening
we talk abut it we speculate with rumours and malicious gossip
Cotogno is given the job of finding out about Valeriana even
though he's not too keen because he knows Valeriana better
than we do and in fact Valeriana gives him short shrift as soon as
he tries asking her questions she chases him away she tells him
to mind his own business and stop spying for all the other shits
which means us Lauro and Lupino have a try with Mora and
Verbena just the same result and I try with China and we end up
having a row everyone's rattled a few days go by and we see a
small group of them at the centre pinning up a poster on a wall
it announces a meeting the next evening they're fixing it with
drawing pins and sellotape talking among themselves as if we
weren't there the atmosphere's hostile some suggest boycotting
the meeting taking a different line from the last few days the

guys in couples are more bewildered more cautious and less sure of themselves but the others are more incensed Cotogno is particularly at a loss Nocciola yawns with indifference only remarking women's stuff sometimes tempers erupt what are you playing at but the meeting comes round full of tension when I arrive they're already there all lined up grimly sitting in a row as we wait none of us says a word ah well it was about time we got down to this says Gelso breaking the silence and doing his best to act cool yes it was about time snaps Menta because we're really fed up with your shitty behaviour

what shitty behaviour we all look at one another in amazement our eyes meeting Menta goes on you treat us like dirt and you even pretend to be surprised but as from today it's over unless there are some changes we're leaving well leave then shouts Ortica losing his temper what's keeping you back ok it's still Menta speaking but first we want to make it clear what shits you are what pieces of crap no different from other men despite giving yourselves airs as revolutionaries and the vanguard of the proletariat but in your relationships with us you're the rearguard about the same level as my father and my grandfather Lupino is genuinely surprised but what's going on what's happened what's this all about this is a funny way of doing things a funny way of discussing things you disappear for a week and you turn up again with a poster for a meeting ok and then you come here and tell us that we're all shits I really don't understand

Valeriana starts speaking and she starts staring straight at Cotogno we've had separate meetings we women on our own have talked about things among ourselves that's how it started without being planned then it became something more serious it became a need to bring out everything we had inside us how we've lived our relationships with you here in the collective and to make comparisons with the relationships we'd had before well we've discovered that there's no difference being comrades should mean being different from normality being better more advanced culturally and most of all in terms of human relationships but you're not a single millimetre more advanced than other men in relationships you have with women

in our meetings we've managed to bring it all into the open it's been hard lovely sometimes but nasty too we've talked about things that are personal intimate and private what people call fears guilt feelings inferiority complexes all that we experience in relationships with you with each one of you then in individual ways with the men that we're with she's interrupted by Lauro it must be too much for him okay okay you confess everything to one another like we used to do with the priest but Mora doesn't let him go on but how can you be so crude you're crude like when you touch me up like when you fuck me have you never noticed how crude you are Lauro freezes he feels all eyes on him but Mora hasn't finished

you workers' vanguard acting the trade union lover boy because I know very well that you prefer making your smart-alec interventions in the factories where there are women workers that way maybe you get to fuck one of them after the mass meeting you and your partner Ortica because instead of just talking about forty hours pay for thirty-five why don't you tell us about the goings on in the factory the bottom pinching the fucking in the toilets only once upon a time it was the foremen that went after women in the assembly shops while now it's the workers' vanguards like you Lauro is ashen he can hardly stammer what's this have you discovered women's liberation in telling the whole world that I don't fuck you properly well then why don't you go and get yourself fucked by somebody else seeing as it's the only thought you've got in your head

Mora's arm lets fly on cue with a half-peeled orange she had in her hand it's aimed straight at Lauro's face but it misses and lands smack on Aglio who's behind him at first he doesn't move in the general silence everyone's waiting for him to get mad but all he does is to take a handkerchief out of his pocket and quickly wipe his face a couple of little pats to smooth his moustache again then he gets up and goes into another room now Verbena starts speaking she's a bit tense to begin with I'd like to say that it's not that relationships between men and women in the factory are any different from the ones there are in our collective it's the same crap the same roles and you Nocciola you'd better cut out that sarcastic laugh of yours you really had better seeing that you go to whores to fuck and then when you come here you act as if those things were of no interest to you

I interrupt her I'm sorry for Nocciola I say I don't think it's right to insult him and it seems to me it's going too far to attack people personally like this China must be annoyed with me because she attacks me right away you too you'd better shut up you're the one who's always thinking of something else the revolutionary cause comes first and sex comes later maybe on the side I'm convinced you wouldn't care which one of us you fucked while you were thinking of something else thinking about restructuring thinking about the crisis the decentralization of production what does it matter we're a step below you we come in handy for things like that just as we come in handy for using the duplicating machine and handing out leaflets there we go it's my turn I'm thinking how boring it is they're all just repeating the same thing I get up and leave the room I don't even pretend to be insulted I leave them to it

five more minutes go by and in comes Cotogno who hasn't even opened his mouth and he stands in front of me and Aglio sitting there in silence on our chairs Ortica arrives with Nocciola Ortica's fuming they could all do with a couple of good slaps that's what I think and Nocciola remarks maybe they've become lesbians but Cotogno shakes his head I thought he was thinking about Valeriana and that he was afraid of how their relationship might end up but then I realized we all realized that this wasn't just about little personal affairs it was about a much bigger affair as we understood later it was about a trauma a big trauma a big rupture maybe bigger than all the other things we were doing and that changed us all later

31

To the left is a guard inside a bullet-proof glass booth and above this are the closed-circuit cameras covering the different sections of the courtyard all separated by solid gates very small sections no bigger than the cells above each section is a heavy iron grating at the end under a small concrete shelter a tap with a wash-basin and a stand-up toilet dirty but still better than the stinking bucket now at last I can have a shit even if there's no privacy because a few yards away on the other side of the gate the guards are patrolling carrying their truncheons and there's the one in the booth and the closed-circuit cameras then from the wing of the prison that I can see from there voices reach me and I realize that they must be together in the cells up there they're not alone like me

I've never experienced solitude or at least I've never had a feeling of solitude and I had no idea that the fact of being made to be alone and not seeing anyone else could be a hard ugly and depressing thing they put you there deliberately to scare you to make you suffer an enforced solitude that you haven't chosen that they justify with the story that this way you won't mess up their enquiries and that you can reflect you can think about things it's hypocritical crap they put you there to scare you to intimidate you to unnerve you to make you suffer to give you a taste of their strength to make you feel bad without being able to do a thing about it you can only put up with it and if you make any show of rebellion the guards are there outside with their truncheons fingering them so as to let you know what to expect if you give them any trouble

no toilet paper and so I tear up my handkerchief and wipe myself with it I walk backwards and forwards here instead of four and a half paces there are nearly seven but at least there isn't the stink of the cells the guard with the truncheon comes up to the gate and he taps with the keys on the bars to indicate that time's up that it's time to go back inside three quarters of an hour it's not long and it felt even shorter then they made me take my exercise time early before the others so that I'd have it completely alone they lock the others up alone in a section too but they let them have their exercise all at the same time in two or three shifts

shortly after I go back to the cell the working prisoner brings me the watered down white coffee another day begins another day just like the first marked by the same things the guards' cell check and the working prisoner bringing you food and the guard coming by for the next day's shopping after lunch suddenly I heard a voice calling me from the next window it was a guy who was next door to me and whose face I never even saw I only heard his voice though when he started asking me questions asking me why I'd ended up in prison I hesitated I held back because I didn't trust him I thought it could be somebody they'd put there just to loosen my tongue

however the doubt subsided because he struck me as someone totally sincere he began by passing on useful information he told me he could see it was the first time I'd been in prison and so he saw it was important to tell me things to explain to me how things worked there because the more things you know the more you feel secure he told me not to worry he told me prison isn't like this this isn't normal prison because upstairs you can make pasta you can cook whatever you want they have all the books they want they're in cells with other people in short he explained how it was upstairs and then he also gave me some legal advice he told me that after the investigating judge's questioning I'd be able to have visits from my lawyer and my relatives too

and he told me that if I wasn't married and I wanted to see my girlfriend I could fill in a form saying we cohabited and how this was done and all these things and in fact none of the guards interfered to make us shut up to stop us talking and this really amazed me and then a few days later he also managed to pass me a book through the working prisoner who brought the food it was a pulp thriller sex and guns however this book was all written in French and I didn't know French and he was amazed that I didn't know French he said but how come you politicals are all teachers and you don't know French well you must know English then no I told him I don't know English either he was quiet for a minute he was really astonished that I didn't know any languages

then that evening for the first time something happens that later I'll see happen dozens of times in gaol I hear the sound of an insistent voice from one of the cells it was maybe six or seven o'clock there's a voice raised I can't manage to make out the words however I can hear him calling the guard he goes on calling guard but obviously the guard doesn't come because the guy goes on calling insistently with an insistence that's unnerving and it's impossible for the guard not to hear because I can hear him walking up and down the voice is raised higher and higher and it becomes a shout followed by insults then this guy in the cell starts beating against the door probably using his feet because it makes a loud noise against the metal that reverberates in the corridor

the guy screams hammers curses and calls out maybe he's ill he calls the guard maybe because he's ill I'm shaken and uncertain whether to do anything I can hear no other sound but the noise he's making and I sense that everyone else must have stopped talking because I can hear no other voices no other sounds from the other cells I'm uncertain my first thought is that I ought to start hammering too because if he's calling with such insistence there must be a good reason I'm surprised nobody else is doing it while I'm still hesitating about whether to start hammering on the metal door too I hear a rapid shuffling in the corridor feet running fast a lot of feet like a group of people running along the corridor it's easy to picture them because the corridor is empty and every sound reverberates amplified

then the shuffling stops a few cells past mine and I can hear the door opening this guy's screaming even more but now the screams are different they are like screams of fear but I still don't understand what he's saying then I can hear confused sounds piercing screams of pain and it suddenly dawns on me that they're beating him up now along with the voice that's scream- ing louder and louder I can hear other voices and muffled blows against the wall as if they were bashing him against the wall they're beating him up there's no mistake the thing goes on for a long time or at least it seems to me that it goes on for a long time because every one of those sounds I hear makes me think they're still beating him they haven't stopped beating him and there are a lot of them beating him and I picture a bunch of guards hitting somebody inside that hole hitting one another so as to get at him there inside that cramped space

then the sounds and the blows stop suddenly I can hear the clear sound of voices two or three people in conversation and a continuous moaning then the gate and the door closing with a heavy clang that reverberates through the corridor then nothing else for a minute or two then metallic sounds it's the spy-holes being opened briefly and then banged shut they're going round the cells and opening the spy-holes I hear the one next to mine then mine is opened too I'm beside the gate beside the spy-hole I've been there standing still from the first moment I hesitated whether to beat against the metal door as well or not I've been there standing still waiting

the spy-hole is lowered a face a young dark face with eyes staring wildly that at first I think is the sergeant of the guard but it's not the sergeant it's someone else also dark skinned and with dark eyes but younger his face covered in sweat he looks inside for a second disturbed excited by the violence he looks me straight in the eyes for a moment his eyes wild then immediately slams the spy-hole shut a feeling of hatred wells up as the blood goes to my head the feeling wells up a feeling I'd never had before a feeling of hatred an extremely violent desire to kill wanting to kill him right then and there something unknown to me which was a very violent desire wanting to crush wanting to smash that face wanting to murder

I felt ill then at once I also felt low like a feeling of weariness like a great depressing weariness that made it hard to stand up any longer that made my legs weak I stretched out on the bed the graffiti get all jumbled together a web of indecipherable signs confused with the stains of dampness with the blistered crumbling plaster the cracks in the floor with the bright light that hurts my eyes I roll on to my side with my face towards the wall and straight in front of me are the brown stains those specks and splatters on the damp yellowing plaster and now I no longer have any doubts about what they are about what made all those stains now I know what that colour is those brown stains splashed all over the walls of the cell

32

In the isolation cells people often just can't stand it and so they injure themselves because once you've been shoved in there alone inside that hole injuring yourself giving yourself injuries becomes the only weapon you have to attract attention to yourself to protest against the long term of isolation so as to get the judge to carry out the interrogation some people manage to get razor blades and cut themselves with them some swallow bits of glass bits of iron some break their own fingers and things like that the forms self-injury takes are varied and inventive everyone has to make do with what he has or what he can manage to get hold of some bang their heads against the wall it seems incredible but there was even someone who took a run at the wall and smashed his head against it splitting his head because it's the only way some injure themselves because they're depressed or also often just to get treatment if they're ill and they're not being treated

or else some injure themselves to avoid a beating from the guards some do themselves damage in advance to limit the number of blows from the guards they turn up to beat the hell out of you and see you there covered in blood so they control themselves because they're afraid that somebody who's already injured might not recover if they pulverize him and then there'd be no way of avoiding enquiries and there could be trouble I'm reminded of the stories people used to tell to get a few days off sick Pepe got Olivo to slam one of the doors of his *cinquecento* on his hand and Ortica too used to talk about how he'd broken a little finger with the classic system used by conscripts numbing the finger with gas from a lighter and then sticking it in the neck of a Coca Cola bottle you take the bottle in your other hand and you twist it back in one clean movement that way the finger breaks and it doesn't hurt then you go to the doctor and you get time off these struck me as crazy stories but then I too realized when I went to work in a factory how things were I'd never had a job before but now in our affinity group the only one still working was Valeriana and the money wasn't enough to keep the house going Cotogno had lost his job he was working as an electrician but he didn't get on with his boss because the guy thought he should always be available even for small jobs outside working hours in the evening and on Saturdays too then the problem had got worse when Cotogno had brought home a colour television while he was working on a job in an electrical goods shop the owner of the shop had no proof but he talked to Cotogno's boss about it and he found an excuse to fire him

Valeriana had been working in the hospital for two years now when she'd finished secondary school she hadn't been able to find anything else but hospital work as a nurse though in reality they got her to do cleaning they made her wash the floors and do the laundry she'd enrolled in the arts faculty at the university but she'd never attended or taken any exams she was fed up to the teeth with doing that job and she couldn't wait to give it up but China was still going to secondary school and so it was up to me and Gelso to sort things out we started delivering advertising bills for an estate agent we should have covered whole districts putting the bills through the letterboxes shit wages we spent half an hour delivering and then we threw the still unwrapped parcels into rubbish bags then in the evening we went to the company's offices to collect our money

after a few days they noticed that we weren't delivering any and they didn't give us any more work they did checks they sent someone round to check on whether the bills had been delivered and they made random telephone calls to people for proof we couldn't have cared less after us there'd be others and they'd do the same thing then I got a chance of a job in the celluloid factory because I had a relative who'd worked there until retirement and they took people on there on the basis of family recommendations the management only took on people who had a relative who'd worked there for years usually it was the father who'd already been working there all his life and then they took on the son that way it was more reliable easier to keep checks easier to put pressure on people

but this rule of thumb for taking people on didn't apply to every section of the factory the management used this rule of thumb only in what it regarded as the central sections then there was the ordinary production sector which was the most shattering work where they took for granted a high turnover and so in these sections they took on an unskilled labour force particularly young southerners who they knew would take it on for a few months and then leave because it was an intolerable job very unhealthy and with productivity targets that were impossible to maintain and it was the work they did on the calenders which were huge machines consisting of a kind of big tall funnel that conveyed the blocks of celluloid heated up to high temperatures between two huge steel rollers that rotated inwards and brought out the sheets of celluloid at the bottom

the section where I worked though was the research department that's what it was called and in a way it was the heart of the factory where new products were tested where proto-types were made well there they made combs and spectacle frames the research was to do with the different colours of celluloid for the combs and the spectacle frames it was regarded as a prestige section to work in not only because the speed of the work wasn't shattering like it was in production but most of all because you worked alongside technicians and engineers and this was something to be proud of for those old workers who believed in the work and all worked hard like imbeciles the workers in that department were all old there were only two as young as me

I didn't have any really clear idea about that factory I saw it from outside as a vast dirty monstrosity that disgorged fumes into the air and stinking liquids into the river that ran alongside it the impression I got on the first morning of work was a grim one there was this business of getting up while it was still dark because it was winter taking the bus that goes through the small villages to pick up the workers and then stopping in front of the gates the line that went in through a kind of tunnel and then punching my card and when they showed me where I had to go there and then I already felt like leaving turning my back and away getting out of there and taking off when I saw my section a kind of long narrow corridor without windows there were only big skylights way up high and a terrible stink of solvents methylated spirits petrol and so on

the workers were all in black overalls except the foreman who had a white overall and who was in his office at the end of the corridor behind the glass screen from where he could keep an eye on the whole section the foreman showed me the machines he told me to buy myself a black overall and to watch what the other workers did for the first few days to give me an idea of the work and so I started looking about making the most of every chance I had to leave the department to go and collect material and so on and see the layout of the factory there were these big dark corridors that branched out in different directions suddenly opening on to the production sections where the noise was deafening where the atmosphere was suffocating where the heat and the stink were unbearable I felt sorry for the people who worked there

I also discovered that there was an interior courtyard with a door that led on to a little hall no bigger than twelve feet by twelve where the workers went to have a smoke because the materials used were highly inflammable and so the management allowed the workers to go there occasionally to smoke a cigarette it was an area with not even a single window and it filled up with cigarette smoke so that you couldn't even see people's faces there was only a bench or two against the peeling walls it was mainly the older workers that went there with their worn out resigned faces not a word passed between them they'd smoke their cigarettes in that posionous smoke-filled hall and then they'd go back to the sections which were extremely unhealthy because the substances used were all carcinogenic especially the colourants and in that place after they retired they all died of cancer within a year or so

after the probationary period the work that they gave me to do along with the two other young guys was just insane they took us into an area where there was a big tub against one of the walls the iron tub was full of boiling water heated by gas ovens that ran under the tub over the tub there were iron rings where you had to place the glass flasks containing the solvent and the powdered colour prepared by the technicians running from the cork-stoppered flask was a rubber tube that ended up in a glass coil they gave us elbow-length rubber gloves because every so often we had to shake the flask over the tub of boiling water to help the colour get well mixed

the wall behind the tub was all red and the old workman who took us there hooted with laughter when he told us that one of the flasks had exploded a few months before and the guy who was holding it is still going round now in a shade of red because the colour is indelible I took the glass flask in my hand and I had to be careful not to knock it against the iron ring and I also had to be careful not to bend the rubber tube otherwise the pressure of the liquid would build up and it would all explode and every time I took out a flask to shake it I'd break into a cold sweat as soon as I shook it the liquid would spurt up the tube and fill the whole coil up to the maximum level and if it went any higher the whole lot would just explode after a few days I made up my mind to finish with the whole business we got hold of some colourant and we added it to every formula they gave us and so in the end the colours came out all wrong and the damage was substantial because every wrong formula meant a lot of money down the drain at that time it was wholesale chaos everywhere in the factories and outside in the city whole streets were erupting as demonstrations of tens of thousands of people went by extremely violent clashes with the police armouries broken into factories and universities occupied trade-union leaders thrown out it was clear that the least we could do in that factory of zombies was a bit of sabotage and then get out and so one morning we stopped going and in no time all the young people who worked in that factory also left one after the other they preferred unemployment to a slow death there like their fathers

33

After I'd been ten days in isolation a sergeant arrived and told me to get my things together because they were trans-ferring me to the wing upstairs and as soon as I'd been taken upstairs and they opened this big door leading on to the corridor of the wing I immediately realized that there in the wing the situation was completely different I heard an incredible din all the armour-plated doors of the cells were open or rather I should say they weren't even armour-plated they were just heavy wooden doors the wooden doors were open and only the cell gates were closed there was a lot of movement a lot of noise and behind the gates I could see people cooking and playing cards so there was lots of movement lots of noise and this was the thing that struck me most after ten days in isolation

there was the sound of prisoners' voices and there was television all the televisions turned on in all the cells with the volume up really high I could hear the shoot-outs in the spaghetti westerns that the private stations put out at all hours of the day and night one characteristic of the non-politicals that I found out right away is that they lived by night because they were awake all night playing cards they played for money and the debts were later settled outside by friends and relatives because in prison you can't have money they were awake all night playing for money with the televisions turned on at top volume and then they slept in the daytime they taped newspapers over the windows and they put blankets over them and so there was never daylight in their cells if they needed light they switched on the electric bulbs

they were real old lags in prison this term *old lag* is used to define this kind of behaviour this way of living your imprisonment this style that's also expressed through dress the classic old lag is always in his dressing-gown or dungarees or pyjamas no in fact dungarees are already a good bit smarter these guys were always in pyjamas and dressing-gowns they always went down to exercise like that pyjama trousers with a dressing-gown over them slippers and socks never shaving while on visiting days they'd undergo a transformation perfectly shaved shampoo cologne and after-shave smart suit white shirt and tie even one or two in double-breasted pin-stripes patent leather shoes polished till they shone that's how they got dressed for visits from their wives their families while the rest of the week they were in pyjamas

I was taken to this wing they took me right up to the gate of my cell which was a big cell where there were three comrades already three politicals while in the next cell there were two other comrades in all there were six of us politicals in that wing of non-politicals but we didn't have exercise together we had our exercise time on a different timetable from the non-politicals as soon as I got into the cell the thing that struck me was the amount of stuff piled up in the cell which unlike the isolation cell was a furnished cell and there were groceries and clothes piled up everywhere it was a very colourful cell the walls were blue they'd painted them blue which seemed to me a very odd colour for a prison cell

I went into this cell where there were these comrades who saw I looked a bit lost right away they made me some coffee and then right away they got some food ready in the cell ravioli in broth for virtually ten days I'd been eating only the disgusting prison food and I thought the ravioli were delicious the comrades wanted to know what had happened to me and they gave me some legal advice they gave me the impression that they knew loads of things that I knew nothing about at all in the cell they also had a copy of the penal code and sometimes they'd look it up when they disagreed about something and gradually they helped me to understand how the prison apparatus worked they showed me which were the softest guards and which were the meanest shits and how to behave accordingly

in that wing I also began to understand what kind of relationship there is between us and the non-politicals or at least the non-politicals of that wing because it's not as if all non-politicals are the same and with the demands they made of us through the working prisoner or shouting to us from their cells they never stopped asking us for things they asked us for food cigarettes everything all the time and the comrades in my cell explained that these non-politicals were convinced we had more money than them because for them we were like a big family for their reasoning was I'm a small-time criminal with no money and here in prison I've maybe got to go to incredible lengths to eat and to get hold of money for the family and for the lawyer and so on

whereas you are one big family you have the solidarity and the material support of so many people outside because when they arrest you people protest on your behalf they sign petitions they make a lot of fuss they collect money for you and they send it to you in prison and you have lawyers who are your friends that cost you very little or even cost you nothing at all and all these things are things we don't have and you're never short of money and so if we ask you for cigarettes it should be easy to let us have them in short what they were asking for was an indirect share for them too in this solidarity that they saw we had they were asking for some sign of a bit of this solidarity coming their way too

something else they asked us to do was the writing involved in filling in application forms for visits for transfers for remission for parole applications of all kinds that they kept on sending to the magistrates to the judges to the courts to the lawyers to the prison administration to the ministry etcetera and they also asked us to write letters to their wives and girlfriends maybe not whole letters but at any rate suggestions or nice ways of putting things poems because we were educated we were people who'd studied here in prison I became aware of the importance of writing I'd hardly ever written letters before I'd never regarded it as a means of communication whereas now besides weekly visits it was the only way if you want to maintain relationships if you want to keep them going

it happened to me once there that a guy asked me to write to women for him he'd found addresses in the classifieds of some magazine in this wing there were also pimps who kept their work going from inside trying to set up new connections and they wrote to women with the aim of meeting them later outside they'd ask the governor's permission to have themselves photographed wearing their double-breasted pinstripes or they'd have a photograph sent from home that showed them posing dressed in the height of style with one foot resting on the wheel of a big bright red car so as to send it with the letter and then they'd ask us to make up some story about their lives a biography full of excitement however we never complied with requests of this kind

another thing for example was that the working prisoners inside showered us politicals with favours there was the laundry worker who offered to wash our things personally because he too regarded us as privileged prisoners who should be given favours then there was the one who worked as the baker who made disgusting bread always either overdone or underdone but as an extra he gave us pizza and *focaccia* that he cooked separately for the sergeants, and the warrant-officers too so as to get on the right side of them or in exchange for favours because he thought in terms of hierarchies and he'd picked out us politicals as the most important in our wing and he gave us the pizzas however people like that more often than not are bastards they're people that the administration uses to get information they're scum pimps surly slippery bastards

but what struck me most of all in those first days in this world of the prison I was discovering was television it was years since I'd watched television except for the news while there I started enduring television because it really is a case of enduring it of swallowing it the whole twenty-four hours out of twenty-four hours a day and to begin with you just let it happen to you with no standard of choice you watch it all indiscriminately because it gives you the illusion of being less aware of time of taking your mind off it after a while though you find yourself sucked into it like an idiot you find yourself completely cretinized and then if you turn off the television you feel worse because you've no longer got a clue what to do to pass the time

34

At the centre the pickets against Saturday overtime had become a routine and it wasn't only the workers directly involved who went on them but to some extent everybody did and the first few times everybody enjoyed it too there in front of the factories at six in the morning with grappa music and bonfires of rubber tyres but then after the first few months the first contradictions erupted we started wondering why we were doing it standing there talking to these shits who've been made apathetic by work and who only listen to us because they're more scared of the picket than of the boss and who go back to doing overtime again the next time if you're not there you can't keep going forever explaining to them that if they do overtime they're doing the dirty on the unemployed that they're opening the door for restructuring the decentralization of production repeating everything over and over again like a broken-down record

so in the end we stopped getting up at six in the morning to go on the pickets in the end four or five car loads of us would go at ten or eleven o'clock and go round the factories and if we saw people were working we'd immediately start knocking out all the window panes from close range and then it was even better if we managed to get our hands on the cars belonging to those shits who were working or the factory lorries it was quicker to do and more fun and did more damage and the workers and the employers had to calculate whether they earned more with their Saturday overtime than what we took away from them then of course the union made its statements of condemnation and the *carabinieri* started going round on the lookout for us except that they could only bring in a single bus load in an area where there are two hundred factories and so within a month overtime working comes to a halt in that area

the news of the struggles reaching us from the cities in the south where the unemployed have organized gives rise to a new collective in the centre made up of unemployed people the majority of the collective doesn't consist of people who are strictly unemployed it's more a case of casual workers who work on and off or work off-the-books in workshops or at home there are many who've deliberately chosen not to have permanent jobs and to work only the absolute minimum to live on and then of course there are also people with qualifications and even the odd graduate I'm a member of the unemployed collective too because I've been genuinely unemployed since I left the celluloid factory the first meetings we hold are really chaotic because it's difficult to have a definite identity given that there are so many differences

and then we get the idea of starting an investigation into the organization of production in the region we gather information through the comrades in the factories we collate the data and at the same time a comrade who works in the town hall gets us a huge heliographed map of the area which we hang on one wall of the centre and on it we colour-code the different links in production connecting the big multinationals with the small factories with the warrens of the black economy and with the network of middlemen who organize it who hand out the work to the families and home-workers and who enable the bosses to make a huge saving on labour costs making it possible for them to pay for the work at a tenth of the rate with the added advantage of easy restructuring by cutting down on jobs and still being able to continue production whenever there's a strike

we launch a propaganda campaign in all the villages of the area we vilify the middlemen attacking them by name on posters and then we decide to do the rounds against the organization of sweat-shops in the same way as we did against overtime the first time about twenty of us went to one of these basement sweat-shops with our red kerchiefs round our faces and one or two sticks because you never knew China took the aerosol and wrote on the wall close down the sweat-shops you felt sorry for the people working there they were terrified except for an old pensioner who wasn't in the least perturbed he sat where he was without moving as if nothing was happening not put out at all

there was a pregnant woman though who started screaming because she thought we'd come to rob the place Valeriana and China tried to explain to her what we were doing and what we wanted but she didn't understand a thing she nodded her head but she didn't understand a thing you could tell from how pale she was and the way her eyes stared there were two young kids who caught on right away they didn't mind us and they said that the boss wasn't there that he was always out and about to do with work Nocciola and I slashed open the big boxes containing the plastic materials and we threw them all over the place switches screws and plastic sockets then we told the kids to tell the boss to put a stop to the sweated labour or the next time the basement would go up in smoke and so we started our rounds against the sweat shops

but meanwhile there was another problem hitting us all of a sudden this was the heroin which was spreading like wildfire and even in the movement it was starting to get people we discussed it over and over for days on end clearly this situation is quite convenient for those in power there's already a big toll of dead and zombies who drag themselves around the fountains in the squares with their syringes and their little spoons it's clear that heroin in general messes up the most rebellious and the most dissatisfied people those who are most disaffected with this system and can't cope with it any more with heroin they're simply offered a personal and self-destructive way out of the wish to change things out of the anger that we have inside

the fact that heroin is spreading rapidly among young working-class people represents a potential defeat because it's spreading on that same ground of people's needs of the will to change life the addicts are living through exactly the same problems as us someone's an addict because he can't cope any more and because he doesn't believe any longer that you can struggle for a different life for this reason we must in no way marginalize addicts nor should we hand over the problem to the institutions it would be a mistake and it would give them a pretext to increase control over us to repress us all the more the greatest weapon we have is solidarity and we must make all the more use of it when it comes to those who are worse off

but at the same time we also decided that it was worthwhile starting to make the rounds against the drug hang-outs we picked out a bar where they pushed heroin and where we knew that the owner of this bar was also tied up in the business because he also extracted a nice fat cut from the deals and so one night China and I Nocciola and Ortica went to set fire to that bar we'd got four petrol bombs ready we'd made them very carefully because we were determined that the whole thing should burn down we'd dissolved expanded polystyrene into saltpetre solvent and we'd added it to the petrol with over-heated oil this way it doesn't burn instantly but it forms a sludge that sticks to things to walls too and it burns for a very long time wherever it sticks we got to the place at one a.m. the bar was closed using a builder's sledgehammer Ortica battered into the glass frontage and we heard a shattering noise like nothing on earth and from the force of it Ortica ended up inside the bar with all the glass falling down on him but he didn't get cut China told him to get back outside come on come on hurry up and she lit the fuse of her bottle Ortica leapt outside and China threw it there was a muffled thud a blaze that lit up the whole interior of the bar we threw the other bottles without even lighting the fuses everything went red then a big cloud of black smoke started drifting slowly out of the broken shop-front we ran away everything in that bar was burned there was nothing left not even a single glass nothing

meanwhile summer had come and plans were underway for going on holiday we were heading for the south for the coast in groups of cars we'd make haphazard stops and stay as long as we felt like it and then we'd take off again for somewhere else we'd get to know other people like us other comrades who do the same things who also talk about the movement nobody went away on their own nobody was on their own any more even couples weren't on their own any more it had become the normal thing to travel in caravans all together even just to go out to the country on Sundays and every evening we all met together in the centre the majority turned up after dinner and when you arrived outside the centre there was always the same scene the great beam of light crossing the street the comrades' cars motorbikes mopeds filling the whole roadway people in groups in the street and around the benches

a continual coming and going a great bustle the noise of cars coming and going the music from the car radios parked outside and the music coming out of the centre the twanging music of guitars the sweet sounds of flutes the whistling of pipes the rhythmic drumming of bongos every evening there are new faces every evening new things to see to hear to do greeting all the people you know going round all the rooms the new posters and leaflets to read the sharing out of news information opinions the meetings to be held the mass gatherings the posters to be put up in convoy the debating and joking the awkwardness and shyness of newcomers the self-assurance of the old comrades the arrival of some weirdo or drunk

all round the centre the streets are busy all the time with groups of comrades the evenings are high-spirited lively noisy with our sounds shouts songs music they're made colourful by our jackets scarves skirts hats the walls are one long stretch of graffiti drawings writing all muddled together all with slogans one on top of the other against the bosses against sweated labour against all work against the ghettos against the clergy against the mayor against the trade unions against the parties against the city council against men against heroin against fascists against cops against judges against the state against poverty against repression against prison against the family against school against sacrifices against boredom

35

A few days after my arrival I had my first visit from relatives my brother and my mother came because my father was ill my brother had a message from China who'd told him to tell me the lawyer was optimistic because it could be proved it was a long time since I or China either had really lived in that house belonging to the solicitor and in fact China hadn't been bothered at all and so what it all came down to was the question of the lease that had stayed in my name the lawyer said he'd asked for bail for me and that he thought I'd be out of there in a few weeks so he was optimistic and then there was news of the comrades who all sent me regards and of the centre and so on

my mother was very upset and she kept asking me how I was whether I was eating and telling me that she'd brought parcels with food and clothes however I was only interested in what my brother had to say I asked him things to give me an idea of how the situation was outside what the comrades' state of mind was like the visit took place in a long narrow room with a long marble table down the middle the length of the whole room we had our visiting time along with the non-politicals there was a terrible racket about fifteen prisoners on one side of the marble table and at least three times that number of relatives on the other side mothers grandmothers aunts children a deafening babble screams shouts of joy weeping hysterics rage desperation abuse for the wives suspected of infidelity slaps scenes

the guards triple-lock the door and they stand behind a window on the relatives' side to make sure there are no serious irregularities there were always too many people and despite the controls things always went on notes and letters were passed no doubt that's something they take for granted that you'll pass stuff across for them the main thing is that you don't pass weapons visiting time is a fun-fair a market whole families with grannies and children all shouting to make themselves heard and I too had to shout to make myself heard but I was unnerved by it while I could see that the others were perfectly at their ease the marble table was four and a half feet wide to prevent contact but sometimes children were passed for a minute or two from one side of the table to the other

the surveillance wasn't very strict I happened to witness some amorous encounters that went pretty far there were people virtually managing to fuck during the visit there were all kinds of special contrivances big overcoats even in the summer that could be opened in a special way then maybe the guy next to them gets mad because there's the kid or the granny there who can see everything in other words a real mess people insulting one another hitting one another everyone shouting the situation is such that in the three quarters of an hour spent like this you can't have a conversation about anything the time passes in an instant you hear a bell like in school and visiting time is over and then they take you into an adjoining cell where they search you all over again

after a while we were transferred to another wing where the difference between us and the non-politicals wasn't enforced so we had our exercise time along with them the non-politicals in this new wing were different from the ones before who were pretty dubious characters I don't mean outright bastards but pretty shady though they were the lowest criminal class pimps and people of that kind in short whereas in the new wing the non-politicals were of a different kind all very young gangs of small-time thieves people who got on very well together and so we came in touch with these non-politicals grouped together in gangs every gang had its leader and when you had to talk it was the leader who talked for his whole gang during exercise we were given a very good welcome just as if we were another gang and there were no problems in our contacts with them

then there was also the fact that we started playing football and volleyball together and we started making friends and we saw that contact with these non-politicals was of a different kind because these guys weren't always asking you for little favours like the others these guys seemed very proud they acted very self-assured just the opposite they never asked us for anything instead it was them who kept on offering things to us right away they started asking us if we needed this or that with the implication that they had a network of connections inside and outside the prison through which things could be had messages got out and contacts made with other wings and so on

gradually we understood that between these gangs there were kinds of equilibrium based on whatever they dealt in on their zones of influence from their traffickings inside the prison for example pushing cocaine and heroin there's no doubt that some of the guards were no strangers to this trafficking because stuff comes into prison mainly through the guards these guards who do this job of bringing stuff inside to sell it to the prisoners are called mules they'll bring anything inside for payment especially drugs and knives and in fact we saw that among these non-politicals a lot of them were using drugs especially cocaine they used cocaine in a big way and the higher-ranking guards were no doubt aware of it they offered cocaine to us too but we refused it whereas we accepted a smoke and for them giving us a smoke was a sign of friendship

on one occasion there was a rumpus with these guys from the gangs down in the exercise yard one afternoon it was an exercise period apparently like any other some were playing football some were talking as they walked along or sat on the benches however you could see that there was a bit of unease in the air and at one moment two little gang leaders pulled out sticks from under their dressing gowns these must have been made from stools or the legs of tables in the cells and they started hitting one of the working prisoners in the wing and this in full view of everyone with no warning it was the first brutality I saw in the prison even though I knew it was a normal thing in prison that it was a daily thing that it was part of the law of prison part of its normal mechanism and so they hit this working prisoner pretty hard while everybody stood there watching without a move and then they told him to go up and get his things together and to go to the isolation cells for you could make a request to go there by choice because otherwise the next time they'd kill him we politicals didn't react in any way we didn't ask any questions but they must have realized that we'd been surprised that we didn't expect this particularly since this working prisoner that they'd clubbed seemed to us to be somebody who just minded his own business but there's no doubt that since they'd clubbed him he couldn't have been somebody who just minded his own business then the next day they told us that this working prisoner was a bastard he was one of those who gave information to the administration about what went on in the wing

a bit later something else like this happened what happened was that a very young boy arrived he never spoke he was very shy he must have been a bit backward he was always there on his own and he never spoke this kid came out of isolation and he came into our wing where he was put in a cell with four others and what happened was that one of these four cellmates of his raped him but we found out about this later on after this shit who did this vile thing was beaten to a pulp what happened was that the other three hadn't realized at the time because it happened in the toilet that's separated from the cell by a curtain and while this shit was doing it he was threatening him with a knife at his throat

afterwards he made it clear to him that he wasn't to say a word about it otherwise he'd kill him so this kid got scared and he said nothing but the other three were suspicious and they started putting the rumour about the wing that they had these suspicions and so a decision was made to test them out and one of the gang leaders went up to the shit during exercise time and with an air of complicity said to him so you had the kid then and so this shit who also happened to be an idiot told him boastfully that he had then all hell broke loose because they took this guy and they literally beat him to a pulp so that even his own mother wouldn't have recognized him they smashed in his whole face and his head stamping on him and clubbing him till his nose was flattened they totally pulverized him

it was during this period that one day I was washing dishes in the cell and every so often glancing at the news on television but I could hardly hear anything at all because of the water running suddenly I thought I saw something familiar on the screen an image that reminded me of something but I wasn't sure what the television camera was going round a room that was all messed up chairs overturned an unmade bed with a big metal bedstead then on one wall I saw a poster with Humphrey Bogart and immediately it dawned on me immediately I recognized that flat where we'd had that famous meeting with Scilla and the others then in the middle of the room you could see a sheet covering something up a motionless body you could see a leg sticking out a naked foot without shoes motionless

I stopped washing the dishes and I went right up to the television set I turned up the volume someone was talking about a terrorist killed in a gunfight with the *carabinieri* the terrorist was held to be responsible for the murder of a *carabiniere* that had taken place a few months before another familiar image came up on the screen the body of the *carabiniere* shot down beside a yellow petrol pump that I'd seen on television with China one evening not long before they arrested me the arrests of other accomplices were expected shortly then a huge black and white photograph came up on the screen it was Cotogno's face an identity card photograph unsmiling and hair neatly combed but I recognized it at once it was Cotogno who was there now motionless under the sheet

36

The car stops in a dark courtyard surrounded by dilapidated old houses half-empty going by how few of the windows had lights on with me is China and Ortica and Nocciola right after that Scilla's car turns up with Cotogno Valeriana and Gelso in it the ring of light from the electric torch skims over tufts of grass pieces of wood bits of broken bottles and tiles then we go up a steep wooden staircase with a shaky banister and treads that creak Scilla turns the key in the lock it's stiff a shove with a shoulder and we're inside there's a musty smell Scilla turns on a light that's hanging from the ceiling on a threadbare cable a few old bits of furniture damp patches on the wall and a poster with Humphrey Bogart over a bed with a big metal frame

we sit down around the table on the straw-bottomed chairs Cotogno and Valeriana sit on the bed there aren't enough chairs for us all Scilla takes a bottle of whisky out of a crooked side-board and puts it on the table with some glasses you know the purpose of this meeting says Ortica we're here to weigh up the different organizational options that have developed inside the movement there are some people carrying out vanguard actions with the use of arms under the illusion that they on their own can influence the growth of the whole movement well we aren't opposed in principal to these practices because we all know very well that you can't claim to be consistent revolutionaries without tackling the problem of the exercise of force of the necessity of building a counter-power equivalent to and even more violent than that exercised daily by the state

but our criticism of these comrades comes from the fact that this creation and exercise of counter-power all has to happen inside the movement we're now in a phase of mass consciousness you only have to look at the news reports the use of force is spreading rapidly wherever struggles are taking place mass disregard for the law is now common practice so it's a question of debating the possibility of a further mass leap forward for the whole movement which must consist in organized force or if you prefer the question of armed struggle Cotogno gets up from the creaking bed he takes the bottle from the table and pours the whisky into the glasses Scilla too has got up and has gone to rummage in an old chest in one corner of the room

now there's no point in me going over every single detail of all that happened in that meeting that went on until dawn and that turned out to be the last one because there was a split between us then and we never met again things got out of hand that time a row broke out that nearly ended in blows at one point Cotogno started shouting there are people now who refuse to see that we're now objectively in a war situation refusing to see this is pure opportunism by those who don't want to accept their ultimate responsibilities as revolutionaries which means that those who refuse to see that we're now objectively in a war situation will be fought and marginalized

but what do you mean by war shouted Ortica the war you're talking about and thinking about is the war they want and it has nothing nothing in the least to do with all we've been doing and all we've been thinking so far you believe you're convinced that the goal is the conquest of power as it is and so now for you the whole thing has become a question of winning or losing Scilla has come back to the table and on it he has laid two pistols a big one with a cylinder and a smaller one why did you need to bring the pistols here China said Scilla scowled at her one's a revolver the other's a pistol he said he lifted one of them in his hand handling it with skill with ease he pressed the butt-end with his thumb and took out the magazine and then took out the bullets and put them one by one in a row on the table the whisky poured in the glasses stayed on the table no one gave a thought to drinking as the tension mounted in the room the divisions were clear on one side Scilla Cotogno Valeriana on the other Ortica Nocciola China and me there was only Gelso who wasn't clearly on one side or the other he was very nervous he didn't speak at all he just kept cleaning the lenses of his glasses and biting his nails we maintained that it was madness to decide in the name of the movement on a leap into clandestinity with one stroke to wipe out everything that had been achieved so far to abandon a movement of thousands of people in struggle for a war waged by twenty or thirty

it ended at dawn with screams and abuse Scilla kept on playing with his guns and when at one point Nocciola told him to stop it in a flash Scilla grabbed the revolver and pointed it at him I'll put a hole in your head he told him we all stopped you could have heard a pin drop the only sound was the tap dripping in the wash basin we all looked at Scilla his arms stiff held in the air the pistol aimed at Nocciola we all knew it wasn't loaded but that wasn't what mattered we got up and we left Ortica Nocciola China and me the others stayed there around the table Gelso too never stirring his head lowered biting his nails staring at the table where the guns were and the glasses of whisky that nobody had drunk

after that evening we never saw them again they'd certainly have moved to another town because with that big step they planned to take they couldn't stay on in our area where they were too well known I never saw Valeriana Cotogno or Scilla again though once I ran into Gelso by chance but both of us avoided speaking about what had happened I thought Gelso looked pathetic he'd always been a real drop-out and now he was dressed in straight clothes with a jacket and a tie and hair cut short and his spectacle frames changed from round to square and then we never saw him again either and so our affinity group came to an end and what happened to them became another story that's not up to me to tell here now

those of us in the collective set to work with even more enthusiasm than before it was as if behind us we felt something monstrous and destructive closing in on us more and more and maybe also because there was a kind of need to prove to ourselves that the choice we'd made to stay inside the movement was the right choice the repression grew with every day that passed armed actions were followed by indiscriminate mass arrests but the repression wasn't only *carabinieri* and police it was also the press and media siege combined with the smashing of our communication network the difficulty and often impossibility of bringing out our newspapers because of arrests confiscations lack of money

a relentless campaign to criminalize the whole movement was set in motion every morning I'd read the newspaper any newspaper and there was no difference from the lowest hack journalist to the most distinguished intellectual sociologist philosopher psychologist historian novelist and so on they all wrote that the movement was nothing but a convulsive disturbance by displaced adventurers fascists schizophrenics criminals who should be locked up as quickly as possible in order to save democracy and civil harmony we felt a sense of powerlessness in the face of that systematic and total falsification but we believed that all the same we had no other option but to accept the challenge in the arena of media information and so we decided to set up a movement radio station

we dealt with the financial problem the way we'd always done before all the comrades set about finding money as best they could without being too choosy about how they did it and in this way we started getting hold of the stuff to set it up Nocciola borrowed a van and with two other comrades he went round the local building sites and helped himself to fibreglass polystyrene sheeting and other useful material and then we also got hold of several hundred pieces of cardboard packaging for egg boxes and with all this stuff we started soundproofing a room in the centre and then we partitioned it with chipboard panelling and sheets of perspex the recording studio on one side production on the other

now we had to get hold of equipment the mixer the amplifier the recording console and the stereo decks but the biggest problem was finding room in the frequency jungle either buying our way in or forcing our way in because either people had a lot of money and could buy a powerful transmitter that drowned out the other stations or else you had to make room for yourself simply by elbowing in shutting up the other stations and we had no scruples about doing this because our argument was what the hell are these commercial radio stations putting out besides advertising they put out shit music shit quizzes shit news bulletins and anyway who do these stations belong to in any case they're enemy radio stations participants in the destruction of our communications being carried out by those in power

so we started making night-time visits to the aerials and the transmitters of the local commercial radio stations that bothered us and we sabotaged them we pulled down the little pylons supporting the aerials and if we could we took away the transmitters or any other apparatus that might be useful for our radio station it was easy to carry out these actions of expropriation and sabotage because in general these things are set up in more or less isolated spots the aerials were placed on small hills or the roofs of tall buildings even ten or fifteen of us would go along without taking any special precautions there were metal cases with the transmitters in them and we'd open the lock and the padlocks with an electric drill and if we couldn't manage that we'd pour one or two litres of petrol under the door and toss a match at it and so gradually we cleared a space for ourselves in the frequency jungle where only the strongest could survive

37

The sergeant turned up it was eleven o'clock at night he called me through the spy-hole speaking the way they usually do as if he had a picture postcard for me instead it was a telegram from the ministry with the order for my transfer to a special prison we were laughing in the cell a bit tipsy then everyone went silent special prison those words scared us there were still six hours to go before it was five o'clock the time I was to leave the time to get my rucksacks ready and to exchange presents to stay awake and talk up until the last minute the news gets round the cells yells from the spy-holes people yell their good wishes because they're putting me on the road at five and there's not even the chance to give me a final hug in the exercise yard

at five sharp the guards arrive to collect me they're in a hurry they're sleepy and edgy because it's their last detail before going off their shift I hug my cell-mates who help me to lift the packs onto my back well see you outside this is what people always say when they're separated even guys who've got three life sentences still to do say it a lot of comrades are awake and I do the rounds of the armoured doors to shake the hands stuck through the spy-holes we have our last conversations give our last bits of advice I collect messages and good wishes to be taken to the comrades I'll meet down there then the section gate closes behind me and I follow the guards through the silent corridors of the sleeping prison

in the registration office we go through the whole series of particulars to be passed on to my new destination this is the most critical moment for if they've got a beating to give you that's when they do it it's the time for settling scores if you had any set-tos with one of the guards they put the word around about who's being transferred there are guards who even if they're not on duty the morning of your transfer are capable of getting up at five o'clock just for the pleasure of giving you a beating if they've got any score to settle with you they wait for the transfer to give it to you particularly in cases when they're not up to giving it to you on the spot in the heat of the moment in the cells but I'm lucky because they make do with a few provocative shoves and threatening reminders of some things I've done

once the registration business is over with they start the search the guards pull the stuff out of the rucksacks and they inspect it much more carefully than usual then I meekly put everything back in its place but then the *carabinieri* who're to be my escort arrive and everything starts from scratch another search they do two of them when you're leaving the guards do one and the *carabinieri* who're to escort you do the other because neither lot trusts the other then they take me to the van the armoured van is parked outside ten yards away from the registry gate in the centre of the prison but all the same the *carabinieri* handcuff me with a long chain they put me in chains for the ten yards I have to go from the gate to the armoured vehicle

outside it's still dark it's cold and the fog is so thick the headlights of the armoured vehicle turn it yellow without managing to cut through it the leader of the escort walks in front of me holding up the chain with my handcuffs linked to it the others walk behind me we advance like this in procession towards the van that's waiting shrouded in the yellow fog with the engine running and the doors open it's the first time I've seen inside an armoured van it's divided into three compartments in front the driving cabin in the middle the cell with two iron benches facing one another along the sides at the back seating for the escorts six men altogether they put me in the cell removing my chain but leaving on the handcuffs tight around my wrists then they close the grating with a padlock

on the first stretch as far as the entrance to the motorway they're extra careful up to there I'm also escorted by two flying-squad cars one in front and one behind with which they're also in radio contact Hare calling Kangaroo and that sort of thing the *carabinieri* are tense they turn out the inside light and peer intently through the port-holes to me all this deployment of forces seems absurd not to say ridiculous just for me but it's the rules they take the rules seriously and this morning I became a special case I mean as far as the rules are concerned I'm an extremely dangerous individual I try peering at the road through the port-holes but I can only see the ends of buildings the windows and cornices of buildings I stand up between the two benches but I can't manage to keep my balance because of the handcuffs maybe on the motorway where there are no bends I'll be able to look at the road ahead through the glass behind the driving cabin

on the motorway the *carabinieri* relax they take off their hats loosen their ties unbutton their jackets make themselves comfortable three of them get down to playing cards they play *sette e mezzo* and they play for money ten lire a card putting the coins inside their upturned hats laughing and losing their tempers the escort leader stays aloof he just keeps an eye on his boys' game they're different from the guards they do a different kind of job and this also changes the kind of contact they have with you they're merely transporting dangerous packages they do thousands of kilometres up and down the length of Italy continuously transporting prisoners up and down in their armoured vans for transfers from one prison to the other the goat path as we're accustomed to call these transfer routes

from time to time out of his bag the kind of bag tram conductors have one of them will take a sandwich made in the barracks or made by his wife the night before great big sandwiches stuffed with mortadella with salami or cheese he eats it slowly with the paper it was wrapped up in over his knees so as to avoid messing up his trousers and then he sweeps up the crumbs with a shovel and a little brush that are part and parcel of the armoured vehicle's equipment they seem more like commuters than warriors I sleep a little the handcuffs are hurting me and I'm hungry perhaps if I ask to have them taken off they'll take them off but I don't feel like asking them any favours as far as they're concerned I don't exist I'm only an object a package to be transported they take no notice of me but from time to time they take a quick look at me to check I'm jolted about up and down and from side to side I ache in every bone of my body

shortly after my arrival there at the special my father was taken into hospital and they took me on the same journey in the armoured van in the opposite direction to go and visit my father for the last time for he was dying of cancer I did the trip in a ten-hour stretch all over again and when we arrived my hands were quite numb because of the tight handcuffs around my wrists we arrived in the morning and after a short stop in the *carabinieri's* barracks they took me to the hospital they took me out of the van in the hospital courtyard and around me I saw a long line of *carabinieri* and a long line of police all carrying sub-machine guns and pistols there were the dogs there were the squad cars with the doors open and the blue lights on the roofs in one of them was Donnola giving orders through a walkie-talkie they put a chain on my handcuffs and they dragged me towards the big glass door of the hospital entrance hall full of people in pyjamas people in white shirts with white overalls white shoes who stopped to watch in amazement and surprise to the right and the left the lines of *carabinieri* cleared the way pushing puzzled onlookers back against the walls I could feel the chain pulling on my wrists I couldn't see where we were going then I stumbled the chain kept me from falling it was the first step on the stairs the procession started going up funnelling closer together I couldn't see the steps in front of me I lifted my feet but I kept on stumbling on the edges of the steps I was being crushed by people around me the chain was pulling me at last we reached the landing

suddenly all round the landing behind the *carabinieri* who hemmed me in I saw faces lots of faces all the faces of my comrades staring at me all the faces had the same expression eyes staring they said nothing no sign of greeting no gesture they all stared straight at me expressionless then a wrench on my wrist and they pulled me up another flight of stairs I slipped forward I was falling the *carabiniere* beside me caught my elbow but the sub-machine gun slung over his shoulder slipped down his arm and ended up between my legs without looking the one in front gave another tug at the chain and I lurched forward and the *carabiniere* holding on to me fell on top of me and so did all of those coming behind us in a heap on the stairs with the chain twisted round our arms and legs

finally we got to the top we came out into a big ward with patients in beds in a row along the white walls the resounding tread of the *carabinieri* the rattling of the chain the curt orders of the escort leader the protests of the doctors and the patients' relatives through that muddle I saw my mother and my brother coming towards me in tears my father was already dead when later they took me back in the armoured van the escort leader heaved a sigh of relief as he banged shut the door of the van and while we were waiting for the engine to heat up I saw him through the grating taking a small bottle of hydrogen peroxide out of his bag he poured a few drops on a wad of cotton wool and started rubbing it hard on his fingers and his hands he rubbed them for a long time and then we set off again for the special

Part Four

38

After the revolt in the special after they'd put us in those empty cells on the ground floor of the wrecked prison there was no more mass brutality and in every dormitory cell the debates began about what had happened of course the positions people took differed a lot but the fiercest debates developed as time passed because at first everyone was taken up with licking their wounds because the ill-effects of the beatings were starting to hit people and the atmosphere was more like a field hospital than anything else by now they'd started letting us have newspapers and what you read in the newspapers was absurd really absurd not a word of it was true it was as if nothing had happened all the news was distorted and it was utter lies to boot

as far as the press was concerned the special services operation had gone without a hitch with no bloodshed whatsoever the impression was that they'd boxed a few ears and everything had been resolved as peacefully as anything we started to demand visits from our relatives which was the only way of breaking this press blackout on what had really happened in the end they let us have a few token visits lasting no more than minutes with the glass screen in the middle what this achieved was that we managed to show ourselves to our relatives for a few minutes behind the screens so that our relatives could see the state we were in there wasn't even any need to speak to convey how things were how things had gone

since the only things that we had were the clothes that were on our backs when the special services burst in our relatives saw us in these blood-covered clothes with our plaster-casts our wounds our cuts our injuries and so on and this was enough in other words with these visits we were able to make a crack in the blackout wall that was meant to blank out the whole business especially since we'd naturally made sure of visits for those comrades who were most mangled up in the worst physical condition which meant the people who'd been brutalized most then the relatives in their turn made a real effort trying to pass on this news to the press

the very first days were extremely hard just at the level of basic survival in these bare cells but gradually we got ourselves together to cope with living even in those conditions and we even launched another protest with the aim of getting out of those bestial conditions in which we were reduced to living ten to a cell and instead of being nipped in the bud as it could easily have been in those conditions this protest succeeded in so far as after the very first days during which even exercise time had been abolished the administration had to allow us exercise time separating us into groups and letting us have one hour of exercise

the revolt was a blaze that had burned up all the strength that we'd accumulated it had been consumed by the revolt so now what we had to do was recover step by step to regain every-thing we'd lost and naturally the first steps were those that would secure us greater control over our lives inside the prison control over our lives means a lot of things it means for instance demanding to have visits again because visits are our links with the outside world it means demanding to have exercise time again because apart from it being physically necessary to go out into the fresh air at least an hour or two every day exercise time also means renewing internal communication between comrades

since we'd all been put on the ground floor some communication was possible for even if the armoured doors were locked the spy-holes were open so by shouting into the corridors through the spy-holes people exchanged information the administration had expressly abolished the working prisoners' role to stop us from circulating information and discussion about what to do now there were only the guards about in the corridors but with shouting and with the notes that people managed to pass from cell to cell collective discussion was possible then once exercise time was restored everything became much easier

some time later they allowed us to shave we could do it with a plastic razor they gave us each time and that we had to hand back immediately afterwards we could only use ordinary soap and we had no hand mirrors and so we shaved one another in turn and in my cell at that time there was a comrade who had both his hands in plaster and who could do nothing at all and at night before going to bed we had to take off his shoes his trousers his sweater and dress him again in the morning we had to put his food in his mouth when he ate we had to wash him clean him and wipe his bum when he had a shit we had to do everything for him and all the time he'd be saying thank you comrade thank you comrades

relationships with the guards have changed for in the rare moments when they could get away from under the noses of the NCOs the sergeants and the warrant-officers who were always in the corridor at least one of them whenever there was no NCO about for a minute the guards would talk to us saying over and over again that they hadn't been the ones who'd done the beatings that they hadn't been there that they'd had no part in that blood-bath and that in fact they totally disagreed with what had happened and they even said all the guards who'd taken part in that bloodbath had all been transferred

but of course this wasn't true at all and there were a number of occasions when comrades thought they could identify some of the guards who were in the corridor on duty and they were sure that they'd been among the guards who'd beaten us up and there were also some tense moments every so often a row would break out when somebody thought he could identify one of the guys who'd beaten us up because then the ones who'd had the worst of it got really mad and then there'd be serious threats made and that kind of thing it's inevitable one day a comrade who was certain he'd identified one of the guy's who'd beaten him up told him just wait one day I'm coming to get you even if you hide under the ground and I'll cut your head off

the sergeant who turned up in the corridor just then reacted by transferring the guard who'd been threatened somewhere else right away so as to make things simmer down afterwards however they remembered this business of the threats because later when all these comrades who'd threatened the guards during that time when all these comrades came to be transferred to another prison weeks and months later then they were badly beaten up all over again because that's how things always work in prison retaliation isn't always immediate things vary from moment to moment according to who's got the upper hand it can maybe happen that they'll make you pay for things even many months later

the guards reckon that sometimes there's no need to settle scores by beating somebody up right away in the heat of the moment because there'd be an immediate response in solidarity from all the other prisoners and then there'd be havoc it's much more convenient for them to mark the name in the black book and later on when it's time for a transfer and a guy's taken out of his cell because he's setting out for a different destination and he won't go back to that prison for at least a good while then they beat him up that's it things like this also happened during that period but the general mood was very good the morale of all the comrades was very high and that was a proof of the great solidarity that existed between all the comrades over and above the different political positions

39

At any rate during the first days we spent in these bare cells after the revolt all crammed together in those conditions the very first things to be done were to see to the treatment of our injuries to look after the comrades who were in a bad way and most of all we were still very afraid of another show of brutality from the guards because we'd started to fight back again and so the comrades put their minds to finding at least some minimum of weapons for self-defence which amounted to getting hold of some blunt instruments at least which wasn't very easy because they'd left nothing in the cells they'd left nothing at all not even stools or tables nothing

and so the first things to be seized on were the windows which were literally dismantled under the guards' very eyes and the iron bars were pulled out of these windows and in those first days even though they saw all this not only did the guards not interfere when they saw what was being done but they no longer dared even to come into the cells in other words the head count the entry of a group of guards into the cells to count the prisoners was suspended for the count the guards made do with opening the armoured door and doing the count through the barred gate but they were perfectly aware that the weaponry was there in the cells because they saw that the windows had been dismantled

but then when they allowed us to have our exercise time again naturally people thought that this was a move to get the cells emptied and that during the exercise period the guards would go inside and clear the cells of all those bars and so we were left with the dilemma whether to go to exercise and leave the cells unattended allowing the guards to go in and disarm us or whether we should choose to forego exercise which most of all meant giving up our means of communication inside the prison but there was no doubt that what mattered most was communication and just as we'd anticipated no sooner had they given it back to us than the guards took advantage of the exercise period to dash into the cells and carry out a general search confiscating all our weaponry the bars and everything else

from that moment there was pressure from the comrades pressure to get out of those conditions though in those conditions there weren't many things to be done the least constructive course given the conditions was to take more guards hostage seeing the way things had turned out earlier for if these guys had come in even when we had nineteen guards hostage it meant they were willing to fight it out on that ground on the assumption even that some people would die our conditions now were very harsh and we absolutely had to get out of them and the only way to get out of them was to fight but it had to be a fight that got somewhere and the conditions we were in meant we had to invent an altogether novel way of fighting we had to find a way of fighting with the only weapons we had available and in the first place we had to invent potential weapons since we had nothing naturally the shopping orders had been done away with every means of buying food had been done away with the food they gave out was the prison food a reddish liquid mess that was handed out at mid-day and in the evening with plastic containers and plastic spoons and then pressure was started with the demand to be allowed to buy at least some items of food stuff you could eat without cooking food like milk biscuits fruit and that kind of stuff because there was still no way these guys would let us have our primus stoves and saucepans and so on

we succeeded in gaining the right to buy these things and the chance to buy food to order gave us our foothold for this protest because now we had the option of not eating the prison food and so the prison food became our weapon in this struggle because every day litres and litres of this red coloured mess were piling up in the cells and then suddenly at a prearranged time all of us together poured the entire mess into the corridor a real river of sickening red-coloured liquid mess that was poured back out of all the cells into the corridor and this became what was known as bacteriological warfare

the guards who were in the corridor had been virtually doubled because they had to be able to maintain their surveillance of us every single minute of the day so there were always a lot of guards in the corridor they were always huddled together in big groups we were on the ground floor which wasn't even well ventilated and so all that sickening mess poured into the corridor naturally produced a certain unpleasantness for the guards and being in the corridor had become virtually unbearable so the guards came up with the obvious solution which was to bring in the working prisoners from the special to clean out the corridor but the working prisoners refused of course out of solidarity with our struggle saying we're not going to clean up this is a protest we're no scabs and we're not going to go against a protest by other prisoners

the working prisoners refused to clean all this mess out of the corridor it stayed there and every day there was more and more of it and we started flinging out not just the mess of broth but all kinds of rubbish as well that accumulated there and people also started shitting in plastic bags and paper bags or in newspapers and flinging them out into the corridor through the spy-holes the war we were waging was bacteriological warfare in earnest because with this mountain of dirt and rubbish and excrement that was building up out in the corridor from day to day there was now a real risk of disease and epidemic there was the risk of viral hepatitis and that sort of thing we were running the risk but so were they

then the guards turned to the working prisoners in the judicial prison instead of those in the special clearly they went and picked out the worst elements from among the working prison- ers in the judicial they went and picked out the worst elements and all the informers the spies in the service of the prison admin- istration and they brought them into our corridor to clean it out then no sooner had they arrived than all the comrades shouted insults from inside the cells from behind the spy-holes we shouted threats saying if you're here cleaning this block the day they move us out of these conditions you'll pay for it and you'll pay dearly this threat was enough for the lot of them took to their heels at once and then the guards found themselves back where they started

by now the situation had become pretty rough it had become intolerable because the guards couldn't lower themselves to the same level as the people who clean the corridors with their own hands because it wasn't their duty it wasn't their job and for them to start cleaning meant giving in while on the other hand the fact was that too much shit was building up in the corridor and they were really in danger of catching some infection or other like hepatitis there was the real danger of an outbreak an epidemic by now they were having to go round with handkerchiefs over their faces in the corridor they had handkerchiefs over their faces they came and opened your cell with handkerchiefs over their faces

since there was no way out of it the ministry decided it had to resolve the situation by sending an outside cleaning firm into the prison they took out a contract and they paid the top rate to an outside firm a company that operates in exactly the same way any firm working in the prison operates a construction firm or a firm of fitters an electrical firm when there are repairs to be done and this was a firm of cleaners and when the firm arrived the guards suddenly closed all the spy-holes of the armoured doors and within a couple of hours these contract workers with all their cleaning equipment and disinfectants had cleaned away the whole lot

40

And so the outcome was the build-up of these cycles where we would fill up the corridor with shit and they would bring in the cleaning firm to clean it out again and so it went on but in the end they allowed us to have visits as a way of relaxing the tension a bit the prison administrators or rather the ministry because with the way things were it was the ministry that made the direct decisions they allowed us to have one visit a month with the visitors behind a glass screen and so China turned up one visiting hour she turned up without them giving me any notice she was coming they called me and they took me into the visiting room with the glass screens in it it was the first time I'd seen that room they'd rebuilt it completely and China was already there waiting for me she was there sitting behind the screen when I went in

there was an intercom under the screen behind a little square grille I bent down to speak into it but across from me China signalled that she couldn't hear anything she also tried to speak into the intercom on her side but I couldn't hear her either I punched the grille a couple of times but it made no difference it was clear that they'd cut off the intercoms they'd cut them off deliberately so that to make ourselves heard we needed to speak very loudly we almost had to shout and so the guards could hear everything the situation was impossible China had travelled a thousand kilometres to come and see me and she had to travel another thousand to get home and we couldn't even talk to one another we had to shout to make ourselves heard

she looked smaller and thinner she was dressed in smart clothes not as I'd remembered her I'd never seen her like this she was wearing a skirt and a smart jacket with big padded shoulders which must have been the current fashion she'd had her hair cut she'd had it cut short it was over a month since I'd seen her she was wearing little earrings and a little wrist watch she who'd never worn a watch she was sitting there on a block of concrete a concrete cube that was supposed to be a stool the glass was thick it was double thickness and it was dirty it was virtually opaque and had a greenish tinge through it China's face was a bit distorted and I shifted around this way and that to try and get a better view of her in the room there were four visiting positions with screens like the cashier's windows in a bank and the guards were in a room just behind us looking at us through a square opening in the wall

as soon as she saw me come into the room she smiled at me from behind the plate glass then when I got closer her expression changed her eyes narrowed into a stare but she didn't look me in the face she looked down a bit I realized that she was looking at my sweater that was all bloodstained it was the same sweater I'd been wearing since that night and then I said it's not my blood but China went on staring staring at the sweater and it dawned on me that she hadn't heard it dawned on me that she hadn't even been aware I was speaking it dawned on me because then she spoke she moved her lips but I didn't hear her voice

I decided there was really no point in even making a fuss I could call the sergeant and the warrant-officer but I knew in advance what would come of it they'd have pretended to follow the rules they'd have said that the intercoms were broken that there was nothing they could do about it but that's how it was for the time being I could make do or if I preferred I could give up the visit and all this would only have wasted the visiting time which was already very short just then a comrade came in he had both his arms in plaster he had a cut on his head they'd given him a load of stitches and to do the stitches they'd cut off all his hair we only nodded in greeting for we disliked one another I really disliked this guy when his parents came in and saw him in this state they were shocked

he by contrast was quite unsubdued in his usual style and he started shouting right away a grin appeared on his still swollen face and then he shouted things like our fight continues and intensifies the struggle goes on tell everyone don't worry about me I'm really fine in a few days I'll be just like new for another struggle his parents were two tired old people and they looked at him in shock and with tears in their eyes China too looked at him with some astonishment I didn't even listen to what the guy was saying because he always talked like this the parents could make no sense of it they nodded their heads in agreement but they didn't take their eyes off the cut with the stitches on his shorn head China now turned back to look at me again with a sad expression I signed to her that the blood on my sweater wasn't mine now she was looking at my nails blackened by the coagulated blood from the truncheon beatings I spoke loudly I'm fine and you and she forced a half smile and shrugged then she asked me what now I shook my head to indicate I didn't know she started telling me that so-and-so and so-and-so sent their regards I listened to the names all the names and nick-names of the comrades who were sending their regards but it made me feel peculiar it made me feel very distant from them almost as if they were strangers or dead people that I'd never see again and I realized that I really couldn't care less about their regards more than that it pissed me off but I was sorry that China was aware of this because she'd come a thousand kilometres to get there and I was sorry

I tried to smile but I felt we were squandering the whole of the visiting time which wasn't much time anyway because the things we were saying were pointless but I didn't even know what she could have said to me what could have helped me my nerves were getting the better of me I only half heard what she was saying but I didn't even ask her to repeat what I couldn't make out then suddenly she stopped talking I stared at the greenish wall behind her soft padded shoulders I didn't know what to say I was getting more and more nervous about the time passing about the time we were wasting but I had no idea what to say what to do to make use of it we were silent for a bit then China looked at her watch a gesture I'd never seen her make before and I said why don't you write to me and she said why don't you write to me when China left it occurred to me that this business of cutting off the intercoms didn't make sense for if they really wanted to hear everything that was said during the visiting hour instead of making us shout it was much easier much more productive for them to leave the intercoms on which would allow them more easily to hear everything even without people thinking they were being overheard and if they wanted they could even record everything we said during the visiting hour after this visit I didn't see China again I only got a letter from her a week or two later that began with her saying she wouldn't write to me again for a while

41

After this we then tackled the problem of how to get another protest going however just then the immediate problem was our reduced exercise time which had been cut down to just an hour in the morning and also the fact that there were no regular working prisoners in the corridors which kept our opportunities for internal communication to the minimum and therefore our possibilities for agreement on how to take joint action so by then it had become essential to find a way of improving our internal communications so in the cells people got the idea of drilling through the walls from cell to cell so that we could communicate directly I mean not pulling down the whole wall but at least making some holes you could talk through from one cell to another

and people started doing it and in fact holes were made in nearly all the cells and so there was a way for us to communicate directly you made a hole in the wall with the remaining bars that could be dismantled from the windows or from the beds or with iron bars that the working prisoners who just came to bring our food managed to pass on to us though it was really risky but of course it took hours and hours for instance to dismantle the beds that were fixed into the concrete floor to get the bars out of them and get the holes made in the wall clearly the guards knew what was going on we'd be banging away all day and so everything was going on right under their eyes

there was the worry the doubt all the time about them coming in and if they came in there could be another bloodbath however there was no other way though bearing in mind the very fact that the guards could come in we took another precaution and this precaution consisted in barricading the cell at night and taking turns at standing watch so as to avoid the risk of being surprised by them breaking in some time while we were asleep the cell barricade consists in jamming some object perhaps no thicker than a biro or a splinter of wood between the gate and the armoured door because the gap between the gate and the armoured door is just a few millimetres

which means all you have to do is fill it in I mean jam something between the gate and the armoured door so that when the guards outside put the key in the lock the door presses against what's blocking it and they can't open it when it's like that they can't come in and therefore there's plenty of time to organize some resistance inside of course they have their own means of removing anything that's in the way for instance taking one of the hydrants that are installed in the corridors of each section and uncoiling the big hose to direct the jet through the spy-hole and then naturally with this powerful jet sweeping the cell you can't do a thing no resistance because it pushes you back against the wall and at the same time they get rid of the obstacle without you being able to do anything about it so the business of barricading the cells became a nightly routine and so did taking turns at keeping watch to keep an eye on what was happening in the corridor we also got hold of some fragments of mirrors again through the working prisoners who brought our food and we were able to place these mirror fragments outside the spy-holes and in this way we were able to see the whole corridor as far as the end and to keep a check on the movements of the guards this procedure of barricading the cells at night and taking turns to keep watch was routine for a good while and we'd spend the time playing cards for we'd been allowed to have cards we were in the cells for twenty-three solid hours and things went on like this for a good while in the cells

when the bacteriological warfare protest eased off then through this communication channel through the holes that we'd made between the cells discussions began so as to decide which new form of struggle should be taken up to put pressure on the prison administration about other things and then it was clear that the maximum goal this whole crescendo of protests was moving towards was to destroy the prison literally in the sense of destroying it as a physical structure but in fact this was absurd because the conditions they'd placed us in meant that we had nothing to destroy nor did we even have anything that could become an implement for our struggle in the meantime because the cell wasn't furnished it was quite empty and so you couldn't threaten to smash it up there was nothing there and what could you do if there was nothing to smash up

then the next stage in the offensive was flooding and so from bacteriological warfare we moved on to operation Niagara in all these protests what was implicit and decisive was always the store of memory preserved most of all by the non-politicals the accumulation of knowledge of a science of struggle inside the prison of a science built up over time and what was decisive was most of all were naturally the suggestions of the old prisoners of people who'd been in prison for ten twenty years and who'd gone through all kinds of things in protests so now we'd moved on from bacteriological warfare as a form of struggle to operation Niagara which was our new form of struggle

operation Niagara consisted in flooding the section flooding the section meant that at the previously agreed time all of us together all of us using rags made from tearing up the sheets that we'd finally been allowed to have and the blankets we made wadding and with this wadding we blocked the toilets we blocked the toilet bowls and we blocked the washbasins after this we used strips of foam rubber ripped from the foam rubber mattresses and we wedged them in the space between the bottom of the armoured door and the floor and we even padded out the foam rubber with strips of blanket so as to stop the water from running out of the cell and running into the corridor

after this we turned on all the taps and we fixed the flushing mechanism so that the water flushed out continuously and we did this during the night in the periods when there were fewer guards on duty and when at the same time it would create greater problems for during the night a general state of alarm in the prison causes much more trouble than a state of alarm in the daytime because all the guards have to get out of bed and everything becomes more of a nuisance so during the night maybe around three or four a.m. we'd plug everything up we'd plug up the washbasin we'd plug up the toilet bowl and we'd flood the cells and in every cell there were gallons and gallons of water pouring out until the water reached our knees

the water mounted inside the cell which was completely hermetically sealed just imagine how many gallons of water there were the water kept pouring out and when it got to your knees you removed the wadding from under the door that closed up the gap between the door and the floor and the water gushed out in a flood from every cell gallons and gallons of water came gushing out in floods into the corridor and within minutes the whole section was waterlogged making it a protest that did real damage for being on the ground floor the water built up in the corridors and stayed there and the result was a quagmire and what's more we did this while we were still going on with bacteriological warfare which made the quagmire well and truly foul indescribably foul

now the guards had to make their way through a quagmire as well as having handkerchiefs over their faces now they had to wear rubber wading boots as the water poured out of the cells we also threw in some detergent making a huge amount of foam and some people also made little paper boats out of newspapers they threw the boats out of the spy-hole and they sailed along the corridors borne by the tide of foaming water it was a genuine flood and this was another form of struggle that we launched and naturally it created a lot of problems for the guards another form of struggle we used was setting off short circuits that made the lights fuse all over the prison this was operation blackout the whole prison went dark

there was one comrade who was an electrician and he knew all about electrical systems which meant he could set off short circuits by disconnecting something or other I'm not sure what I never did it myself he made things short-circuit and when there was a short circuit for a few seconds you'd hear a very loud noise it was the sound of the outside generators going on and putting the lights back on at once there were moments of panic though for when the lights go out in the prison in the middle of the night the guards start running around with torches it was all pretty unnerving for them but naturally it was unnerving for us too for we'd anticipate retaliation at any moment we'd be anticipating some large-scale operation against us

42

All this built up and built up these small everyday protests built up all the time until naturally the prison administration was faced with the question of some decisive major operation to put a stop to it once and for all but among the guards there were two camps whereas over and above our political distinctions and different opinions on the outcome of the revolt we were now struggling over basic issues issues affecting our survival which meant that now it was clear that unity was the sole requirement for achieving this survival we were struggling for

for the guards however the problem was posed differently and the result was that they were divided into two different camps there was the interventionists' camp in other words those who maintained the need for immediate intervention by force and on the other hand those who maintained that there was no need for intervention by force and inevitably this disagreement touched the hierarchies too there were interventionist sergeants and warrant-officers and non-interventionist sergeants and warrant-officers but the interventionists had deliberately stirred things up what had happened for instance was that guards had burst into one of the cells one day because a comrade had insulted a sergeant by throwing a cigarette-end in his face

what had happened was that while the majority of the comrades were having exercise time one afternoon a group of guards turned up with shields and helmets and truncheons and burst into the cell and they seized this comrade and took him away to the isolation cells that's when tension rose to boiling point and naturally the comrades made all kinds of threats they'd carry out if this comrade wasn't brought back to this section at once then the guards thought it over and they gave permission for some other comrades to go and visit the comrade however the prison administration said that since a charge had been made by this sergeant who'd had the cigarette-end flung in his face there would be a hearing which meant that they couldn't remove him from isolation until the day of the hearing

however the date of the hearing was fixed for just two or three days later and so this comrade went to the hearing where of course he was found guilty and straight away went home again that's to say to his section what's more he made the most of the opportunity at the hearing to make a public denunciation of the conditions we were still being held in after more than a month and our situation of daily struggle for survival then the Ministry of Justice formulated its plan for solving the problem which like all plans for solving problems when what's involved are unified and solid struggles there's always just one solution to the problem splitting up prisoners and breaking up this solid unity

in other words what they always do in these circumstances is to try and pick out the ones they think are the ringleaders in the protests and separate them from the others and also to create distinctions as a basis for different kinds of treatment and so one day while we were all at exercise a great throng of guards turned up they'd brought christ knows how many hundreds of guards from other prisons too it was terrifying and our first thought was that they'd come to sort things out again just the same way as before and all the comrades there were still suffering from the after effects of the bloodbath that followed the revolt an unbelievable number of guards came but right away they told us what they planned to do we have to split you up and take some people to the first floor we're only going to split you up

they told us what they planned to do there in the exercise yard then they took out their list and said either you come out or we'll go in and there'll be trouble there were really so many guards with so many shields truncheons water hoses and so on so we thought it was better to concede and all those destined for the first floor went upstairs they let themselves be taken to the first floor there was no violence but the first thing the comrades did as soon as they got up there was to test the strength of the new plate-glass windows that they'd put there and with the stools they found up there they smashed one or two of them just to test the resistance of the new plate-glass windows they'd put in

they left the other comrades downstairs on the ground floor their plan was to break the internal circuit of communication again by putting people on two different floors because with people on two different floors they could break the flow of communication that we'd achieved so far but people found a way round this too for the comrades upstairs tore up their sheets into strips and dropped messages down from the first floor windows to the ground floor the torn sheets with the messages would be weighted with a lemon and they'd dangle the lemon and the messages in front of the first floor window

however this division also coincided with the start of the first mass transfers in record time the Ministry of Justice had carried out the complete reconstruction of that other special prison that had been totally destroyed a few months earlier they'd re-estab-lished this prison and so on the basis of their lists of those they regarded as the ringleaders of the revolt the mass transfers began people were transferred in batches of ten they began first and foremost with those they'd put on the floor upstairs then the transfers went on until a score or so of us altogether were left in the prison after all these transfers

a few days before the transfers the administration had given everyone permission to go up to the first floor that had been wrecked by the guards one at a time escorted by guards they took us up there to collect our things from the cells that we'd occupied before the revolt when I went up I saw the holes made by the grenades in the floor of the rotunda and the metal gate blown out and propped against the wall it was almost pitch dark in the corridor I could feel water underfoot where there must have been big puddles and there was also water dripping from the broken pipes in the corridors there were radiators lying up-ended broken tables cupboards that had caved in stools strewn all over the place all broken and in pieces

bits of television sets mattresses books strewn everywhere food leftovers clothes sodden with water and there was a stink of dampness and putrefaction lingering on in the corridor there was light in my cell in the doorway I stumbled over the violin gutted with its strings torn off I went inside and I saw the wreckage of my cell everything smashed up everything uprooted everything shattered everything lying on the ground in an inch or so of water a sludge that had been rotting away for two months now the guards looked and said nothing I didn't know where to start I didn't know what to do there was nothing recognizable anymore there were shirts sweaters rotting with stains of green mould I'd left everything there all my shirts and sweaters

I took two sweaters that had been saved because they were on top and some other stuff then I also took a pair of trousers half mouldy and ripped too at the bottom but I really needed them in one corner I saw a little pile my letters ripped crumpled and torn I recognized the little yellow square of China's last telegram her letters were there and other letters I gathered them up in a handful I saw her writing on the pieces of paper and I put them in my pocket I searched for my books one or two of them were still in good condition although wet I dried them a bit and I put them with the sweaters after trying to dry them a bit

I searched around a bit longer but halfheartedly I raked around a bit kicking aside the plastic plates and the sodden newspapers

I stood there staring about the guards didn't seem to be in any hurry I looked through the broken window pane and I started wondering what was the point of this I dropped the books I only kept the sweaters and the mouldy trousers then I put my hand in my pocket I pulled out the shreds of the letters and without looking at them I dropped them on the floor too even her letters and before I left I also took off the red scarf that I always wore around my neck and threw that down too and I hurried away with the guards because by now nothing mattered to me any more at all

43

The date of the trial came round and I was transferred to the prison where I'd been the first time after my arrest we were in a small transit block for people who like me were there for trial a small block that was really awful a small block in continual darkness buried in a corner where the sun's rays never reached that was where I understood because for the first time I saw it for myself about all these stories of *pentiti** that had started just at that time I became aware then that the worst things about this whole business were still to come that everything that had happened so far had been nothing by comparison with what was starting to happen in fact it almost looked good by comparison for with all these things happening now it seemed to me that not only was it all over and done with but also that the whole thing

---

* *Pentiti* (literally *penitents*) was the term used to describe those in prison who collaborated with the judiciary, giving evidence against comrades or associates, simultaneously rejecting their former allegiances.

had been futile that it had all been utterly futile every single thing everything that all of us had ever done

it so happened that in this block of the prison there was someone who was reputed to have talked to have sent other people to prison what had happened to this guy was very unusual because he'd been captured as a result of a *pentito*'s statements and then early on he'd admitted to everything this guy had accused him of there was a murder involved too he admitted everything but went no further than that made no accusations against anyone else however his comrades in prison judged these actions of his to be an admission of the *pentito*'s statements and they gave him the option of getting himself sent to a prison where there were *pentiti* and taking a *pentito* and killing him

when his comrades forced this on him he cracked in the face of this proposal he reacted by cracking up and he decided to become a *pentito* in earnest then he justified it by saying that this proposal had struck him as monstrous this thing they proposed to him in other words a murder to purify himself he cracked up and spent a few days in this state then he made up his mind he called the investigating judge and he talked in earnest and came out with a load of names he told them a lot he even told them the name of a guy who was his best friend the only one who defended him in prison and so further incriminating evidence turned up against his comrades who were in prison who were incriminated all over again by what he'd said

when he finished his statements the judge told him these statements mean that you can't go back to the special again with all the rest because they'll kill you right away so they sent him to a prison for *pentiti* he went to this prison for *pentiti* sure that there he'd at least have the chance to discuss these experiences but once he'd got there in this prison for *pentiti* there came another shock even worse than the first because what he saw and heard in his talks with these *pentiti* was even nastier for he explained in the letters to his friend that I read too that these individuals weren't *pentiti* at all but were just people making calculations about when they'd get out on the basis of the number of statements they'd made how long it would take them to get out on the basis of that

and then he freaked out again and once more he called the same investigating judge to whom he'd made his statements and he withdrew the whole lot saying I know very well that the retractions I'm making are unlikely to exonerate the people I've incriminated but all the same I want to leave this prison because I don't want to stay here any longer then the judge told him listen now if you go back where you were before they'll kill you they won't give you any option this time this time instead they'll kill you as soon as they set eyes on you and that's the end of it but he said it doesn't matter I'm going there even if they kill me for I'm not staying here

at a loss to know where to put him the ministry parked him in this block and he was there just when I arrived for my trial he was in isolation he even went out for the exercise period alone they put him on his own in one of these enclosed segments however as soon as his comrades arrived he started sending them notes and letters telling them about all his goings on and saying that what he was hoping for was to go back with his comrades despite having done what he'd done and saying that he was ready to accept whatever judgment the comrades would make on his decisions and his actions saying that he preferred the risk of being killed because he was aware of what he'd done and he preferred the risk of being killed

he set out all these self-critical arguments and sent them to his comrades from isolation but they were all rejected he received no replies and then one day after these futile attempts to establish a dialogue he made a decision he went down to the exercise yard and spent half an hour pleading with the sergeant who was on duty to put him in with his comrades he pleaded and pleaded the sergeant was doubtful however in the end he let him go through and then he started talking to his comrades telling them his story which they knew already the comrades told him don't come in here again tomorrow or we'll kill you and then he said he'd come anyway tomorrow because if that was what they decided whatever it might be he accepted it

and then his comrades discussed what's to be done and if the guy really does come to the exercise yard tomorrow they really do have to kill him otherwise he'll stay there and it'll blow over and besides in the end word would get round all the prisons and it would get known that this guy that they regard as a bastard is having exercise with them in their yard quite undisturbed and so the next day this guy does in fact turn up in the exercise yard the comrades had a blade but they decided not to knife him but to strangle him with knotted shoelaces they'd woven a cord from shoelaces and then right on time he turned up in the exercise yard as on the day before he'd had himself taken into the section where the comrades were and he knew that they were going to kill him and he was there waiting for them to kill him

and in fact they put him against the wall and they put this cord of shoelaces around his neck and he didn't put up the slightest resistance he didn't say a thing he didn't struggle at all he didn't move he let them go ahead he let them put the cord around his throat when one comrade started pulling the cord around his neck the last thing he said was no not like this the guy who was pulling it was a friend of his he said no not like this I beg you use the blade do it with the blade and the guy kept on pulling the cord and by now the other one was turning blue he was purple he was quite purple his eyes popping out of their sockets he was gradually suffocating because the whole thing was taking a long time then slowly he fell to his knees

then suddenly the cord broke the cord made of shoelaces broke all of a sudden and the guy pulling it was left standing there with the broken cord in his hand and by then the guards who'd followed everything from their booth on the closed circuit cameras had rushed up and this guy on his knees stayed there huddled there on the ground they could have gone ahead and killed him with their bare hands he wouldn't have put up a fight but they left him there they all looked horrified the guards arrived with their dogs with their helmets pulled down their truncheons their shields this guy was there huddled on the ground half-conscious but his body was jerking I don't know he was coughing he was trying to get his breath there was froth coming out of his mouth then he vomited I don't know but what a fucking shitty business I was watching what a shitty business I'm telling you about

only the story wasn't over there because after the guards took him away and as soon as he recovered this guy was talking from the window of his cell to the guys in the next cell saying tomorrow I'm going down again tomorrow I'm going down and they were saying but the guards won't put you with us again and he was saying I've tried to kill myself but I can't kill myself you have to kill me and so in the end he went down to the exercise yard the next day too but the next day that friend of his had arrived the one he denounced along with the others the guy went down to the exercise yard and the guards naturally put him on his own the guards were very tense for these weren't nice things to see and when they see scenes like this they tell themselves they're dealing with murderers people who'll kill at the drop of a hat they become even surer of this

his friend arrived he'd heard about what had happened in the exercise yard and then the first thing he did was he went up to the gate the other guy was at the next gate and by wriggling their heads through they were able to speak face to face the first one went over there wriggled his head outside and started talking to the other one and this action led to a certain amount of embarrassment among their comrades however the last thing they could do was set upon that guy who was much too impeccable a comrade much too blameless just for having said something to him and the guy didn't just make this gesture but then he also took off a ring he took a ring off his finger and gave it to him through the gate the guy had denounced him but they were friends they'd been friends since childhood

then the next day this guy still talking through the cell window told his comrades that he planned to call the investigating judge and attack him and so he asked them to give him a primus stove so that he could make a skewer and then the comrades told him okay but don't imagine that if you do this your problems are over if you want to do this do it but it doesn't change a thing the blood of a judge won't wash away your problems this is exactly what they said the blood of a judge won't wash away your problems however at the same time they gave him the primus stove and he'd made the skewer he sent for the judge to whom he'd made the statements and the judge came probably thinking that he had more statements to make and in the visiting room he managed to stab him in the arm after which the guards intervened and put a stop to it

44

A few days before the start of the trial Gelso and Ortica arrived in this block too I was very excited about them coming because it had been so long since I'd seen them Gelso had been arrested at the same time as I'd been arrested but right away he'd been put in a special even further south and in all this time I'd had no more news of him whereas Ortica had only been arrested a few months before and he'd ended up in the same special as Gelso I was very excited and emotional about seeing my comrades again through the spy-hole I saw them arrive at the end of the corridor surrounded by guards Ortica was loaded down with rucksacks Gelso carried nothing at first I didn't even recognize him he was very thin short hair no glasses he looked straight ahead without returning the greetings from the spy-holes of the cells

then I called to them and Ortica heard immediately he knew who I was even though he couldn't see me because the guards were putting them in a cell quite far from mine I heard Ortica's voice calling to me saying where are you then pressing my face to the spy-hole I saw him for an instant in the middle of the corridor waving to me in greeting as a guard was pulling him back by the other arm as soon as they'd locked them in I called the sergeant and told him they were my co-defendants and that they were there for the same trial as me and I immediately put in a written request to have them come into the cell where I was on my own the sergeant told me that he would take it to the administration and that maybe the cell transfer could be made that same evening

meanwhile right away I set about preparing supper for Gelso and Ortica I didn't have much stuff in my cell I called the working prisoner and sent him to other cells to get things for me wine in particular meanwhile I swept the floor and I also washed it with a rag I lifted the mattress off its base because were was no table in the cell just a bit of metal shelving fixed to the wall when the working prisoner came back he brought me three plastic mineral water bottles with a quarter of red wine in them which is the way they sell them to us and other food which didn't amount to much so I was at a bit of a loss because I wanted to make a nice supper for my friends

and then I thought of making a dessert in my cell I had two packets of instant pudding I made two puddings a chocolate one and a vanilla one heating the milk in a saucepan on the stove and then I put them on the window sill to cool down in two plastic bowls I made coffee and mashed up some dry biscuits in it and then I layered the pudding and the biscuits on a plate I beat up the white of an egg with some castor sugar to whip it into a white cream that I put on top and on the bed base I put a clean white sheet then I unscrewed the gas stove and round it I wound a cone of tin foil so that the flame came out like a candle

I put out the light and I was setting the table when the guard opened the armoured door and let in Ortica but Gelso wasn't there and Ortica told me he'd explain later we hugged one another and as soon as the guards had left he told me that Gelso was sick he was sick in the head he'd been ill for a good while already prison was too much for him to begin with all he talked about was escaping and then he stopped talking altogether he no longer seemed to recognize people he no longer wanted to talk to anybody and then during exercise time he also started going around the courtyard on all fours growling and making faces like a crazy man muttering that if he was a dog they'd let him out

to start with I'd cut some bread with slices of salami and some mayonnaise we started eating and Ortica started telling me about Scilla I'd already heard the story a rumour was going round but I hadn't believed it what they were saying seemed impossible that Scilla had become a spy a police informer who'd betrayed his comrades even though I'd never liked him but Ortica told me that by now all the comrades outside were convinced that Scilla had turned informer to the *carabinieri* that he'd had a whole lot of comrades arrested it had all started when the *carabinieri* had carried out a search on him and maybe because they found arms on him or whatever nobody's sure exactly how the fact is that they took him to the barracks and he stayed in the barracks for a whole day and then they released him during the night

Scilla had explained this business telling his comrades that the *carabinieri* had spent the whole day threatening him but had to let him go because they had no evidence the comrades had believed this they were even pleased because nothing had come of it but nobody had even the slightest suspicion it didn't occur to them that that was the start of a collaboration with the *carabinieri* Scilla was quite above suspicion everybody would have staked their lives on his honesty yet the fact was that when the *carabinieri* asked him to collaborate he agreed and they released him and shortly after this there was the ambush and death of Cotogno and then once he'd denounced all his comrades Scilla disappears nobody knows maybe they gave him a passport and money and he's vanished abroad

Ortica brought direct proof that Scilla was to blame for Cotogno's death from Valeriana who he'd met shortly before being arrested he'd run into Valeriana outside a chemist's shop it was a while since he'd seen her and hardly recognized her he'd heard that she'd become a junkie but he was really shocked when he saw what a state she was in clearly that day she was going through withdrawal because she couldn't get her hands on any stuff I can't tell you what a mess she was in Ortica told me she was crying and screaming she was outside the chemist's screaming help me nobody will give me any methadone I've gone round all the chemists in all the villages nobody will give me any

methadone none of these bastards these shit pharmacists I'll kill
the lot of them I feel rotten I'm going crazy

it was another week before I saw her again then one day she
was waiting for me in the street outside my house she was
dressed like the time before with the same black woollen cap
pulled down over her forehead she asked me if I could find her
some money because she owed Nocciola a million lire Nocciola
had become the local pusher this was something else I found
out from Ortica Valeriana had been selling heroin for him but
she'd spent all the money on her own habit in short she was in
real trouble and there was nobody else to turn to any more she
was in debt all over the place she talked without stopping
saying that she wanted to kick it that now she was taking methadone because she wanted to kick it but first she had to sort out
the debt with Nocciola

she wasn't afraid of him so much as of his crowd of friends who
were the sort to come down hard on people who didn't pay
they'd already threatened her and Nocciola had kept out of it
he'd washed his hands of it and he'd no doubt let his friends go
ahead we went into a bar she took off her anorak but she kept
on the woollen cap it seemed stuck to her head to her hair do
you remember what nice hair she had long and blond now it
was falling over her shoulders in sticky dirty clumps her face
was sweating and yellowish her eyes sunken and circled with
shadows so deep that they looked like furrows she talked non-
stop all the time running her nails up and down the sides of her
velvet trousers

it was that time in the bar that Valeriana told Ortica about
Cotogno's death they'd arranged to meet in the flat where we'd
had that famous meeting Cotogno had told Valeriana before
going that he had an appointment with Scilla but Scilla didn't go
to the appointment the *carabinieri* went instead they came into

the flat shooting obviously they wanted revenge for the *carab-iniere* who'd recently been killed and it was just then that Scilla went out of circulation and there was a series of arrests all comrades who'd been connected with Scilla and finally Ortica too he'd never had anything to do with Scilla's affairs but it was probably because Scilla hated him

we ate the rice salad that I'd scraped together and some tinned sardines Ortica told me that nobody had had any news of China for some time now she'd completely vanished into thin air the last time he'd seen her was at the centre when they were doing test runs on the radio I preferred not to talk about China we ate the pudding it was disgusting then Ortica grinned and from his jeans pockets he pulled out a pellet of dope he looked at it against the light saying can you imagine the lengths I had to go to to get it in here we sat down on the mattress and we made a joint the dope was really good and we both started laughing Ortica's laughter got louder and louder he was laughing like a madman tears came into his eyes

tomorrow we've got the trial do you realize tomorrow they'll take us over there and they'll give us a nice trial I haven't got the least idea do you have any idea what we're going to say to them he stopped laughing though without altering his expression his face was set in a grimace I said whatever it is they'll give us all a heavy sentence all the same whatever we go there and tell them or don't tell them the candle flame from the stove was going down gradu-ally the little gas cylinder for the stove got weaker until it went out completely now I could hardly see Ortica there in the dark-ness I spoke to him I ask myself sometimes now that it's all over I ask myself what did it all mean this story of ours what was the meaning of all we did what did we achieve with everything we did he said I don't believe it matters that it's all over but I believe what matters is that we did what we did and that we think it was right to do it I believe this is the only thing that matters

Ortica passed me the joint for the last toke and I asked him about the radio station what had happened with the radio station Ortica started laughing again the radio was all ready we had all the equipment we had the frequency we even had the telephone we did all the voice tests with China's voice one two three testing he laughed all we managed to say was one two three testing everything was there ready we only had to press a button and speak but we had nothing to say any more nobody went to the centre any more by this time there was a new disaster every day somebody being arrested somebody having a breakdown a disappearance a suicide everybody vanished there was nothing to say any more and so it all stayed there gathering dust the transmitter the console the stereo the amplifier the microphone and China's voice

45

Won't you answer the voice of the investigating judge addresses me through the microphone and I can hear it reverberate behind me I look up and I look at those faces watching me from behind their dark glasses up there I feel as if I'm slumped in my chair with the *carabinieri* standing behind me and that serried row of faces above me behind the bench staring at me with contempt and hostility everyone in the courtroom is staring at me the lawyers the journalists the scanty public made up of relatives the comrades in the cage the carabinieri dotted about everywhere they're all staring at me they're all waiting for me they're waiting for me to speak I'm waiting too it feels as if I've always been waiting that time has stood still and now what do I do what do I say there I was standing still waiting for something I don't know what

I nodded to say that I'd answer and immediately without so much as looking at me the investigating judge asks me if I pleaded guilty or innocent and then I had to start speaking since I'd indicated that I would I made a great effort my mouth so dry it was burning and without looking at anyone only fixing my eyes on the wooden bench right in front of me I said that before I answered we needed first to agree on the meaning of these words because it couldn't be taken for granted that these words guilty or innocent had the same meaning for me as for them and so there was a need first to clarify to understand this was more or less what I was saying when I heard a shout from the public prosecutor who interrupted me saying I was obliged to answer the question and not to make pointless quibbles over words

my first reaction was to get up and to go back into the cage I didn't do this because I felt nailed stuck to that chair now there was silence around me then I waited a moment then I went on saying well let's put it like this you're the ones who're talking you're accusing me you're saying armed band that I've been that I've taken part in an armed band that I'm a subversive the investigating judge interrupts me no no he says that's not it I'm not the one who's saying this and with the flat of his hand he hits the pile of files he has in front of him I'm not the one who's saying this these are the indictments and he hits the files again its from all these indictments that the penal code arrives at the crime of armed band it's on the basis of these indictments that we must argue and that you must answer me because it's on the basis of these indictments that we're conducting this trial

just then I hear my lawyer speaking up behind me if the president of the court will permit I'd like but the investigating judge does not permit on the contrary he loses his temper and he shouts at the lawyer that for now he will permit nothing that the lawyer must wait the lawyer tries to insist once more saying I believe I have the right what right shouts the investigating judge I'm the one to say who has the right in here I'm the one in charge of this session from the cage come a few shouts and whistles the prosecutor gets on his feet and points towards the cage shouting but I can't hear what he's shouting because now everyone's shouting the investigating judge is shouting louder than anyone into the microphone the *carabinieri* are shifting to and fro outside the cage the investigating judge is shouting louder than anyone that's enough silence another word and I'll clear the court

and again they're all waiting for me to resume speaking the investigating judge has calmed down he waves a hand come on come on let's get on with it then I say I was saying that I don't understand what sense there is in my stating that I'm innocent or guilty because I don't want to deny or rather disavow what I've done what I've been because if I thought that this society we're living in has to be changed the presiding judge interrupts me but you must realize that we're not here to put ideas on trial but actions actions regarded as crimes under the penal code but then I say why do you start by accusing me of being a terrorist these are ideas don't you think these are ideas I said the investigating judge raises a finger

but they're ideas that lead straight to bloodshed that have led to a lake of blood you forget or you deliberately put out of your mind all the dead there have been that have been the natural consequence of subversive ideas and behaviour then I say apart from the fact that in any case I don't believe I'm being accused of any death of any act of bloodshed but the public prosecutor interrupts me with a shout of indignation this is an attitude of cynicism and contempt there's a shout from the cage buffoon I recognize Ortica's voice the investigating judge says he won't put up with interruptions and with that kind of language and he orders Ortica's expulsion from the courtroom there was bedlam everyone shouting inside the cage the lawyers protesting the prosecutor waving his arms about rumblings in the public gallery until the investigating judge was heard shouting recess and with this my questioning came to an end

everything we've heard so far is a senseless story but above all it is a criminal story with this the prosecutor began his summing up at the end of the trial from his bench on high standing upright wrapped in his black gown beneath the vast and horrible mosaic with the triumph of the blue forces of evil his mouth pressed to the black head of the microphone and his voice reverberating in the silence of the courtroom in that cage is locked the madness of these years the jurors all turned their heads towards the cage in unison we must dismiss every temptation for social political or cultural justification the direct or indirect responsibility for the criminal actions that have bloodied the country we must the jurors' heads turned back again to face the prosecutor

seeking to engender chaos in the fundamental institutions of our democracy the family education work before you you have not revolutionaries but men and women transformed by hatred against society into savage wild beasts the jurors' heads turn again towards the cage with no ideals but those of destruction and death behind these individuals there is no culture there is the pedagogy of violence mark my words the heads of the jurors turn again to face the prosecutor in unison sowing hatred in the immature and unprepared minds of the younger generation basely exploiting the freedom that our democracy offers indis-criminately to all to hatch their subversive schemes aiming to destroy the foundations of a peaceful and civilized way of life

but whoever sows the wind shall reap the whirlwind the pros-ecutor has raised his voice and appears to be eating the micro-phone he leans forward supported by the tips of his fingers on the edge of the bench there is no culture in this story there are no ideas in these ravings that have neither rhyme nor reason there is only the preaching of ignorance and violence of total refusal of pure negation the prophets of ill fortune who have schemed behind our backs with impunity for years who have put weapons in the hands of these wretched young people who have brought so much mourning to honest innocent hard-working families here they are before you the heads of the jurors turn in unison towards the cage for a moment then turn back to stare at the prosecutor who is now shouting with his arms up in the air

all of us who rise up in defence of democratic institutions and their laws must acknowledge the evidence of irresponsible laxity the stance of open complicity and consent the jurors crane forward because the prosecutor's voice is reverberating so much that his speech is becoming incomprehensible unmistakable fellow-travelling yes today self-seeking intellectuals it must not be left unsaid that they presumed to make history no doubt no mercy these individuals will be condemned by history punished to the very roots the ignorant instrument of these perverse minds our warning to the healthy element of the youth of this country will end up in the dustbin of history for those who come after us to crush this monstrous dragon

46

I made the return trip to the special along with a guy who was later killed in prison and who earlier on had himself murdered someone else in prison and was going to one of the first units they were trying out then for murderers he was being sent there because he'd just killed somebody in a special as a settling of scores between *mafiosi* I don't know what exactly it made me feel strange to think that he was a murderer he seemed quite a harmless young guy maybe even a bit of a softie he had a big colourful dragon tattooed on his chest we talked for the whole of my trip back to the special prison after the trial later things worked out badly the following year this young guy was murdered he had about thirty stab wounds

before we left we were in neighbouring cells he'd come there for a trial too and through the window he passed me some roast chicken that his sister had sent him I made the return trip in the usual armoured van and the weird thing is that I was happy to go back down there to the special and see all my comrades my friends I talked to this young guy in the armoured van and he was pretty desperate about ending up in this murder unit he said that life there was impossible there was nothing he was in total isolation he couldn't write to his relatives it was even difficult to get in touch with his lawyer the prisoners never saw one another a state of utter and total isolation

through the port-hole of the van I can see the prison complex looming ahead of me then the image shrinks to detail the outer wall behind the mesh of the wire netting a high fence with barbed wire round the top the bullet-proof glass of the sentry posts rushes past us then the van stops in front of the first gate it feels like coming home I'm handed over to the guards and then begins the usual ritual of the search of my belongings of my rucksacks they x-ray me because now there was this new thing since the minister had sent an x-ray machine for they'd always had trouble whenever they wanted to do rectal searches there were always commotions and fuck-ups because people resisted which meant that there were always punch-ups and commotions and fuck-ups over this so the minister made this technological leap he sent the specials these x-ray machines and after that they x-rayed you they put you behind a screen to see if you've stuck anything up your bum inside a container blades explosives and so on because for people in the specials opportunities for escape only occurred during trials because of the transfer and so there were people in the special who'd been there for years and who regarded this as a good chance to try and escape so if they had blades or explosives they could maybe exploit the opportunity to try and break out and so they took them with them on transfers

I recall that as I'm getting dressed again a sergeant made some remark about my trial that he'd been reading about it in the newspaper then he asked me if I knew that while I was away there'd been a murder among the non-politicals I said yes I know I read it in the paper and then he started giving me all the details about how this murder had happened because he'd been there right on the other side of the gate I cut him short okay okay I'm not interested because anyway what he wanted was to see my reactions or maybe not one of the ways things are distorted in prison is that you end up trying to give a meaning to everything trying to interpret everything everything must be a sign of something else you have to be able to read the logic of it while in fact if you think about it you realize that there are always loads of things that just happen like maybe that sergeant was just in a talkative mood

after that murder an order came from the ministry to separate the politicals from the non-politicals but the murder was just a pretext it was a plan already in the pipeline to make a clear separation between politicals and non-politicals in the meantime however after the revolt there'd been an easing off of relations between politicals and non-politicals there'd been a general changeover of non-politicals and there wasn't one non-political brought in who sympathized with the politicals and who could therefore be a link between the two groups so that way there was a reduction in the contact there'd been between politicals and non-politicals before the revolt there'd been no resistance on their part and the non-politicals even put the word round that they were really pissed off with the politicals because with the troubles they'd caused they'd worsened conditions in the prison and they didn't want any more trouble from us

and in fact the sergeant put me in the picture about what had happened you don't have exercise together any more he told me the non-politicals are pissed off and so on the sergeant kept up his non-stop talking as he took me to my section all the way along the corridor and whenever we stop at locked gates and going up the stairs also telling me that a whole lot of new people had come in and now they'd rebuilt the second floor after a year of building works they'd rebuilt it all and so in the end everything had been re-ordered back to the way it was before the revolt working prisoners on the ground floor non-politicals on the first floor and politicals on the second and that way they'd been able to fill it up with new people and when I got to the rebuilt second floor I saw how it had been transformed

the section had a completely new look the look of a bunker even more of a bunker than before there were a lot more guards in the corridors there were a lot of gates filters on the corridors not just the rotunda gates any more but other filter gates there were elevated closed-circuit cameras that filmed the corridor in sections the closed-circuit cameras switched on with their red lights the armoured doors are closed and through the spy-holes I see unfamiliar faces the sergeant tells me take my advice he tells me in a fatherly way listen to me take my advice it's in your interest to have a cell on your own for with other guys in a dormitory cell you know that you're in for trouble you've been here a while and you know that take my advice go on your own I said no I want to go back to the dormitory cell with my friends the sergeant shakes his head it's up to you though for tonight you'll have to sleep here you'll have to be on your own for now there's no room in your dormitory cell but tomorrow there's a guy leaving for a trial and when he leaves you can go into the dormitory cell and take back the place you had before you left going along the corridor I saw a lot of people I didn't know but then I got to the cells with the old comrades I'd left behind so there was the usual ritual of kisses through the spy-hole with noses poking through the spy-holes and this sort of thing shouts greetings that were kept up when I went into my cell I stood for a bit shouting through the spy-hole then ending with see you tomorrow at exercise and then the comrades sent me things to eat too much food everybody sent something

when the greetings were over I had a better look round the cell and in fact the cell was completely transformed from the way it was before for instance they'd taken up all the floor tiles and they'd just concreted it over as well as the double row of bars already at the window they'd added a new grille of special bars made of thick criss-cross cylinders I'd already heard about these new bars for these are the famous anti-saw bars for they're made of a special alloy and inside they have a core another steel cylinder that turns on its own axis so even if you break through the bars with a saw when you're halfway through you find the swivelling core and the hacksaw can't get any grip on the swivelling core

so besides the double bars that were there already they've put an extra grille with these special bars and on top outside they've put an iron grille with such a tight mesh that you can't even get your little finger through it and then the next day I realized that hardly any light came through and then I also saw that they'd replaced the washbasin it wasn't ceramic any more but made of iron and steel completely embedded in a block of cement the same went for the stand-up toilet also embedded in a block of

cement the little wardrobe was also made of steel and bricked in
the armoured doors were kept locked for practically the whole
day only the spy-hole was open and naturally the armoured
doors were always locked at night

I spent the first night after my return in this cell but before I
went to bed something else happened for in the cell opposite
mine I had an old comrade that I knew well and who'd also been
in prison for a long time and in the cell next to his I saw a face at
the spy-hole a young comrade that I didn't know he greeted me
I greeted him then I talked for a bit to this old comrade and the
new arrival was there at the spy-hole listening to us and wanting
to talk as well but the old comrade would make strange faces at
me whenever the new arrival tried to get me into conversation
the other guy would make strange faces then he made a sign to
me with his hand as if telling me to be quiet at the time I didn't
understand I understood there was something wrong but I didn't
understand what it was

47

The next morning I went down to the exercise yard and I ran at
once to hug my old comrades so there were hugs and kisses for
everybody and then they started talking about everything that
had happened in my absence especially the arrival of these new
comrades all of them very young and judged by the old comrades
to be very childish and inexperienced they'd just been impris-
oned they still didn't know the way things worked in prison
besides there were rumours that among them there were suspect
individuals people who'd been arrested on the statements of

pentiti and who during the judges' interrogations had made total or partial admissions and so had backed up the *pentiti* even if they hadn't given names or added anything else and then there were others who themselves had been *pentiti* and then had thought better of being *pentiti* and had retracted

I felt all the contradictions and tensions of this new situation because before the atmosphere of the prison had been an atmosphere of community for there were excellent fraternal relations and so on with these newcomers there were really big problems because many of these newcomers had weird histories they were the last generation of combatants all of them really young their biographies all very similar they'd had no experience of a movement also because by now the movement had been swept away which meant their experience had amounted to reading some document or other the clandestine distribution of some leaflet or other slogans on walls a banner pinned up on a fly-over and then maybe somebody killed on one of their very first actions and then arrest on the statements of some *pentito*

they were now living through a dreadful dispersal for they now no longer had any political project and their comrades who were left outside were now small groups trying only to escape hunted down with *carabinieri* and police on their trail all over Italy but even there in prison they held on stubbornly to their connecting bonds of clan and band that for them were like family ties I asked about this new comrade in the cell across from mine who the night before I'd been warned not to speak to and they told me he was one of those arrested a couple of weeks earlier I'd followed his story on television and his and his comrades' arrest wounded and on the run through the woods and countryside these scenes of a large-scale manhunt with *carabinieri* pursuing in helicopters and on horseback after a robbery that went wrong they captured them and what had happened was that this guy had been tortured and he'd talked under torture and had brought about the arrest of other comrades of his who were now there too in this same prison for the first week this guy had stayed in his cell he hadn't gone down to the exercise yard his comrades tried to argue with the others and they spoke up for him saying he was tortured he named names but it's us if anyone who should have a say for we're in jail because he gave them our names but since he talked under torture and they tortured us too even though we didn't talk we can still very well understand what he did so after a week of arguing it out a decision was made that the guy could come out to the exercise yard and it was all settled

in the exercise yard the atmosphere had changed there was no more football it had become a neurotic scene of endless discussions where every day there arose the problem of someone who was maybe an infiltrator a bastard and so on and as in all prisons there was this argument about grassing and torture that had become routine with anybody they captured then the comrades of that guy who'd been tortured and who'd talked told him it would be good for this experience of yours to be written about and passed round he took it as a duty and spent a week writing this document just when he was going to have others read it he said he'd had second thoughts that that draft wasn't right that he had to do another one a few more days went by he did a second draft he circulated it among his comrades as far as his comrades were concerned it was fine

but then he decided to withdraw this second draft too and not to circulate it any further and then one day he came down to the exercise yard he called a meeting he came down to exercise with an extraordinary expression very tense very nervous he called all his comrades together the rest of us couldn't figure out what the hell was going on what was happening he called his comrades together in a corner of the yard and he started talking to them however we saw that once he'd stopped talking there was no discussion they let him finish then they all walked away and they left him there alone without a word and they went away

we went and asked these others he'd talked to and we found out that he told his comrades that he'd never been tortured but had been threatened with torture which had scared him and he'd talked and named names without being tortured we were all flabbergasted this was really serious because we were in the middle of arguing about how to halt the spread of grassing and something like this turns up and there are guys who've ended up in prison because of this guy people who've really been tortured and haven't talked and this guy here on the other hand was only threatened and he talked in other words there was hell to pay it was clear that the situation was out of hand

then the first thing they do is remove him from the dormitory cell and put him in a cell on his own in quarantine when the guy went down to the exercise yard nobody talked to him any more and we asked his comrades what they planned to do they said we're conducting an enquiry into this business and since we're part of an organization we're also asking the other comrades in other prisons what they think as well as the comrades outside before we make a decision and in the meantime he stays as he is that was their answer then they started their investigation which consisted in sending out word of the problem to get a response from people in their organization who're in other prisons or who're outside in clandestinity through a complicated system of codes through letters and telegrams written in code

the guy kept to his cell he spent the whole time on his pallet reading the sports pages in the newspaper watching films on television like any other convict he spent all his time like this waiting for the solution to his problem talking to him was pointless all he did was reiterate I'm not leaving here it's right that the comrades who are in prison through my fault should have the right to judge me he'd say he was ready to die if this in some way would make up for what he'd done he talked about suicide and some of his more cynical comrades thought that this would be the best solution for everybody because it would save them the trouble of killing him and it would also mean more politically than them killing him

there was no doubt that what his comrades preferred was not to have to kill him they weren't at all happy about having to face this problem and having to come up with this solution of having to kill him it was perfectly clear that if they did it it wasn't in the least from conviction but because they were compelled they were compelled in the face of their comrades in the other prisons and outside from whom there began to arrive telegrams with decisions that were all unanimously for killing him and they were compelled in the face of the other combat groups who otherwise would accuse them at once of openly covering up for a *pentito* a bastard just at that time when the struggle against the spread of grassing is the main thing which means that if you come face to face with a *pentito* you have to nail him straight away without hesitation

I was ambivalent because on the one hand I was already in a psychological state of preparation for my eventual release I really believed that now there wasn't much longer to go so it wasn't the right time to be drawn into this whole business with any strength of feeling because anyway I'd be getting out pretty soon but also because the truth is that when I heard about this business I didn't like it at all not because I despised him because I'd been scared at the prospect of torture I'm in no position to judge they never threatened me with being forced to drink gallons of salt water with being given electric shocks on the testicles with being systematically beaten with truncheons with being kept standing on one spot for days on end with being cut up with razor blades with having my fingers burned with lighters they never threatened me with these things and I know very well that these things are done

the weird thing was that this comrade went down to the exercise yard and without fail every day he went up to his comrades who ignored him they even avoided looking at him and he'd say to them well have you decided and they'd say no he'd go back to his corner then despite everything I decided to talk to him however the guy was completely out of his head I told him go away go leave here what are you doing here what are you waiting for for them to kill you he kind of smiled at me shook his head and then walked on so I walked beside him and went up and down the yard a couple of times beside him the yard had gone silent they were all watching us I was taking a risk it was a challenge but then two other old comrades joined me and walked along with me and the guy it's not as if I thought it achieved anything it was a gesture a gesture that was all

maybe it achieved nothing in that situation of general lunacy but at least they didn't kill the guy they gave him a thorough beating once and made him go into isolation and as far as he was concerned it all ended there but afterwards things like this happened one after the other things it was hard to make sense of any more or find solutions everything seemed crazy to me now everything seemed really crazy everything now was possible like your cell-mate maybe your best friend suddenly one day will crack you'll come up from the exercise yard and he's not there anymore and then you realize that he's gone into isolation where a judge will be summoned and he'll sing to him and he'll sing your name too and for us this was the end of the solidarity that had been our great strength the only thing we'd had left

48

When I got the news of what happened to Gelso the winter was
nearly over above the reinforced concrete pit of the yard there
was a luminous blue sky the air was sweet when the wind blew
you could smell the sea nearby down in the exercise yard we
started wearing fewer clothes taking off our sweaters and shirts
we lay down in the sun our white bodies breathed but then we
looked at one another and on our pale necks our torsos our backs
our arms we saw a mass of darker marks we were all covered in
those fungus marks and we pretended not to look at one another
not to see those marks that covered us all it was in that period
that I got the last letter from outside it was from Malva and it
was about Gelso

in the end with some pressure from the prison doctor who no
longer had any doubts about Gelso's unbalanced mental state
his plea for release had been accepted he'd been put under
house arrest because they'd come to believe that he couldn't be
treated in prison he only got worse there and so he'd gone
home he'd gone back to live with his family and at first his
friends his comrades people who knew him well who were also
his childhood friends and who were fond of him went to visit
him they tried to get close to him to help him any way they
could but it all seemed futile it seemed that Gelso no longer
recognized anyone he didn't want to talk to anyone he didn't
want to see anyone

he'd asked his parents not to let anyone into his room and he
himself never left his room he also had his food brought to his
room and within a few days he turned the room into a cell he
took out all the furniture he only wanted to keep a bedstead a
table and a chair he always kept the window closed and the light
on even during the day and he started fixing it up like a cell with
the same things prisoners use cardboard boxes that had contained

detergent or pasta hung on the walls to make do as shelves and then one evening he acted out an escape he tied the sheets together and dropped down from the window they found him in the yard with a sprained ankle

he spent a month without once leaving his room he lived like people in prison and he had no wish to see anyone and if he saw someone he didn't recognize them he hardly even recognized his parents who of course were in despair they were at their wits' end but they preferred to keep him there even like that since it meant that at least they could keep him out of a criminal asylum and a month later one day they found him hanged in his cell which was his bedroom one morning they found him there he'd hanged himself with the sheets tied together that he'd used to act out the escape that he'd always had on his mind and that even now had failed him

Malva's letter ended by saying that we had to realize how things had changed now outside and that we had no idea how different things had become outside like everything outside the air had changed the atmosphere the mood how people talked we weren't to imagine that things had stayed the same now the great fear had passed the bosses had regained their confidence they were flaunting their money again their Rolls Royces in the streets their furs their jewels at La Scala and now everybody including many old comrades thought only about working to make money forgetting everything that had happened before when they thought that maybe everything was going to change

in the evenings after supper there's a strange silence we no longer call to one another from our cells you can see the blue rectangles of the spy-holes uniformly lit up by the reflections from the television sets you can only ever hear the same monotonous rise and fall of music mingled with voices the ceiling is patterned with the beams of the yellow floodlights cutting through the huge window grid pinning you to your bed you're inside an enormous tin of sardines squashed pressed together you're inside a sealed tin hermetically soldered shut what is there outside this tin who is there outside what are they doing what are they doing now why do they go on doing things doing all the things they're doing without me where am I what am I which is my face now that all I have left is my face here crushed flattened squashed

I broke the mirror with a leg of the stool I threw all the pieces down the toilet I flushed it I flushed it five six seven times I kept on flushing it staring at the black hole of the toilet that black circle where the water rushed down I put my hand inside it then deeper down to feel the bottom I put my head in it I pushed my head down but it wouldn't fit it wouldn't go through the hole to come out somewhere else to see out to see where I am where you are when we were a thousand ten thousand a hundred thousand it can't be true that there's no one outside it can't be true that I feel nothing any more that I no longer hear any voice any sound any breath it can't be true that outside there's only a vast cemetery where you are can you hear me I can't hear I can't hear you I can't hear anything any more suddenly the floodlights cut through the darkness they fill the cell with light

when the opaque morning light slid through the bars and the window grids things in the cell regained their usual banal ordinary appearance we began again to think and imagine how we could see how we could make ourselves seen outside that prison that was becoming a cemetery the place of greatest silence where no message no voice no sound passes in or out any longer we looked at the problem of how to regain communication with the outside world and we decided to launch new protests to break that deadly silence we began by beating the bars during the night we'd agree on the time for this at exercise we had no watches we had no alarm clocks but we could see what time it was on the television sets that were kept on all night

and so simultaneously in the middle of the night all of us together started beating on the bars with wooden ladles with broom handles with stools most of all with pots and pans and pandemonium broke out because everybody was beating harder and harder even people on the other floors who heard our battering started battering too along with us and in that closed place all the cells all the corridors reverberated in the night it was as if the prison would explode it was as if everything would come down but in the end when gradually the blows died away a great sadness came because we all realized that we were only beating for ourselves and for the guards because the prison was in the middle of the countryside lost in a great expanse of boundless emptiness with no one around who could hear us

then we thought that maybe we could attract more attention by making torches but it was more complicated to make torches there were greater problems because there were the grids on the windows there were the iron grids they'd put outside the bars to prevent anything being passed from one floor to another and so we had to make holes in the grids we broke the stools and we made pieces of wood with sharp points and with these pieces of wood slowly and with difficulty we managed to widen the mesh and make holes in it and then make the hole bigger until we could pass the torches through the hole

we made holes in all the wire mesh grilles and then we made the torches the torches were made with bits of sheets tied tightly together and then soaked in oil and for this too we agreed a time in the middle of the night we all lit the oil of the torches and we pushed these brands through the holes in the grilles but there was no one there to see this either the torches burned for a long time it must have been a beautiful sight from outside all those torches flickering against the black wall of the prison in the middle of that boundless plain but the only ones who could see the torchlight were those few people driving their cars that sped like tiny darts in the distance on that black ribbon of the motor-way several kilometres from the prison or maybe an aeroplane flying above but they fly very high up there in the silent black sky and they see nothing

CPSIA information can be obtained
at www.ICGtesting.com
Printed in the USA
LVHW091451130820
663080LV00002B/324